CAPTURED

CAPTURED

ANONYMOUS

Carroll & Graf Publishers, Inc.
New York

Copyright © 1991 by Carroll & Graf Publishers, Inc.

All rights reserved.

First Carroll & Graf edition 1991

Carroll & Graf Publishers, Inc.
260 Fifth Avenue
New York, NY 10001

ISBN: 0-88184-714-3

Manufactured in the United States of America

CAPTURED

1

Maya lay on her back, her face to the afternoon sun, her oiled legs bent, one arm stretched outward. Her plump toes were half-buried in the warm sand, and with one hand she absent-mindedly stroked her sun-reddened belly. The only sound was the rhythmic crashing of the waves, the slow trickle of foamy water on the deserted beach.

Maya was glad to be alone on the beach, to be able to lie in any position she chose without attracting unwelcome attention. She had grown to despise the city with its dark-suited men always staring at her, staring at her breasts, her belly, her buttocks, their eyes greedy and suggestive. Once, a man on the subway had gone so far as to grind his hand deep into the cleft of her buttocks, and when she had turned to face him, a look of disbelief on her face, he had only smiled at her, as if he had expected that she would thank him.

She had even grown annoyed at Peter. Was it possible that she would marry him? He was so nervous lately, so moody. He had always been strange, had always made strange requests of her. Once, he had wanted to cover her belly with whipped cream and lick it off, and another time he had wanted to tie her to the bed and blindfold and gag her. She always refused, and long arguments always resulted, but she couldn't bring herself to leave him. There was something so beautiful about him, so boyish and beautiful. She loved to look at his slender body, his round little boy's behind, his almost hairless belly. But he was growing stranger by the day. What had it been this morning? Yes, the pictures, yes, yes, yes. He had wanted to take pictures of her, nude pictures of her, and as if that wasn't unreasonable enough, he had wanted to take pictures of her masturbating.

"You're so *childish*," he had said when she refused. "You're such a little girl . . ."

How could he ask her to do that? Why in God's name did he want to take pictures of her masturbating? He was growing stranger, more restless, by the day. And he was growing more distant. Often, when they made love, he would just stop all of a sudden and roll over on his stomach, his head buried in the pillow. When she asked him what was the matter he would just say, "Nothing . . ." and turn away from her. At first, she had tried to excite him. She would stroke his back and buttocks and thighs and rest her hand between his legs and tickle him, but he never responded. Once, he had told her to leave him alone. Now she didn't even try. She would just lie quietly on her back and stare up at the pale yellow ceiling of the bedroom. Was it possible that she would marry him? Maya didn't want to think about it. She was glad to be alone on the beach.

Maya glanced down at her red-brown belly and thighs. She edged her dark green bikini down another inch on her hipbone and studied the contrast of brown and white. A few strands of pubic hair curled over the edge of her suit. Maya smiled and squeezed some tanning lotion from a tube and rubbed it over the white strip of her belly. She stared out at the ocean, at the white-capped waves glinting golden in the afternoon sunlight, then lowered the top of her bikini until just the tops of her pink nipples showed above the green fabric. She closed her eyes and took a deep breath, the trace of a smile still on her face, then lay back down, her legs and arms outstretched.

She thought of the little country house in Vermont where she had spent most of her life. She remembered the feeling of moist earth between her bare toes, the cold brightness of the lake where she had swum, her clothing folded neatly on a rock. She remembered the night sounds of owls and crickets, the day sounds of sparrows and frogs; and for the thousandth time, Maya remembered the day she took her longest walk through the woods, the day she met the boy...

It was the day after her sixteenth birthday. It had been raining for two days and nights, and when the sun rose on the third day, the woods almost sparkled with freshness. Maya awoke early and stood naked in front of the dresser mirror. The cool morning air made her flesh tingle, and the sight of her erected nipples in the mirror made her shudder with delight. She spent thirty minutes brushing her long golden-brown hair just to be able to watch herself in the mirror. She put on a faded pink-and-white checked dress and turned to leave the room. She stopped at the crude wooden door and turned to face the dresser once again. The trace of a smile on her lips, she walked to the dresser and picked up a little white box that lay next to the mirror. The box contained a strand of simulated pearls that her father had purchased for her birthday. Maya fastened the pearls around her neck, stared at herself for another minute or two, and left the room.

Downstairs, Maya could hear the sound of her father's snoring as she baked a half-dozen biscuits and packed them in a brown paper bag. She wrote a note saying that she had gone for a walk in the woods and would be back in time for dinner, and, as an afterthought, she thanked her father once again for the pearls.

Outside, Maya walked slowly at first, watching the moist earth squish between her white toes, listening to the distant chirping of the birds. The forest was filled with little orange salamaders, brought out by the rain, and Maya stopped once to run her little finger along a salamander's leathery back. The salamander darted into a pile of damp leaves.

After an hour or so, Maya came to a narrow stream winding through the woods. She waded in up to her smooth muscular calves and followed the stream deeper into the woods, watching the silvery flashing of minnows darting to and fro in the water. The combination of the cool morning air and the iciness of the stream made Maya's nipples powerfully erect so that the elongated tips strained against her tight cotton dress. The friction of nipple against cloth was at once a delightful and painful sensation, and after a short time, Maya decided in favor of unbuttoning the dress. There were six buttons down the front of the dress and Maya undid them slowly, without breaking her slow pace through the water, first watching her jutting breasts bounce free, the unbelievably elongated nipples pointing proudly upward, then belly, bush, and thighs, the silky hairs covering her tight lips sparkling golden in the morning sun.

Maya delighted in her exposure. As she walked, she couldn't resist running her hand along her smooth, round belly, couldn't resist touching the tips of her pink nipples with the tip of her little finger. Impulsively, she stooped down and cupped the clear stream water in her hands, dousing her breasts and belly and thighs with it. She watched the water bead in the golden bush that covered her plump mound. She smiled and wandered further down the stream.

A mile or so downstream, a group of fallen trees, probably struck by lightning, blocked Maya's path. She stood before the trees for a time, one hand resting on her naked hip. Just prior to quitting the stream, Maya wrenched the pink-and-white dress from her back, and mounted the slippery bank stark naked, the morning winds softly drying the faint moisture that dripped in the dark crevice between her buttocks. Her senses reeling with new and vaguely forbidden pleasure, Maya stood upon a huge gray rock, her legs spread wide, and parted the cheeks of her tight rump with her fingers, delighting in the soft breezes that caressed her tingling openings.

After a short time, Maya folded her cotton dress and placed it in the brown bag with the biscuits. Naked but for the single strand of pearls that her father had given her, she resumed her walk through the woods, breasts and buttocks bouncing lazily with each slow step.

She came to a small clearing in the woods, a grassy place surrounded by three tall trees, and lay down in the grass, her legs spread apart and bent at the knee, her white toes digging into the moist earth, one hand absent-mindedly stroking her smooth belly, the other fingering the precious strand of pearls that adorned her naked throat.

Maya lay with her eyes closed, remembering her birthday party. Uncle George had gotten her into a corner, his heavy arm around her, his eyes wild with the party punch.

'She's getting to be such a big girl, Sammy," Uncle George had said to her father. "A big, big, girl," he said, staring down at her heaving breasts, and he grabbed one of them and squeezed it with all his might. Uncle George laughed and laughed, and Maya's father laughed uneasily. It made Maya feel so strange, like loving and hating all at once.

Impulsively, Maya rolled over on her stomach, her head tucked into her arms. Without actually willing it, she began rubbing her throbbing mound against the grassy earth. She pictured Uncle George tearing the party dress from her breasts, squeezing them, squeezing the nipples, taking them in his mouth, kissing and sucking them. Maya could feel the sticky foam oozing through her vagina, moistening the parted lips. She could feel her pink clitoris stiffening, sliding through the soft blades of grass, her buttocks rising and falling, contracting and expanding. She pictured Uncle George on his knees behind her, spreading the tight cheeks of her smooth rump, lapping at the little pink hole with his long red tongue.

As she rubbed her twitching vagina harder and harder against the moist earth, pouring her hot juices over the twisted stalks of grass, Maya could hear all the sounds of the forest, the rustling of leaves on the trees, the clatter of falling branches in the distance.

Suddenly, Maya became frightened. Something was out of place ... a sound ... a strange sound ... a sound that didn't belong. Waves of terror crept over Maya's naked body as she slowly made out the nearby sound of human breathing. Gasping, Maya spun quickly around, throwing her weight on her elbows. Her large breasts heaved up and down, up and down as she lay on her back, eyes wide with fear, facing the source of the sound she had heard. At a distance of four or five yards, a boy crouched under one of the trees that surrounded the small clearing. The boy was barefoot and naked from the waist up, wearing only a faded pair of denims, cut and frayed at the knees. He seemed to be adjusting his pants, and Maya caught a flash of something long and pink, but the boy's hands hid it from view. The boy's skin was dark and hairless, his face perfectly smooth and quite thin. His long, tousled black hair waved slightly in the wind, and he had the darkest eyes that Maya had ever seen.

Maya grabbed for the brown paper bag that contained her dress, edging backwards, away from the boy, holding her knees tightly together to keep her foam-covered mound from the boy's view.

"Don't be afraid," the boy said. "I won't hurt you ..." His voice was soft and low and hoarse. He made some final effort with his pants and stood up, facing her. Maya couldn't take her eyes from the boy's denims. A huge bulge reached nearly halfway down the boy's thigh and seemed to be throbbing rhythmically against the thin, faded fabric of his denims.

Maya still lay on the ground, her weight on her elbows. Both an explosive curiosity and an overwhelming fear possessed her as she watched the boy walk slowly toward her, his thumbs hooked in the belt loops of his denims.

"I'm sorry if I surprised you," he said. "I couldn't help watching you . . ."

He lowered his gaze from Maya's face to her heaving breasts. Again, Maya lurched for the bag, this time tearing it open and removing her pink-and-white checked dress. She held the dress up in front of herself and stared down at the boy's bare feet.

"You shouldn't cover yourself," the boy said. "You shouldn't act like there's something to be ashamed of . . ."

The boy crouched down again, his face close to Maya's.

"You're the most beautiful thing I've ever seen," he said, "You shouldn't be ashamed . . ."

The boy's voice was the softest that Maya had ever heard. Very, very gently, the boy reached forward and tugged lightly on the cotton dress. Maya resisted at first, holding it tightly to her smooth belly.

"Don't be afraid," the boy said. "I won't hurt you . . . Don't be afraid . . ."

The boy continued to pull on the dress, gently but steadily, until finally Maya relinquished her hold and lay naked before him.

"You're the most beautiful thing I've ever seen," the boy said again. "I could watch you all day and all night . . ."

Gently, the boy touched Maya's ankle, his eyes wandering across her white belly and golden triangle. Maya tensed as the boy's hand travelled upward, swept her calf and knee.

"Don't be afraid," the boy said. "If you relax, I can make you feel very good . . ."

He stared directly into Maya's hazel eyes as he ran his hand along her thigh and hip, caressed her smooth belly, then brought his hand down on her other thigh. He made slow circles around and around her throbbing vagina, pausing to squeeze her soft flanks and heaving breasts. The boy lay lengthwise on the ground and took one of Maya's breasts in both his hands, pulling it toward his mouth. His lips closed over the nipple while he squeezed the breast as if he expected to draw milk from it. He sucked harder and harder, taking more and more of the firm breast into his mouth. Maya closed her eyes and let out a soft moan. She listened to the sound of the boy's heavy breathing, her buttocks, tautening in time to the rhythm of the boy's insistent squeezing. The boy put his face to Maya's chest and pulled her breasts against the smooth sides of his face, nuzzling them, squeezing them. He licked one, then the other, his thick pink tongue pausing at each of Maya's tingling nipples. Then he buried his face in the soft blonde hairs of Maya's armpits and lapped up the tiny beads of perspiration that gathered there. He licked her shoulder and neck and throat, finally inserting his tongue deep in Maya's open mouth. Maya moaned and rubbed her tongue against the boy's, then pushed past it, exploring his lips and teeth, the roof of his mouth, then his throat.

The boy sat up and placed his hands on Maya's knees. Slowly the boy parted her knees, his eyes fastened on the moist lips of her vagina. He pulled her legs as far apart as they would go, until the twin mounds of her buttocks, spread wide on the moist earth, were clearly visible. Gently, he stroked the fine silken hairs, sparkling with moisture, that surrounded her small hole. With both hands, he spread the plump lips. Holding the lips open with one hand, the boy slowly fingered the inner lips with the middle finger of his free hand, making slow circles around the narrow opening. Gradually, he pushed his long middle finger into the pink hole until it was halfway in, then withdrew it, covered with Maya's thick foam. In and out, in and out, he moved the finger, deeper and deeper, until it had gone as far as it could go. Smiling at Maya, he swirled the finger around and around against the slippery walls of her vagina. Maya made little whimpering sounds in her throat. Her whole body arched against the boy's strong hand. Her eyes were fixed on the gigantic bulge at the side of the boy's thigh, threatening now to tear the thin fabric of his denim.

Maya's obvious curiosity excited the boy. He got to his feet, breathing heavily, unbuttoned his denims and pulled them down. His huge penis pointed to the treetops, twitching violently. He smiled at Maya and knelt beside her, the thick penis twitching just above her face. Maya stared at it, her eyes wide. The boy took her hand and guided it to the head of his penis. She took it lightly in her hand and felt its strange bumpy texture.

"Squeeze it," the boy said.

Maya squeezed the head and a drop of clear liquid formed at the tip. She watched, fascinated, as the liquid dripped from the tiny hole as if in slow motion, then fell across her full upper lip. She licked at it with her tongue, tasted it; her eyes closed, then swallowed. She raised her little finger to the tip of the boy's twitching penis and wiped the remainder of the liquid from the tiny hole, then lifted the finger to her lips and licked the liquid from it.

The boy closed his eyes and held the huge head of his penis to Maya's lips.

"Kiss it," he said. "Kiss it and then put it in your mouth and suck on it . . ."

Maya held the boy's penis with both hands and planted a slow, wet kiss on the head of it. Then she held the head in one hand, squeezing it every so often, and kissed and licked up and down the long, rock-hard shaft.

"Put it in your mouth," the boy said. "Put it in your mouth and suck on it . . ."

Maya had to open her mouth as far as she could to take in the heart-shaped head. The boy moaned softly and held Maya by the ears, forcing his swollen penis deeper into her throat, thrusting it in and out of her warm, wet mouth. Suddenly, he shoved it all the way into her throat and Maya made a choking sound and pulled the throbbing penis from her mouth. She held the saliva-covered penis with both hands, watching it gleam in the midday sun, then squeezed it with all her might. Another droplet of crystal-clear liquid formed at the tiny opening. Maya put her lips to the swollen opening and sucked the liquid into her mouth, smiling up at the boy.

Suddenly, the boy flung himself on top of Maya, his face to her dripping hole. His buttocks rose and fell in the air a few inches from Maya's face as he rubbed his heavy penis in the sweaty valley between her soft breasts. Maya grabbed the boy's tight buttocks in her hands, squeezing them in rhythm to the boy's thrusting penis. The boy plunged his tongue into Maya's pink hole and swirled it around and around, his saliva mixing with the thick liquid that poured from her vagina. Then he lapped up and down her fleshy slit, pausing to suck on her stiffened clitoris, tickling it with his tongue.

"Pussy ..." the boy murmured, "love your pussy ... tastes so good ... so good ..."

Impulsively, Maya raised her head and licked at the full testicles that hung in her face, the dark, curly hairs tickling her chin. She took one of the heavy balls into her mouth and sucked on it, still squeezing the boy's buttocks. The boy moaned and spread the lips of Maya's vagina with his hands, thrusting his tongue deep into the loosening hole. He grabbed Maya by the backs of her thighs and raised her legs and buttocks in the air. He ran his tongue from her protruding clitoris down to the tiny hole that lay between her plump buttocks, just tickling its furrowed ridge with the tip of his tongue.

The boy got to his feet and stared down at Maya, his dark eyes wild with lust, his hair damp and tangled on his forehead.

"I'm going to fuck you," he said. "I'm going to fuck you till I can't move anymore ..."

He crouched between Maya's extended legs.

"Take off your necklace," he said to her.

Maya hesitated, one hand at her throat.

"You should be naked," the boy said. "I want you

to be naked as naked can be. Take off your necklace . . ."

Maya looked up at the boy, his penis twitching up and down, almost beating against his flat, hairless stomach, his strong hands resting on his bare hips. He had the face of an angel. Maya removed the necklace, stared at it for a second, and flung it into the grass.

The boy cupped Maya's buttocks in his hands and lifted her to the swollen head of his penis. Holding her legs apart with his rigid forearms, he pushed the tip of his penis to the mouth of the vagina and nestled the head in Maya's steaming wetness. She gasped, twisting her head to the side, her eyes shut tight, and let her breath out between clenched teeth.

"Oh," she said, "more . . . more . . . oh, please more . . ."

Overcome, the boy heaved himself forward, tearing through Maya's hymen and lodging his penis three inches into her tight hole.

Maya screamed with pain, scratching at the boy's broad shoulders. She lay still for a moment, the boy stroking her buttocks with the tips of his fingers, then wrapped her legs around his back.

"More . . ." she said, "give me more . . ."

Slowly now, the boy pressed forward, entering her a half-inch at a time. Maya writhed on the ground, twisting her head from side to side, breathing in short gasps.

"Too big," she moaned, "too big . . . tearing me apart . . ."

"Shhh . . ." the boy said.

"No, no," she said, "please no . . . too big . . . oh . . ."

Slowly, the boy slid it in, inch by inch.

"*No*," Maya screamed, "no, no, no, no, no . . ."

The boy made one final thrust and sunk it in up to the hilt. His heavy testicles bounced against Maya's damp buttocks.

"You're splitting me apart," Maya screamed.

The boy withdrew about four inches and looked down at his foam-covered penis, at the dilated lips of

Maya's vagina. Maya let out a sigh of relief. The boy began a light rolling motion and Maya sighed with pleasure.

"Yes," she said, "oh, yes, yes, yes . . ."

The boy increased the tempo of his movements, driving deeper and deeper with each thrust. It felt to Maya as if a hot pipe had been stuffed inside her. She arched her body to take more of his penis into her, felt her sopping bush rub against his smooth belly, felt his large testicles thud against her contracting buttocks. Deeper and deeper, the boy thrust, until the length of his penis slid in and out of her tight-muscled vagina. Their bodies made a loud sucking noise as they pulled apart, a slapping noise as they came together. Maya twisted against the boy, screaming:

"Oh, oh, oh, oh, more, more, more, more . . ."

She squeezed his thrusting buttocks with all her might, biting his shoulder and pressing her breasts to his sweat-drenched face. Again and again, her entire body trembled with the force of her orgasm, until finally, she felt the boy's huge organ throb inside her, shooting great spurts of sticky fluid into the very depths of her. Again and again, the boy drenched the hot walls of Maya's vagina with his steaming liquid. With each plunge, her battered sex emitted a loud gurgle, until finally there was silence.

After a time, the boy withdrew his still-throbbing penis and sat beside Maya. Semen, foam, and blood mixed in a widening pool between Maya's legs. They lay together without touching, the afternoon breezes cooling their bodies, listening to the rustling of the leaves, feeling the blades of grass sway against their nakedness. Finally, Maya turned and put a hand on the boy's smooth belly.

"Can we do that some more?" she said.

And again the boy had entered her, pulling her on top of him, kneeling behind her, propping her against a tall tree, and finally, possessing her mouth, spurting into her until semen dripped from her lips to cover her mouth and chin. She hadn't gone home until dusk had fallen over the peaceful forest.

In the course of her recollections, Maya had turned over on her stomach. She lay with her face pressed into the beach blanket, her slender arms folded around her head. The bottom of her green bikini had slid down somewhat, revealing the deep slit between the apple-halves of her tight rump. The exposed part of her derriere had turned a bright red.

The day was fading softly into evening. Cool ocean breezes wafted over Maya's body, causing tiny little goose bumps to rise on her sunburned flesh. The sound of the ocean was thunderous now, the rhythmic crashing of the waves alternating with the sizzling sound of thousands of tiny foam-bubbles bursting all at once. The tide was coming up. The ocean trickled to within a few feet of Maya's blanket, a wavy line separating sun-warmed sand from ocean-drenched mud.

Maya had never seen the boy again, had never wandered back to the grassy place surrounded by the three tall trees, had never even ventured very far into the woods after that. Recalling the experience in the days that followed, she became afraid to test the reality of her memory, afraid to return to the grassy place and find the boy was but a cold shadow compared to her radiant memory of him, or to return and not find him at all. Similarly, she had been afraid to repeat the experience, to meet the boy day after endless summer day, until her pulsing memory was battered into commonness. And so, she had never returned to the grassy place, but instead, had lain awake at night, recalling every detail of the experience, every thrust and moan, while stroking her dripping slit and fingering her steaming hole through orgasm after orgasm.

Maya stirred uneasily on the beach blanket at the recollection of her reluctance to return to the grassy place. But what could have come of it? she thought. What could possibly have resulted? He had been such a simple boy, such a common boy. Surely, she couldn't have stayed with him for the rest of her life. They wouldn't have had anything to talk about. She would have become quickly bored with him, and they both would have been unhappy. And she would have had to leave him anyway, when Aunt Elena called and offered her a job modeling clothes in the city. No, it just wouldn't have worked out. She had done the right thing.

Involuntarily, Maya's buttocks ground together as an image of the boy's huge twitching penis entered her mind. She tried to force the image away, but it wouldn't budge. She saw a droplet of clear fluid forming at the tip of the penis, falling across her full upper lip. She remembered the taste of his sticky, hot semen. Maya found herself rubbing her stiffening clitoris against the rough-textured beach blanket.

In her fantasy, the boy stood over her, whistling. The whistling annoyed her, and in her mind, she told the boy to be quiet. Maya became confused when the boy closed his lips, and the whistling continued. A vague tension gripped her as she realized that the sound was not coming from her mind, but from the beach. Images of the boy dissolved into nothingness as Maya suddenly sat up, her weight resting on her outstretched hands.

The man stood at a distance of about eight yards, hands on his hips. He wore a pair of white duck pants which contrasted sharply with the sun-tanned darkness of his broad chest, and a pair of wrap-around sunglasses which hid his eyes from view. He seemed to be older than Maya, perhaps in his late twenties, the barest suggestions of creases in his high-cheekboned face. There was a light stubble on the man's face, and he seemed to need a haircut—little curls of hair graced the sides of his neck—but these features only emphasized a strong quality of manliness which he possessed, a quality of ruggedness. Tufts of blonde-brown hair highlighted the darkness of his chest, hung from the hollows of his armpits. In one hand, he held a thin cigar.

"Hello," he said to Maya in a friendly tone, walking slowly toward her, his bare feet making a shuffling sound against the warm sand.

Maya hurriedly adjusted her green bikini, wondering briefly if the man had caught a glimpse of the tops of her nipples, of the golden strands of pubic hair that curled over her suit. Certainly, he had seen her lying on her stomach. Maya blushed. A circle of wetness was visible in the crotch of her green bottoms. She sat with her arms crossed over her tightly closed knees.

"I haven't seen you here before," the man said.

Maya felt no fear of the man, but only a slight uneasiness. Some unpleasantness might develop, she thought. The situation could become sticky. She didn't like to think of herself as a pickup.

The man stood several feet from the edge of the blanket, arms folded across his chest.

"Don't worry," he said, "I don't want to bother you . . ."

He smiled at her. She looked out toward the ocean, still slightly tense.

"Is it all right if I sit down for a minute?" the man said.

Maya looked up at him.

"Just say no and I'll be on my way," he said.

Maya felt guilty for her anxieties.

"It's all right," she said. "I'm sorry if I seemed—'

"No, no," the man said. "Believe me, I understand. I know how it is. Nobody can blame you for being a little nervous . . . the way guys are nowadays . . ."

There was a pause during which Maya and the man stared out at the ocean. The crests of the waves glowed orange in the fading light of the sun. The ocean was a patchwork of shimmering color: orange, green, blue, black, gold, white; it seemed to hold all the colors of the universe.

"The beach is so beautiful," the man said. "I come here everyday in the late afternoon. I walk for miles . . ."

"It is beautiful," Maya said, looking at the man.

He removed his sunglasses and looked down at the sand. His eyes were a deep blue color, like the ocean at dawn.

"This beach is usually deserted," he said to Maya. "This is the first time I've ever seen anyone here."

He paused for a minute, staring down at his toes, then looked up at Maya.

"Usually, I'm glad to be away from people," he said.

Maya thought of the men on the subway, in the crowded streets, always staring at her, staring . . .

"I know what you mean," she said.

"What made you decide to come here?" the man said. He took a long puff on his cigar.

"I don't know," Maya said. "I guess I wanted to be alone. It's so crowded in the city. I just got in a cab and told the driver to take me to the most deserted beach that he knew of. He took me to a beach a few miles from here, but there were people there, so I walked and walked until there were no more people, and then I walked some more . . ."

"You must have really wanted to be alone," the man said, looking down at his sun-browned feet.

"Yes," Maya said. "I . . . had a fight . . . with my fiancé . . ."

"Ohhhh . . ." the man said, nodding vigorously, "I see . . . Listen, if you mind my company, just say so . . ."

"Oh, no," Maya said. "Really, no . . ."

"Good," he said. "My name's Phil, by the way . . ."

"My name is Maya," Maya said.

They shook hands, smiling at each other.

"So you had a fight with your fiancé," Phil said after a pause.

"Yes," Maya said. "Sometimes . . . we don't get along too well . . ."

"Well," Phil said, "you'll straighten it out . . . When you're in love, things aren't always easy . . ."

"I guess not . . ."

The man had a strange, sad look in his eyes, a look that spoke of melancholy memories. Maya felt drawn to him, found herself wishing that she could soothe his sadness in some way.

"Believe me," the man said, "it's worth it to straighten these things out . . . Believe me . . ."

He stared out at the sea, a consuming sadness etched into his face. Maya tried desperately to think of something to say, but words wouldn't come to her. She too stared out at the ocean, and both sat in silence for a time. The sun was practically gone and the ocean breezes were becoming harsh, chilling. Maya shivered and the man turned to face her.

"Cold?" he said.

Maya nodded.

"I think it's time for me to go," she said. "I didn't plan on staying this long."

The man stood up.

"How are you getting back?" he said.

"I don't know," Maya said. "I guess I'll find a bus or a cab that'll take me to the subway . . ."

"Listen," the man said, "I hope you don't think I'm being pushy or anything, but the nearest bus is miles from here, and, believe me, you won't find a cab. Why don't you let me take you home? I don't live far from here. We'll just walk to the house, pick up the car, and you'll be home in forty minutes . . ."

Maya hesitated, staring down at the sand.

"If you don't want to," the man said, "just say no, and I'll be on my way . . ."

"I don't want to put you to any trouble," Maya said.

"No trouble at all," the man said. "It would be my pleasure . . ."

"O.K.," Maya said, "but really . . ."

"Really," the man said, "no trouble."

Maya stood up to put on her jeans. She turned her back to the man so that he wouldn't see the circle of wetness on her crotch. She wondered if he was watching the tight cheeks of her rump as she pulled on the tight jeans.

"That's quite a sunburn you have there," the man said.

Maya nodded and pulled on a white sleeveless top.

She held her sandals in one hand and scrunched the beach blanket up in a ball and stuck it under her arm.

"I'll carry that," the man said.

The man took the blanket and they walked slowly down the beach, Maya tossing her long gold-brown hair over her shoulder, sandals swinging at her side.

After walking a distance of about a quarter of a mile, the man named Phil pointed to the concrete wall separating the beach from the street.

"Over there," he said, walking toward a narrow space in the wall that permitted entrance to the street. Beyond the wall lay a cluster of evenly-spaced, white-washed, red-roofed bungalows, each with a small front porch and lawn. Phil pointed to the first of the bungalows. A late model Oldsmobile, painted a conservative dark blue, stood in front of the house.

"Here we are," Phil said. "Ready to go? Or would you like a cup of coffee or something first? If not, just say the word and we're city-bound..."

Maya felt cold and tired and the thought of a hot cup of coffee was very pleasant to her. She was about to nod when she noticed an old woman sitting in front of one of the bungalows across the street. The old woman was leaning forward on the railing of her porch, fixing Phil and Maya with a cold, suspicious stare, the paleness of her face set off by a frayed black shawl.

Phil caught Maya's glance.

"Don't let her bother you," he said. "She looks at everybody like that... Believe me... everybody..."

"I *would* enjoy a cup of coffee," Maya said. "I'm kind of cold."

"Come on," Phil said, a smile creasing his dark, stubbly face as he walked toward the door of the bungalow. With a slight, almost self-conscious flourish, he swung the door open and motioned Maya in.

Maya walked into a red-carpeted living room furnished with expensive-looking modern furniture. A long, low couch upholstered in an orange fabric stood before a wall-length window that looked out on the ocean. Before the couch stood a long wooden coffee-table on which rested a crumpled newspaper and a circular ashtray filled with cigar butts of various sizes. Maya pictured the man spending sleepless, lonely nights, smoking cigar after cigar and trying to concentrate on his newspaper.

"This way for coffee," the man said, still rather self-conscious. He was like a bashful boy on his first date.

He led Maya down a narrow hallway decorated with pastel-colored lithographs. Maya caught a glimpse of the man's bedroom as they walked past it. The bed was unmade, sheets, blankets, and pillow lying in a tangled mess at one corner. Poor, lonely man, Maya thought.

The kitchen was a cheerful little room, the walls and ceiling painted a light mocha. A circular, white formica table stood near a window that faced out on a small garden. Two leather-backed chairs stood at the table, and a narrow vase rested on the window-sill. The vase contained a single dying rose.

"So," said Phil, putting water up to boil in a red enamelled pot, "do you mind instant?"

"That's all I drink," Maya said.

"Good," Phil said. "I never made a real pot of coffee in my life. Believe me, not once..."

A long row of mugs of different colors rested on a shelf above the kitchen sink. Phil chose a red one and a white one and placed them on the white formica table. He took a small jar of instant coffee from a copper-handled cabinet and put a teaspoon of the brown powder in each cup.

"Do you take sugar?" he asked.

Maya raised one finger.

"I always put the sugar in with the coffee," he said. "You know, before the water. Gets mixed around better that way..."

He poured boiling water into each cup, stirring the mixture as he poured.

"Milk or cream?" he asked.

"Cream," Maya said.

He carried the white cup to the refrigerator and fumbled for a while with a small container of sweet cream, mumbling something about it being stupid of him to carry the cup all the way to the refrigerator. He brought the cup back, full to the top, and placed it in front of Maya.

"You take yours black?" Maya asked.

Phil nodded, watching her sip her coffee.

"I could never drink coffee black," Maya said between sips. "Tastes like poison . . ."

"You get used to it," Phil said. "Is yours all right? I usually put in too much coffee or sugar or something . . ."

"It tastes fine," Maya said, taking a long sip. "Really perfect, just the way I like it."

"So, you like the way it tastes?" Phil said. There was something strange in his tone.

"Yes," Maya said, "it's really perfect . . ."

"You really like the way it tastes?"

"Yes," Maya said. There was definitely something odd in his tone, something almost . . . vicious.

"Did you say you like the way it tastes?" Phil said.

For a brief second it entered Maya's head that perhaps she had offended the man in some way, but the thought quickly gave way to a frightening vagueness as comprehension seeped slowly from Maya's brain. The room became flat, one-dimentional, its outlines blurred.

"I mean, 'cause if you like the way it tastes, maybe you'd like to try somethng with it," Phil said. "Say, a piece of fruit . . . a nice, juicy piece of fruit . . ." He stood up clumsily, grazing the table with his hip. Coffee spilled over the sides of his teetering cup.

Maya tried to say that she didn't feel well, but only a brief gasp escaped her lips. She reached for the edge of the circular formica table in an effort to gain her feet, but her arms fell limp at her sides. She heard Phil's voice as if from a great distance. His strange words rang in her ears.

"I really think you'll enjoy it, you know what I

mean? You know what I mean, you dumb cunt, you? It's gonna be a big treat . . ."

Through closing eyelids, Maya saw him unzipping his white duck pants, saw him pull from his fly a long, thick reddish penis and shake it up and down, pushing the foreskin back with thumb and forefinger.

"Here," he said, advancing on her and holding the fleshy organ up to her face. "Like it? Like the way it smells?"

He grabbed her by the back of the neck and forced her nose against the swelling head of his penis. Then he rubbed it against her eyes and forehead, cheeks, chin, and lips.

"Like it?" he kept saying. "Like it?"

Maya could comprehend none of what was happening. The room had dissolved into a dull pink blankness. The man's voice had become like the sound of some mad musical instrument, his stiffening organ like a huge lead pipe being battered against her face.

Phil stepped back for a second, laughing, then pulled Maya's jaws apart and placed the heavy head of his penis between her full lips. Suddenly, he thrust four inches of it into her mouth, wriggling the head in the wet tightness of her throat, ignoring Maya's involuntary choking. With both hands, he grasped her by the back of the head and forced her lips up and down on the red shaft of his penis. He closed his eyes and made a soft, sighing sound which turned to a grunt as Maya's teeth scraped against the base of his organ. He jerked it out of her mouth and stepped violently backward, his hand raised to strike her, then caught himself in mid-swing. He leaned back against the kitchen sink, his long penis twitching in the air.

"Just as well," he said to himself, "just as well. Gotta keep you clean for the main man, right? Right. Gotta ke p you nice . . ."

He stuffed the throbbing penis back into his white ducks and zipped up the fly. He picked up the receiver of an antique phone that rested on the windowsill next to the dying rose, and started to dial. After dialing two or three digits, he placed the phone back on the receiver, staring wickedly at Maya, a smile playing across his wet lips.

"Plenty of time," he muttered, "plenty of time..."

He stood before Maya, gloating at her helplessness, stroking the long penis throbbing against the leg of his pants.

"Don't mind if I just take a little peek, do you?" he said to Maya. "Just a little peek..."

Maya felt her blouse being pulled roughly over her head, felt her breasts spill free, felt the man's hot hands squeezing and pulling at them. She had the vague notion that she wanted to beg the man to leave her alone, but words wouldn't come to her, speech was impossible, and the thought quickly slipped from her buzzing brain as she felt her jeans being unbuttoned and yanked down her long, shapely legs.

Phil stared down at her practically naked body. The cups of her bikini had slipped down to her smooth brown belly, the bottom bunched around her hips. Golden tufts of pubic hair curled around the lowered elastic band of her suit.

"You are too much," Phil muttered.

He pulled the bottom down her legs, sliding his hands along her plump buttocks and the backs of her muscular thighs, then pulled the cups from her stomach. He pulled her legs as wide apart as they would go, exposing the perfect golden triangle to his view. He stood back, leaning against the kitchen sink, taking in all of Myra's stunning nakedness.

"Just too much," he muttered again.

He opened a cabinet above the sink and withdrew a half-emptied bottle of scotch. He unscrewed the cap, tossing it carelessly into the sink, and took a long swig, letting the liquor run down his chin onto his naked chest where it beaded in the thick tufts of blonde-brown hair.

"Ahhh," he said, pulling the bottle from his lips. "Plenty of time..."

He took another long swig, then another, and rested

the nearly empty bottle on the windowsill next to the telephone and the dying rose. He pulled Maya up from her leather-backed chair, holding her limp body tightly to his own. He could feel her large breasts squashed against his hairy chest, the scratchy curls of her pubic hair rubbing against his long penis through the thin fabric of his white ducks.

"Mind if we take a little walk?" he laughed.

Grasping her by the back and buttocks, the fingers of one hand buried in the moist crack of her tight rump, he dragged her through the narrow hallway into the red-carpeted living-room.

He drew the red-and-black striped curtains across the wall-length window that looked out on the ocean, and turned on a dim light, then threw Maya down on the orange couch. One of her long tanned legs fell over the side of the couch, pulling the plump pink lips of her vagina slightly apart. One arm had fallen across her belly, the hand resting in the golden tufts of her perfect triangle, the other across her chest, one finger of the limp hand touching her long, erect nipple.

Phil made a low sound in his throat. He walked back into the kitchen and drained the bottle of scotch. Again, he walked to the telephone and picked up the receiver, this time hanging up without touching the dial.

"Plenty of time," he muttered again.

He walked into his bedroom and opened the drawer of a small ebony night-table, withdrawing a small, German-made camera. Holding the camera by its leather strap, he walked back into the living-room. He stood at a distance of about six feet from Maya, adjusting dials on the camera, then held the camera to his face.

"Don't move now," he said to Maya, who lay in precisely the same pose as when he had left her, her mouth open, pink tongue resting on her lower lip. He snapped a picture of her, then laid the camera on the long wooden coffee-table. He moved the table to the side of the room and pulled Maya from the couch. He placed her on her knees on the floor, full breasts resting on the edge of the couch, head cupped in her slender arms. He spread her legs wide apart, pushing her knees forward, so that her rump, cheeks pulled wide, stood high in the air, exposing the furry V of her plump vagina. He inserted his middle finger in her tight little hole, swirling it around until she became wet, then lubricating the open lips with the moisture thus produced. He stepped back for a second, admiring his handiwork, then approached her again, and again moistened his middle finger with her thick foam. This time, he spread the fluid over the tiny hole that lay between the parted cheeks of her rump. Again he stepped back. Maya's crotch glistened with slippery foam.

"Beautiful," Phil said, picking up the camera and snapping two pictures of the pose.

He placed the camera back on the coffee-table and grabbed Maya by the buttocks, pulling her from the couch. He rolled her over on her back on the red carpet, and once again pulled her muscular legs apart, bending them at the knee, exposing the double crack of rump and vagina. Impulsively, he grabbed her plump sex in both hands and squeezed it with all his might, sticky foam dripping down his fingers.

"You are just too much," he said again, wiping his hands on his hairy belly.

He placed Maya's hands on her heaving breasts in such a way that she seemed to be squeezing her nipples with thumb and forefinger, pulled her tongue between her lips, and rubbed thick vaginal foam across her entire belly, practically filling her almond-shaped navel with it. He took two pictures of the pose, one from directly above her, and one from between her legs.

Again, he placed the camera on the coffee-table, squatting on the floor beside Maya. He took one of her hands and placed it over her dripping vagina. He held the furry lips open with his hand and stuffed two of Maya's fingers into her narrow hole. Then he placed her other hand over her belly so that the forefinger rested on her involuntarily stiffening clitoris. He took a close-up of hands and vagina, then a full-length shot, then ran to the kitchen, returning with the empty bottle of scotch. He took her hands from her sex, pushed her legs back until her buttocks were raised in the air, and stuffed the empty bottle deep into her hole. Maya made a gasping sound in her throat, and Phil pushed the bottle even deeper, enjoying the helpless cry of pain ... Then he placed both of her hands on the base of the bottle and snapped a close-up and a full-length shot.

He sat down on the couch, leaving the bottle inside her, and lit a cigar. He drew on the cigar for a while, then stood up and pulled the bottle violently from Maya's hole. The suddenly contracting muscles of her vagina caused a loud sucking noise. Phil laughed and shoved the bottle in and out of her, delighting in the loud noise.

"Say something else," he said to her gurgling vagina.

Finally, he pulled the bottle from her, and got to his feet. He pulled off his white pants and dropped them on the red carpet, then straddled Maya, his knees on either side of her head, his hairy testicles resting on her chin. His long reddish penis twitched in the air above her face. He guided it down to her lips and forced it deep into her throat, shaking it back and forth with his hand. Then he reached over to the coffee-table and grasped the little camera in his hands. He shoved his stiff penis even deeper into Maya's throat, leaving only two inches of it exposed to the camera, and snapped the picture, then pulled back until just the head of his organ lay inside her mouth, foreskin pulled back and punched against her full lips, and snapped two more shots.

Phil returned to the couch, puffed on his cigar. It was dark outside and he glanced at his wristwatch. Nine o'clock. Getting late. He stroked his cock with one hand, holding the cigar in the other. Finally, he put out the cigar and got to his feet.

"Well, honey," he said, "gonna have to leave you soon . . ."

He turned her over on her side and lay beside her with his face at her sopping wet triangle. He placed his throbbing erection against her full lips and began stroking it rapidly, testicles thudding heavily against her smooth cheek. He squeezed and pulled at her vagina, finally inserting two fingers in the tight hole, whipping it to a froth. He jerked his swollen penis harder and harder, licking at Maya's wetness, biting her stiffening pink clitoris, until huge gobs of semen shot from his penis, covering her lips, nose, chin, and neck.

Phil lay on his back absent-mindedly stroking Maya's warm golden pussy. After a time, he knelt beside her and wiped the semen-covered head of his penis on her soft, jutting breasts. Then he stood up and pulled on his pants. He rolled Maya over on her back, foot pressed against her belly, and inserted his big toe in her dripping hole. He withdrew the toe, wiped it off on Maya's nose, and walked into the kitchen.

Phil took the antique phone from the windowsill, accidentally knocking the vase that contained the dying rose on its side. He dialed quickly, holding the phone to his ear.

"Hello, Johnny? It's Phil . . ."

"Pretty good. You?"

"Listen, I got one . . ."

"Yeah, you won't believe this one. She's got the hottest little pussy I ever saw in my life . . ."

"Naa, you told me I shouldn't fuck 'em. All I did, I took her clothes off, I took a couple of pictures, and I jerked off in her face . . . I swear I couldn't help myself . . . Wait'll you see the tits on her . . . I swear she's got nipples an inch and a half long. She's got the tightest, pinkest little hole I ever saw in my life . . "

"Of course, she's young, what do you think, I'm an idiot . . ."

"Yeah, I pulled the lonely beachcomber shit on her.

Had her eating out of my hand. You should've seen it . . ."

"I told you, I didn't fuck her . . . You told me the main man wants 'em nice . . . All I did, I shot all over her face. I figured, what the hell, I can always wash her face . . ."

"You think it would be all right? Man, I'd love to shove it up her little asshole. Man, I'm telling you, I would love to fuck her in her ass . . . . You're sure it would be all right?"

"Yeah, sure, right. Just wipe it out or something. Sure. Great, great. Look, I'll wait until you get here, right? We'll take pictures . . ."

"Great . . . Listen, wait about an hour before you come, O.K.? That old bitch across the street, I think she's getting kind of suspicious, you know?"

"Yeah, so I'll see you in about a half-hour . . . Bye . . ."

Phil hung up the phone and took another bottle of scotch from the kitchen cabinet and swigged from it, picturing Maya's rump-cheeks being spread wide apart, a huge, hard penis forcing her little pink asshole. Carrying the bottle with him, he walked into the bathroom and urinated. He wet a washcloth with cold water and returned to the living-room. He stood above Maya, rubbing his hairy belly, his cold blue eyes gleaming at the thought of entering her tight little bottom. He stooped and washed Maya's face, neck, breasts, belly, and pussy, pausing to breathe in the lingering aroma of her foam. Then he sat back on the couch, smoked a cigar, and waited for the man named Johnny.

Maya had partially regained her faculties when the doorbell rang. Although unable to move, she was able to hear quite distinctly, and could even raise her eyelids enough to make out the room.

The door opened and closed and Maya could make out the figure of a tall, thin man, seemingly quite young, dressed in striped bellbottom jeans and pink shirt. His hair was long and honey-colored and he, like Phil, wore a pair of sunglasses.

"Wow," Johnny said, staring at Maya's naked sun-burned body, "Look at that goddamned cunt. What a cunt . . . Man, her twat-hair looks like spun gold . . ."

"Didn't I tell you?" Phil said.

Maya felt sick with shame and fear. She knew that she was naked, that her legs were pulled wide apart, that she was powerless to close them, that two men were staring at the distended lips of her pussy, and commenting vulgarly.

"The man is gonna love this one," Johnny said. He squatted on the floor beside Maya. "He's really gonna love you, honey," he said, "He's gonna love you up your cunt, and he's gonna love you in your mouth, and he's gonna love you up your ass . . ."

"You think she can hear you?" Phil said.

"I don't give a shit," Johnny said. "I think I'm gonna take a little taste of her . . ." He knelt between her legs, his hands lifting her buttocks to his face, and lapped at the hot pink slit of her sex.

Maya felt his long tongue probing her deep hole, felt his lips and teeth nuzzling her stiffening clitoris. Despite herself, she felt the juices drip down her crotch and moisten the cheeks of her rump.

"Hold it for a while," Phil said. "Let me take a couple of pictures . . ."

Maya burned with shame as she felt Johnny's tongue thrust deep inside her, tickling the walls of her pussy, heard the clicking of Phil's camera as Johnny lapped wildly, his long honey-colored hair flapping against her belly, his stiff penis rubbing against her foot.

"Man, I'd like to take this bitch right now," Johnny said.

Through nearly-closed eyelids, Maya could see the man named Johnny pulling off his brightly-colored clothing. Finally, he stood naked above her, his thick, bluish penis rising slowly in the air. His body was very white and hairless, his legs and arms long and thin.

Johnny threw himself on top of her, his smooth

chest pressing against her firm breasts, his belly flattening hers, his stiff penis rubbing against the open lips of her hot sex. Phil bent down and placed Maya's hands on Johnny's sweaty buttocks, her fingers just dipping into the crack. Then he stood back. Maya had a sinking sensation as she heard the metallic clicking sound of the camera.

Johnny rubbed his penis harder and harder against her slit, teasing the clitoris with the plump, velvety head.

'Hey, Johnny," Phil said. 'Don't fuck her in the cunt, man, use her ass. Be easier to clean it up, you know what I mean? We gotta keep her nice for the man..."

"Don't worry," Johnny said, "I just want to get the head a little wet..."

Maya felt the man's hot breath on her neck, felt his sweaty cheek against hers. With growing horror, she felt the bulbous head of his penis pushing at the inner lips of her tight hole. Slowly, he eased it into her, until the head and about one inch of the shaft was lodged tightly in her hole. Waves of shame engulfed her as she felt the muscles of her pussy contract involuntarily around the thick penis, squeezing it rhythmically.

"Oooeee," Johnny said, suddenly grabbing Maya by the buttocks and squeezing with all his might. "This little cunt is too much, man. She's out cold, but that little twat of hers is squeezing my dick like a motherfucker..."

"Come on, Johnny," Phil said. "Let me play with her for a while. You've been in her for five goddamned minutes..."

"O.K., O.K.," Johnny said. Suddenly, he thrust himself deep within her, and just as suddenly, yanked his penis out of her. Her pussy made a loud sucking noise, and Phil laughed.

Phil pulled off his pants and squeezed his long red penis. He knelt at Maya's pussy and pushed her legs way up in the air, rubbing his penis in the double crack of buttocks and vagina.

"You got her nice and wet," he said to Johnny.

Johnny nodded and squatted at Maya's head, dangling his thick penis on her lips and chin while Phil worked on her pussy.

Maya felt Phil's penis slipping inch by inch into her vagina, pushing the narrow walls farther and farther apart. A scream formed in her mind, but only a slight gasp escaped her lips, tickling the shaft of Johnny's penis. Phil started pounding into her, his hairy belly slapping against her, sweat from his armpits drenching her breasts. Johnny squatted above her, her small nose pressed into the crack of his buttocks, and stuffed his penis into her open mouth. After wriggling his penis in Maya's throat for a while, Johnny tapped Phil on the shoulder.

"Hey, Phil," he said, "Don't shoot in her cunt, man . . ."

Phil continued pounding, his eyes closed, his heavy testicles thudding against Maya's buttocks.

"Come on, Phil," Johnny said. "Use her ass, will you? He's sure to examine her cunt . . . Fuck her in the ass . . ."

Phil stopped, breathing heavily. He squatted on the red carpet, three fingers stuck in Maya's dripping pussy.

"Man," he said, "I'd like to stick a goddamned flagpole up this little twat . . ."

"I'll choose you who comes off in her first," Johnny said.

"What do you got?" Phil said.

"Odds," Johnny said.

They chose and Johnny won. Maya felt his cold feet rolling her over on her stomach. She was terrified of being violated in this strange way.

Johnny grabbed her by the breasts and pulled her over to the couch. He rested her head and shoulders on the couch's orange upholstery, and bent her knees under her, legs pulled apart, so that her buttocks stuck up in the air. Holding his twitching penis in one hand, he rubbed it in the dripping wetness of her pussy until the head was covered with foam.

"Baby," he said in a hoarse voice, "I am going to fill your asshole to the brim..."

Maya felt his hot hands spreading the tight cheeks of her rump, his fingers probing the little rosy hole. He rubbed his hand in the foam of her vagina, then rubbed the foam around the little asshole. Slowly, he inserted his forefinger. Maya could feel the smooth membrane contracting around the finger, squeezing it invitingly. Her body tingled with the new sensation. Then, panic seized her as she felt the huge, throbbing head of Johnny's penis pushing at the little hole, his fingers spreading her cheeks wider and wider apart. She heard Phil laugh as Johnny lodged the head within the tight hole, causing a loud gurgling sound to escape her. Maya trembled inside as she heard the camera click once again, caught a slight glimpse of Phil, camera in hand, his long penis still wet with her foam. Then pain exploded through her as Johnny thrust another two inches of his stiff penis into her tight hole, then another two, and another, until it was buried inside her and she could feel his scratchy pubic hair rubbing against her buttocks, his testicles tickling her crotch. Slowly at first, Johnny moved his penis in and out of her tightly-contracted hole, then faster and faster, his belly slapping against her rump-cheeks, his heavy balls banging against her juicy crotch. Faster and faster, he thrust, like a dog, Maya's whole body shaking with the force of his blows, his hot hands kneading her buttocks, pulling at her shaking breasts. Panting, he sunk it as deep into her as it could go, his body pressed to her back, and shot spurt after spurt of hot semen into the depths of her, drenching the walls of her hole with his wetness. He pulled it slowly out of her, both he and Phil laughing at the drawn-out gurgling sound made by muscles contracting around a vacuum.

"She's all yours," Johnny said, standing up, squeezing a last drop of semen from his penis and letting it drip into the crack of Maya's rump.

Johnny sat on the couch, his thighs around Maya's

head, his penis and testicles pressed to her face. Phil got behind her and pried the cheeks of her rump apart once again. He slid his penis slowly into her, jerking it up and down as he did so. Maya could feel his bunched-up foreskin inside her.

"Loosen her up enough for you?" Johnny said.

"She's just right," Phil said, "It's like sticking it in a vat of lard or something..."

Phil's penis was about two inches longer than Johnny's, and Maya almost fainted with pain as he sunk it in up to the hilt, balls thudding between her legs, but then he reached around in front of her and grabbed her pussy and started squeezing it as he thrust into her, and Maya became disgusted with herself as slow waves of pleasure began to creep over her.

"Come on, man," Johnny said. "Finish her off. We still gotta deliver her..."

"Be with you in a second," Phil said through clenched teeth.

He pounded viciously at her, his sweaty, hairy belly slapping against her soft buttocks, his body moving back and forth like a machine.

"Here we go," he said, suddenly slapping Maya's flanks as he would a horse. "Giddyap," he hollered, "Giddyap, you cunt, you..."

Huge spurts of semen filled Maya's hole. She felt as if her intestines were drenched in it.

Phil yanked his still-twitching penis from her hole as fast as he could, hoping to hear her make a final noise. He wasn't disappointed: a long, gurling sound issued from her widened hole as gobs of semen dripped from it down the crack of her rump, into the golden tufts of her pussy-hair, and finally onto the red carpet.

"She's too much," Phil said, getting to his feet.

He and Johnny sat on the couch, Phil lighting a cigar, Johnny a filtered cigarette. Maya could just barely make them out from where she lay. They sat stretched out on the couch, feet resting on the wooden coffee-table, letting their swollen organs cool in the ocean breeze.

"Man," Johnny said, "that's the most beautiful asshole I've ever been in in my life. I could fuck that for days..."

"I'd still like to fill up that sweet twat of hers," Phil said.

"Ah, fuck it," Johnny said. "We're gonna have enough trouble cleaning up her asshole. I must have put a half-quart in there..."

"Yeah," Phil said. "I put in the other half..."

They were silent for a time, each man smoking his tobacco. Phil broke the silence.

"How much you think I'll get for her?" he said.

"I don't know," Johnny said. "The usual probably. I don't know. Maybe he'll give you a bonus.."

"You call him up?" Phil said.

"Yeah, I told him we'd be there around twelve. We got an hour yet," Johnny said, casting a quick glance at his wrist watch.

"You think this stuff'll last that long?" Phil said, pointing at Maya's naked body.

"You give her the stuff I gave you?" Johnny said.

"Yup," Phil said. "Put it in her coffee. The bitch didn't know what hit her..."

"It'll last," Johnny said.

Again, they fell silent. Their talk had terrified Maya. Old tales of white slavery and such raced through her brain. She tried desperately to move, but found herself unable.

Then Johnny went into the bathroom and washed himself off, drying himself with a white towel. Phil did the same, and both men got dressed, Phil changing to a pair of gray summer-weight slacks and a blue *Ban-lon* shirt.

"O.K.," Johnny said. "Let's clean her up."

Phil went into the bathroom and returned with a fistful of pink toilet-paper and a damp washcloth. He wrapped a sheet of toilet paper around his middle finger and inserted it in Maya's asshole, then withdrew it drenched in semen. Again and again, he repeated the process until finally the hole was clean and dry. Then he wiped her pussy and thighs with the washcloth and dried her with what was left of the toilet paper. Then he straightened her hair, smoothing it with his hand, and sent Johnny into the kitchen for her clothes.

Johnny returned with her clothes in one hand and a little white purse in the other.

"Where'd you get that?" Phil said.

"Dropped out of her pocket," Johnny said, opening it. "Just some phone numbers and a couple of fives ..."

"Think we should give it to the man?" Phil said, lighting a cigar.

"Yeah," Johnny said. "He always says he wants everything they got with them ..."

Johnny stuffed the purse back in the pocket of Maya's jeans, then helped Phil dress her, first putting on her green bikini, then her jeans and blouse, and finally her leather sandals.

"Beautiful," Johnny said as Phil propped her up on the couch. "Never touched by human hands ..."

"Ready to go?" Phil said.

Johnny nodded, putting on his sunglasses and lighting a cigarette.

"O.K.," Phil said, "Just let me check for the old bitch across the street ... She's really been busting my balls lately, always staring at me ..."

He went to the front door and opened it a crack, peeking through at the darkened street. The street was silent and empty. There was no sign of life in the old lady's house.

"O.K.," Phil said. "Everything's quiet. Want to take my car or yours?"

"Take mine," Johnny said. "I put it in the driveway."

Phil pulled Maya to her feet, holding her by the back and buttocks, while Johnny walked through the house turning off the lights. Then they tiptoed out into the street, Johnny closing the front door quietly after them. Johnny opened the back door of the car and helped Phil ease Maya into the backseat. Then Johnny got into the car and started the engine. Phil walked around the car and sat down next to Johnny. For a second, just before he pulled the door closed, Phil thought he heard a creaking sound coming from the old lady's bungalow, but before he could make sure, he had automatically closed the car door after him, and was unable to hear so small a sound over the roar of the engine. Before he had much time to think about it, they were on their way, loud rock tunes playing on the radio.

II

After a drive of slightly less than an hour, they arrived at a deserted stretch of road on the southernmost part of Long Island. Johnny turned on his brights and squinted into the silent darkness. Just ahead of the car, he made out a battered wooden sign, its lettering concealed by thick strokes of black paint. He drove very slowly for a distance of about five yards, then turned the car sharply to the left, seeming to drive it off the road into a cluster of low-hanging branches. Beyond the branches lay a narrow dirt road that wound deeper into the darkness.

Phil breathed a sigh of relief. "Jesus," he said, "It always blows my mind when you do that..."

"You'll get used to it," Johnny said.

They drove another quarter of a mile into the darkness, finally stopping at a wrought-iron gate, at the side of which stood a small wooden structure in glossy white and black stripes. A man dressed in a gray guard's uniform emerged from the shack. In one hand, he held a compact walkie-talkie sheathed in a leather case, in the other, a shiny automatic revolver. He seemed to recognize Johnny's green Buick, and spoke briefly into his walkie-talkie. Then he stepped to the side of the car and motioned to Johnny to roll down his window. Johnny complied.

"Can't you put that goddamned thing away?" he said, pointing at the guard's automatic. "You know us..."

The guard's face was expressionless.

"I take my orders from inside," he said. He peered into the back seat of the car, glancing coldly at Maya. Then he stepped back and spoke once again into the walkie-talkie. There was a crackling reply, too dim for Johnny to make out, and the guard motioned them forward, opening the wrought-iron gate with the flick of a switch, and stepping back into his white-and-black striped cubicle.

Johnny drove deeper into the darkness.

"Man," Phil said. "When I quit this gig, I am gonna punch that shithead out like he has never been punched out in his life..."

"Ahh," Johnny said. "Look at it this way: Whatever this guy is doing with these cunts we bring him, it's for sure they could hang him for it, right? So I guess they got to take precautions, you know what I mean?"

They drove on in silence for another quarter of a mile, finally arriving at a huge wood-and-stone house, the outlines of which could barely be discerned in the darkness. One side of the house gleamed in the lights of Johnny's Buick, the walls made entirely of glass. Johnny stopped the car in front of a steep stone stairway that led to a huge oak door. He turned off the ignition and both he and Phil pulled Maya from the back seat. They were quite gentle with her now, as they were afraid that someone might be observing their actions. Gently, they carried her up the stone steps until they reached the heavy oak door. Before Johnny was able to knock, the door was swung open by a thin, gray-faced man wearing the uniform of a butler. Johnny started to speak, but the man interrupted him with a wave of the hand.

"Yes," the man said. "Bring her inside..."

They entered a large vestibule panelled in dark wood. The floor was done in mosaic tile of orange, pink, and gold, apparently ending at either of two closed wooden doors, which led to the interior of the house. Dim, recessed lighting caused the vestibule to glow dully.

"Place her on the couch," the thin man said, motioning with a sweep of his hand to a narrow couch upholstered in orange-and-pink striped satin. Gently, Johnny and Phil complied, tucking Maya's hands across her smooth belly, placing her legs neatly together.

"You administered a drug?" the man said when they were done.

"Yeah," Phil said, somewhat nervously, "You know, that like grayish powder..."

"I know," the man said with another gesture of his hand. He reached into his inner jacket pocket and withdrew two envelopes, handing one to Johnny and the other to Phil.

"This is your fourth act of service to our ... organization," the gray-faced man said. "We are grateful to you. We have tripled your payment."

Johnny and Phil turned to each other, their faces creased by broad smiles.

"And now," the man said, swinging the door open and motioning them outside, "Until the next time..."

They walked swiftly down the stone steps and into Johnny's car. Just prior to driving off, Johnny turned to Phil, a look of naked wonder on his face.

"I can't believe it," he said. "We find a good-looking cunt, slip her a mickey, fuck her in the ass, drop her off here, and we get paid six thousand bucks. Six thou, man. I can't fucking believe it..."

"Too much," Phil said as they drove back into the darkness.

Inside, the gray-faced man was sliding a section of wooden panelling along rollers concealed in the wall. A shiny metal plate came into view, dotted with tiny multicolored lights and silvery switches and dials. The gray-faced man pressed one of the switches, waited for a red light to flash on, and spoke into a tiny receiver set into the metal plate.

"She is here, sir," he said.

"They're gone? The men are gone?" a crackling, metallic voice asked.

"Yes, sir. They left several minutes ago."

"How many times is this for them?"

"Four, sir."

"I see. Has the girl been drugged?"

"One of Dr. Shroeder's preparations, I believe, sir."

"I see. Very well, have her brought to Dr. Shroeder. I'll be there in a few minutes to personally deliver my instructions."

"Very good, sir," the gray-faced man said. He flicked a switch on the shiny metal plate and rolled the section of wooden panelling back into place. He walked to one of the large wooden doors, knocked twice, and flung the door open to reveal a long, dimly-lit hallway. In a matter of seconds, two men emerged from the other end of the hallway, both dressed entirely in form-fitting black clothing, and walked briskly toward the thin, gray-faced man. Maya could barely make them out through her still-heavy eyelids. One man was a light Negro, his skin a creamy cocoa color. The other seemed to be a Latin, his features sharp but sensuous, his hair dark and bushy. Both men were gigantic and seemed to be in perfect physical condition.

"You're to take her to Dr. Shroeder," the gray-faced man said. "Be very careful with her."

Maya felt herself being lifted in the air, felt rippling muscles being pressed against her.

The men carried her down the dimly-lit hallway, then up a darkened flight of stairs. They paused on one of the landings and the Negro pressed Maya against his chest, squeezing her buttocks with his large, strong hands.

"I hope we get a chance to service this one," he said to the Latin in a thick Jamaican accent. "I shove it in so hard, it come out her mouth." He rubbed his penis against Maya's thigh.

Again, Maya felt waves of terror seize her. From the feel of it, the man's penis was at least nine inches long, and it wasn't even hard.

"We'll get her," the Latin said. "He likes to watch his athletes fuck . . ."

"I shove it in so hard, it come out her mouth," the Jamaican said. He held her by the hips and rotated her pussy on his huge penis. "Baby," he whispered in her ear, "you just wait till we get you downstairs. You just wait. We fuck you so much, you can't walk. We got ten big athletes downstairs for you, handpicked from all over the world, gonna fuck you good. Ten big dicks for you, ten big dicks . . ."

"Come on," the Latin said with a nasal laugh. "We gotta take her to the doctor . . ."

They carried her up another flight of stairs and down another dimly-lit hallway until they came to a large door with a heavy brass knocker at its center. The Latin knocked twice and the door was opened by a heavy, red-faced man wearing thick, black-framed glasses. He wore an immaculate white smock and a thin cigarette between the thumb and forefinger of his right hand.

"Yes, yes," he said with the trace of a German accent. "Bring her in, bring her in . . ."

The men carried her into a brightly-lit laboratory, its walls lined with racks of chemicals contained in vials of various sizes and shapes. Neatly-placed medical equipment filled the room: hypodermic needles, jars of alcohol, several stethoscopes, and other such apparatus. In the center of the room stood a long operating table and a wooden stool.

"Put her on the table," the doctor said. "Yes, yes, good. Very good. You may go . . ."

The black-garbed men left the room and the red-faced doctor seated himself on the stool beside Maya.

"Yes, yes," he clucked, "you certainly are a beautiful girl, yes. Most beautiful." He ran his hand along Maya's smooth belly, then noticed her partially-opened eyes.

"Well," he said, "you seem to be regaining your senses somewhat, eh?"

He reached forward and pulled her eyelid back with his thumb. For a brief second, Maya found herself staring up at the man's oily red face, his sinister eyes magnified surrealistically by the thick lenses of his black-framed glasses.

"Yes," he said. "Just a matter of time now ... I take it you can hear me, my dear ..." He puffed on his thin cigarette, blew a smoke-ring into the air. "But, I'm afraid it is not for you to gain control of yourself just yet. We wouldn't want to have to deal with any futile attempts at resistance at this early stage of the game. But, in the meantime, since by all indications you have gained the use of your ears, allow me to tell you that you are a most beautiful young woman ... a *most* beautiful young woman. In the near future, I hope to have the pleasure of your *intimate* acquaintance ..." He reached forward and squeezed the lips of her pussy through her tight blue jeans. "For now," he continued, "it is best for you to be patient. Your fate, I assure you, has already been sealed. Mr. Etheus will be here presently, and then, we shall see what we shall see ..."

The doctor sat erect upon the stool, puffing on his cigarette and whistling bars of an old waltz. Occasionally, he would stroke Maya's shoulder or forehead, his touch filling her with disgust.

Suddenly, the door to the laboratory was thrown open. The doctor stood at attention, hands at his sides, as a tall, majestic figure entered the room. Like the men who had previously attended Maya, he was dressed entirely in black, but over his form-fitting black shirt he wore a golden chain from the center of which dangled a large red stone. His face was almost god-like, the nose aquiline, the nostrils flared, the lips full and sensuous, the eyes a blazing green color. Crisp curls of dark hair fell across his high forehead as he bent to touch Maya's slender arm.

Maya felt a tingling sensation when he touched her. She squinted through her heavy lids to make out the man's hand. It was very smooth and quite pale, the fingers long and slender.

"She is still under the inflence of the drug?" the man asked the doctor. His voice deep, but at the same time soft; authoritative but gentle.

"She will remain so for only another short while," the doctor replied. "Already, her faculties return to her."

"She can hear?" the man asked.

"I am quite certain that she can ..."

Maya could feel the man bending close to her, his breath warm on her cheek.

"I am Etheus," the man said in slightly more than a whisper. "For the time being, you are my prisoner. Hopefully, you will soon become my guest. I am sorry for whatever indignities you have suffered, and can only say that, in time, you will understand that they were necessary. For the present, I regret to say that it is impossible to allow you to regain control of yourself, for reasons which you will later understand. You will soon be injected with a new chemical, the properties of which are rather different from that which you have already experienced. In the morning, all shall be explained to you, both my ideas and ... methods ... the latter of which, you will shortly be experiencing ..."

The man named Etheus continued staring at Maya after he had finished speaking. His green eyes blazed as he studied the features of her young, suntanned face. Lightly, he traced the gentle curve of her nostril with his forefinger.

"She is magnificent," he murmured.

Abruptly, he turned from Maya and faced the doctor. The doctor stood at attention, his gaze lowered.

"I want you to administer a drug," Etheus said, "Something that will—"

"Give her the use of her limbs," the doctor said, "but leave her quite susceptible to suggestion?" A devilish smile played on his thin lips. Behind his thick glasses, his cold gray eyes gleamed.

"Precisely," Etheus said. "And when you are finished, have Claudia prepare her and bring her to my study..."

The doctor bowed deeply, and Etheus turned and walked briskly from the laboratory, strong arms swinging at his sides. The red-faced doctor turned on a bright fluorescent light above a long wooden table. He chose several vials of chemicals from an overhead rack, measured careful amounts of each in a calibrated flask, then poured them into a small glass tube. He warmed the mixture over a gas flame, watching it carefully until it turned a bluish color, then added some white powder from a small jar that rested on the far end of the table. The mixture fizzled and turned clear and the doctor turned off the flame and left the mixture to cool.

Maya heard him walking about the laboratory, puffing on a cigarette and whistling off-key bars from an old waltz. Continually, her mind focussed on Etheus' strange words. What had he meant by *methods*? What strange *methods* was she about to experience? She felt that he must be a madman, and yet, his bearing had been more that of a prince.

The doctor ceased whistling and filled a small hypodermic with the fluid, holding it up to the bright fluorescent light as he did so.

"This is a wonderful chemical," the doctor said to Maya, approaching her, hypodermic poised in his gnarled hand. "Etheus is quite fond of it. Once, he said that it was an almost adequate replacement for ... love. He's really quite fond of it, uses it to the exclusion of all the other ... *interesting* chemicals that I have devised for him. Truly, you will seem to love him ... or perhaps, it is better to say, that which he represents ... even more than yourself. It is a most wonderful chemical ..."

Maya felt alcohol being rubbed on her bare arm and the sharp sting of the needle entering her flesh. A warm sensation flooded her as the needle was withdrawn from her arm, a feeling of lightness and peace.

"Open your eyes," the doctor said in a toneless voice.

Maya responded, amazed at her ability to do so.

"Good," the doctor said, "Very good. Now stand up."

Again, Maya complied, sliding from the table and standing in a fixed position facing the doctor. Again, Maya felt a tingle of astonishment at her ability to move, and a slight perplexity at not being able to do so of her own accord, but these feelings only lasted for the briefest period of time. Maya found herself totally engrossed in the present, as if the past had somehow been obscured, and as if the future had ceased to exist.

"Very good," the doctor said. "A most wonderful chemical. Sit down, please," he said, indicating the wooden stool at the side of the operating table.

Maya complied and the doctor walked to a small intercom that rested on his cluttered desk. He pressed a small red button and spoke crisply into the machine.

"This is Dr. Shroeder," he said. "You will please report to my laboratory immediately . . ."

He switched the machine off without waiting for a reply, and turned once again to Maya.

"Very soon," he said, "we are to part, my pretty one. How unfortunate. My work here is so painstaking and tiresome. Always I am seeking the more perfect chemical, always seeking to please the demanding Mr. Etheus. But . . . my rewards are great. Men such as myself cannot be paid in mere gold. Perhaps . . . you shall soon learn the method of my payment. I'm sure you will find it most interesting . . ."

Two sharp knocks on the door interrupted him. He snapped to attention, facing the door.

"Come in," he barked, his accent particularly thick.

The Jamaican Negro and the Latin entered the laboratory, their faces expressionless, their bodies seeming even larger, more magnificent, in the bright fluorescent lighting of the doctor's laboratory.

"Yes," the doctor said, his eyes cold through the thick lenses of his glasses. "You are to take her to Miss

Claudia. You are to instruct Miss Claudia to prepare her for Etheus..."

He paused, glancing at his leather-banded wristwatch.

"Don't waste any time," he said, pronouncing each word with a certain deliberateness, "The hour grows late." Aain, he turned to Maya. "Go with these men," he said.

Maya stood and followed the men as they left the laboratory, closing the door softly behind them, and walked down the dimly-lit hall to another darkened staircase. Suddenly, the Jamaican halted and turned to Maya.

"You want some dick?" he said in his melodic accent. "Want some big dick?"

"That won't work," the Latin said, his hand on Maya's thin waist. "I seen them like this before. You gotta tell them, gotta tell them what to do. Watch..." He turned to Maya. "Get on your knees," he said, pulling a huge, heavy penis from a fly that opened with miraculous ease.

Maya kneeled on the landing above the men, her head at the level of the Latin's groin.

"Now, open your pretty mouth and suck on my beautiful big dick..."

He forced the gigantic head of his penis into Maya's wet mouth, forcing her lips into a perfect O. The Jamaican made a low sound of lust in his throat as the Latin rocked back and forth on the balls of his feet thrusting about three inches of his huge organ in and out of Maya's pliant lips.

"Let me do her," the Jamaican said, pulling his friend's throbbing organ from Maya's open mouth.

The Latin stepped aside as the Jamaican pulled his long, cocoa-colored penis from the slit in his tight black garment and waved it in Maya's face.

"Ten juicy inches for you to suck on, darling," he said. "Suck it good..."

He rotated his hips, twisting the shiny organ around in her mouth as it grew to an incredible size. Then he pulled his penis from her mouth and held it flat against his muscular stomach.

"Lick it, darling," he said, holding it by the head. "You lick every inch of my big brown dick..."

Starting at his huge testicles, Maya ran her tongue along the smooth base of his penis, rising slightly from her knees to reach the tip. Up and down, up and down, she licked, the cocoa-colored penis glistening with her saliva. The Jamaican stood with his eyes closed, his head thrown back, making a moist clicking sound in his throat.

"Come on," the Latin said. "We're supposed to take her upstairs..."

"O.K., O.K.," the Jamaican said. "Just one minute..."

He turned his back to Maya and pulled his black slacks down over his plump, muscular buttocks. With both hands, he spread the cheeks of his rump wide apart.

"Lick my sweet asshole, darling," he said. "Lick that pretty little asshole..."

Maya buried her face in the Jamaican's buttocks, tongue working rapidly up and down, tickling the dank-smelling hole.

"Stick your tongue way up there," the Jamaican said. "Stick it deep in that pretty little asshole..."

Maya plunged her long pink tongue into the hole, swirling it against the rhythmically-contracting walls, licking it clean.

"Come on," the Latin said. "Let's get moving."

"O.K.," the Jamaican said, pulling up his pants and stuffing his penis back into the slit as best he could. "Come on, darling," he said to Maya. "Get on your feet and come with us. Plenty of dick for you later. Ten big dicks downstairs for you..."

They continued up the stairs to another dimly-lit hallway at the end of which was a black door illuminated by a small yellow light. The Jamaican knocked on the door.

An intense-looking woman opened the door, her

shining black hair pulled sharply back from her forehead. She wore tight slacks of dark brown suede with a matching vest that left the tops of her firm breasts exposed to the nipple. In one hand, she held a small white kitten, stroking its fur with her long, pointed nails.

"Yes?" she said, her nostrils flaring as she spoke.

The Jamaican didn't answer her. He stared at the deep valley between her breasts, a leering smile forming on his face.

"We've brought the girl for you," the Latin said. "Etheus wants you to prepare her..."

"Bring her in," the woman said.

The men led Maya into the room. The walls were painted in a light beige color, one wall entirely covered by a mirror. A brown carpet set off the light walls, and golden drapes covered the room's single window. In one corner of the room there was an open closet in which hung costumes of various descriptions. At the opposite wall a doorway led into a large, tiled bathroom, in the center of which lay a sunken bathtub. Beside the entrance to the bathroom stood a huge, ornate vanity. A long black whip rested on the top of the vanity.

"You may go," the woman said to the black-garbed men, putting the white kitten down on the brown carpet and holding the door open.

The Latin started to leave, but the Jamaican remained immobile, staring at the woman's firm breasts.

"What are you staring at?" the woman said after a pause.

The Jamaican hesitated, a smile playing across his lips.

"At your pretty titties," he said after a short laugh, his eyes burning into hers.

The woman smiled a strange smile, cast a glance at Maya.

"Would you like to kiss them?" she said in a soft voice.

"I would love to kiss your pretty titties," the Jamaican said.

"Get on your knees," the woman said, "and I'll let you kiss them."

The man got on his knees and the woman bent above him and pulled one of her breasts free from the suede vest. She held it to his face, squeezing the large nipple between thumb and forefinger. He parted his lips to take it into his mouth, and as he did so, the woman stepped back and kicked him directly in the groin with tremendous force. The Jamaican staggered to his feet howling, one hand pressed to his testicles, the other reaching forward for the woman's throat. With lightning-like movements, the woman stepped back to the vanity, grasping the handle of the black whip in her left hand. The whip cut through the air and sliced across the Jamaican's naked throat, leaving a deep red mark in his cocoa-colored flesh. Again, the man lunged for her, and again, the whip whizzed through the air, marking him across the Adam's apple. The man stood doubled-over in the center of the room, both hands to his burning throat. Horrifying choking sounds escaped his clenched teeth as he shook his head wildly from side to side.

"Now, get out," the woman said venomously, tossing the whip disdainfully upon the vanity. The black-garbed men left hastily, closing the door quietly behind themselves.

The woman took the white kitten up in her arms and seated herself in a plush velvet chair facing Maya. She stroked the kitten in silence for a few moments, then placed it once again on the thick brown carpet.

"All right, my dear," she said to Maya. "Take off your things."

Maya pulled her sleeveless blouse over her head, her motions very slow and lazy, and dropped it to the floor. She undid the straps of her green bikini top and let her large breasts spill free, then unzipped her tight jeans and slid them down her long, muscular legs, finally kicking them to the floor. The little white purse slipped from her pocket.

"Bring that to me," the woman said, pointing to the purse.

Maya complied and the woman placed the purse on the top of the vanity next to the black, bloodstained whip. Maya pulled the green bikini bottoms from her hips and stood naked before the dark-haired woman. Slowly, the woman took in Maya's nakedness, viewing her from front and back and side, then stepping back to view her naked body in the mirror. She approached Maya and stood close to her, holding the undersides of Maya's breasts as if weighing them, then running her hand along the swelling curve of Maya's buttocks. Finally, she ran her fingers gently through Maya's thick bush.

"Gold," she whispered, and stepped back once again. "Go into the bathroom," she said abruptly, "and run the water for a bath. I'll be in presently to wash you ... " She stared at Maya's bouncing buttocks as Maya entered the bathroom and knelt to run the water.

When the tub had been filled the woman entered the white-tiled bathroom and ordered Maya into the sunken tub. She then removed her suede vest and slacks and folded them over a straight-backed chair that stood against one wall of the room. She stared at her naked body in a mirror that hung behind the bathroom door, admiring her dark nipples and clean-shaven vagina, then sat at the edge of the tub, dangling her legs in the warm, scented water.

The woman pulled Maya to her and soaped her neck and breasts and armpits, running her hands greedily along the slippery skin, tickling the golden-tufted armpits and enjoying Maya's strange, drugged laughter. Then she slid into the tub beside Maya and soaped her buttocks, running the bar of soap up and down in the smooth crack. She soaped Maya's legs and feet, pausing to lick the tip of her little toe, then worked up her thighs to the crotch, soaping the pink slit again and again, finally covering her own fingers with soap and inserting middle and forefinger deep in Maya's narrow hole. Suddenly, she spread her long legs over the sides of the tub and pressed Maya's face to her naked vagina, opening the lips with her fingers.

"Kiss it," she said, pressing Maya's lips to her stiffening clitoris.

Maya nuzzled the soft flesh, kissing it again and again.

"Suck it," the woman said, "suck it . . . "

Maya complied, pulling the meaty object in and out of her wet lips, holding it in her mouth and running her tongue around and around on it.

"Put your tongue in the hole," the woman said, pulling the lips of her pussy further apart.

Maya's long tongue slithered into the hole, lapping at the contracting walls.

"Deeper, deeper," the woman said, moaning, sighing.

Maya thrust deeper, tickling the smooth membrane with the tip of her tongue, forcing the tight walls farther and farther apart.

"Yes, deeper, deeper," the woman moaned, her thighs tightening around Maya's neck, pressing Maya's lips flat against her steaming slit. Thick foam spread in the bathwater from the woman's bare vagina. Maya's tongue worked furiously inside the woman, until finally the woman gasped sharply through gnashing teeth and lay still.

After a time, the woman helped Maya from the tub and dried her with a thick pink towel, paying special attention to her breasts and buttocks. She dressed herself in a long white robe and led Maya back into the brown-carpeted room. She sat Maya in the velvet-covered chair and washed her face with a damp cloth, then combed her long golden tresses with a jewelled comb. She sprayed Maya's armpits and pussy with a strange-smelling perfume, and rubbed a small amount of pungent-smelling salve in the crack of pussy and rump. The salve caused an odd tingling sensation, and

Maya found herself squeezing buttocks and thighs together every so often.

The woman withdrew from the closet a silk black costume and helped Maya into it. The costume was a tight-fitting affair, its almost weightless fabric clinging to Maya's naked skin. It left Maya exposed in the front, except for arms and legs, tying at the neck. A cleverly-stitched cut-out revealed Maya's plump buttocks, their whiteness accentuated by the costume's black fabric.

The black-haired woman stepped back and appraised her handiwork, smiling strangely. Once again, she ran her fingertips through Maya's perfumed bush.

"Gold," she whispered. Then she turned and flung open the door. "Come," she said to Maya. "Etheus awaits us..."

They walked down dimly-lit corridors, their bare feet making soft, padded sounds on the cold wooden floor, and down a thinly-carpeted stairway. The darkness became impenetrable, and the woman called Maya to a halt, pulled a small candle from her vest-pocket, lit it with a wooden match, and led the way into the darkness. At the end of a narrow hallway, the woman doused the candle and knocked twice on a heavy oak door. From inside, a deep voice bid her enter.

The room was lit by a number of circular fixtures set evenly into the ceiling. The wine-colored walls were decorated with huge photographs of couples in various attitudes of love-making: here, a young boy knelt between a woman's parted legs, his lips fastened to her moist slit, there, a woman bent forward, spreading her cheeks to facilitate the entrance of her partner's organ. The room's carpeting matched the walls, and set about the room were various leather-upholstered sofas and easy-chairs. In one of these chairs sat a couple making love. The man was young and fair, his long white penis pulled through the elastic slit of his black garment. Like Etheus, he wore a chain about his neck, but the chain was smaller than Etheus' chain, and no stone dangled from it. The girl impaled on the man's stiff penis was completely naked, her body deliciously long and slender, her flame-red hair done up in tiny, intricate ringlets. Up and down, she moved on the man's thick organ, her thighs squeezing his together, her bouncing, pink-tipped breasts pressed to his face. In black leather chair to the left of the couple sat a thin, dark-haired man, the long fingers of his right hand lightly stroking the underside of his thin penis which he held pressed to his stomach with his left hand. His eyes were fastened on the spot where the fair man's penis entered the redhead's foamy hole. At the far end of the room, behind a massive mahogany desk, sat Etheus, his large head resting majestically on his open palm. At a signal from him, the couple ceased their lovemaking, the girl taking a seat in a vacant leather chair, her long white legs spread over the arms, foam dripping from her open hole onto the seat of the chair. Simultaneously, the dark-haired man ceased his stroking, leaving the thin penis lying flat against his stomach.

"Come in, Claudia," Etheus said, rising slowly from his chair.

Claudia proceeded to the center of the room, leading Maya by the hand. Maya remained expressionless as Claudia twirled her slowly around, displaying her pink-nippled breasts and plump buttocks to the attentive group of people. The redheaded girl fixed her eyes on Maya's golden bush and stroked her own foamy vagina excitedly.

"Excellent," Etheus said, his voice soft and low.

The man who had previously possessed the red-haired girl turned to Etheus, an expression of yearning written across his face.

"Yes," Etheus said with a small gesture of the fingers, "You may take her, Eric . . . "

The man called Eric got to his feet, hastily removing his tight black clothing. He stood before the expressionless Maya, his naked body muscular and pale against the wine-color of the room, his heavy white penis rising in the air. Then he removed Maya's garment.

"Lie down," he said to Maya, "and spread your legs wide..."

As Maya complied, the man squatted between her strong thighs and raised her buttocks until the mouth of her vagina met the heart-shaped head of his penis. With a sudden thrust, he buried his organ half-way inside of her, then ordered her to throw her legs over his shoulders. Slowly, he slid the remaining four inches of his penis into her tight hole, then got to his feet, holding Maya suspended in mid-air. Mercilessly, he pounded his throbbing organ around and around in her slippery hole, his buttocks grinding together, his blond-haired testicles thudding against the bottoms of her rump-cheeks. Maya, her inhibitions totally removed by Dr. Shroeder's strange drug, sobbed and gasped in ecstasy, her breath hissing between her clenched teeth.

Tiring of his standing posture, Eric ordered Maya to her knees, then thrust his penis into her wet mouth, ordering her to lick it clean of foam. The dark-haired man watched, sitting at the edge of his leather easy-chair, his thin penis rising to a length of about eight inches. He turned breathlessly to Etheus, droplets of sweat forming at the top of his forehead. Etheus nodded to him and made a small gesture of his left hand.

"Yes, André, yes," Etheus said in a voice that was only slightly more than a whisper.

André divested himself of his black garments and stood behind the crouching Maya, the thinness of his body accentuating the length of his penis. He knelt behind her, spreading rump-cheeks and pussy-lips with his long fingers, and inserting his penis slowly into her already foamy hole. Maya's lithe body worked furiously, first lunging forward to take more of Eric into her mouth, her pussy simultaneously sliding to the head of André's organ, then thrusting backwards to take in more of André, the head of Eric's penis almost slipping from her lips.

At a signal from Etheus, the red-haired girl joined the tableau. First she crouched behind Eric, her hands spreading the tight cheeks of his rump, her tongue tickling the rim of his little hole, then entering it, licking wildly at the contracting walls.

She then performed the same service for André as he thrust his penis in and out of Maya's pink hole, sliding her tongue as deep into him as it could go, causing him to moan with pleasure. Finally, she lay on her back beneath Maya, her tongue lapping at Maya's foamy slit and André's thrusting penis, her small feet squeezing Eric's saliva-coated organ and testicles.

Claudia approached Etheus, withdrawing Maya's white purse from the pocket of her suede vest.

"This fell from one of her pockets," she said, handing the purse to Etheus who laid it aside on his desk.

"Yes, yes," Etheus said, his blazing green eyes intent on the naked intertwined bodies before him, one hand fingering the red stone that hung from the golden chain, "very good. I'll attend to it later . . ."

His eyes still on the thrusting, sweating bodies of his disciples, Etheus pressed a small blue button situated to the left of an elaborate control panel that lay on his desk. Several seconds after he had pressed the button, a small blue light began to flash in the center of the control panel. Etheus spoke into a small microphone.

"Please come to my study immediately," Etheus said. "Bring your equipment with you . . ."

Etheus sat back in his chair and watched the lips of Maya's vagina squeeze André's thin penis, the lips of her mouth slide up and down on Eric.

"May I go now?" Claudia asked.

"Take off your clothing," Etheus said to her.

Claudia complied, blushing, and Etheus flung her naked body over his knees, inserting one finger in her asshole and two in her clean-shaven vagina He worked her to a froth as he watched the glistening group writhe on the wine-colored carpet. Claudia moaned despite herself.

There was a double knock on the door.

"Come in," Etheus said, his voice deep and resonant, without taking his eyes from the group before him, without removing his strong fingers from Claudia's writhing body. A fat, shaggy-haired man entered the room, a thick black moustache curling over his full upper lip. He wore a wrinkled yellow silk shirt, the tails of which flapped over his ham-like buttocks. Over one shoulder, he carried an expensive-looking movie camera and tripod. He stood at the door, staring wide-eyed at the sweating group on the wine-colored carpet, his eyes finally coming to rest on Eric's tight, thrusting buttocks.

Etheus made an impatient gesture of his free hand, then turned from the man, and inserted a second finger in Claudia's contracting asshole. The fat cameraman began immediately to film the frenzied activities of the group on the floor, removing his camera from its tripod and holding it by a leather-covered handle. He moved in on Maya's face, contorted now by the size of the organ which pumped back and forth in her mouth, then moved along her body and came in close on her dripping vagina. He stepped back as Eric and André began moving in rapid unison, their organs thrusting in and out of Maya like pistons. The red-haired girl began laping furiously at Maya's slit and André's foam-covered penis, squeezing and tickling the base of Eric's penis with her bare feet. Moan after moan escaped Maya's squeezing lips, as André and Eric shot spurt after spurt of thick, hot semen into her mouth and pussy. The red-haired girl eagerly lapped at the overflow from Maya's burning hole, foam and semen mixing together in her mouth. Eric pulled his still-twitching penis from Maya's lips, watched the overflow trickle down her chin and neck.

"Swallow it," he said to Maya. "Swallow it all."

Maya licked her lips with her long pink tongue, caught the dripping semen in her hands, lifted it to her mouth, and swallowed every drop. André removed his penis from Maya's pussy, and sank down in a nearby easy chair. The redhead inserted her tongue deep in Maya's dripping hole, and licked it clean of foam and semen, then joined André, performing the same service for his long limber penis.

"Join her," Etheus said to Claudia, withdrawing his fingers from her asshole and vagina, and wiping them off on her raised buttocks.

Blushing, Claudia walked to André's side and sucked on the head of his penis as the red-haired girl ran her tongue along the shaft. Maya remained in her crouching position, Eric squeezing a last drop or two of warm semen into her open mouth.

"Have her lick Suzanne," Etheus said to Eric with a gesture toward the redheaded girl.

Eric ordered Maya into another crouch, this time behind Suzanne, and pushed her face into Suzanne's silk-haired crotch. Suzanne, still licking the shaft of André's stiffening penis, aided Maya by pulling her own rump-cheeks wide apart and rubbing her furry pussy against Maya's moist lips. Maya slid her tongue between the lips of Suzanne's vagina, swirling it around in the foam-smoothed hole. Suzanne squeezed the hole tightly around Maya's tongue, then released it and lowered her buttocks until Maya's tongue tickled the rim of her asshole. The silk-shirted cameraman moved from one angle to another, as Maya's slippery tongue probed deeper and deeper within Suzanne's tight hole. The cameraman's thick penis stiffened as he watched Maya's eager tongue through the viewfinder of his camera, and he squeezed it occasionally between his heavy thighs.

"Have her attend Claudia," Etheus said to Eric. "Have her lick both of them . . ."

Eric directed Maya to Claudia's smooth-shaven crotch, then took a seat behind Maya and inserted his big toe in her sopping hole. Claudia let out a low moan as she felt Maya's tongue slip first into her vagina, and then into her asshole. Her eyes closed, she took more and more of André's long penis into her mouth as Maya drove deeper and deeper into her. Impulsively, Claudia began squeezing and licking André testicles, her tongue touching Suzanne's while Suzanne licked up and down the long, pale shaft. André moaned and discharged, his hot semen filling Claudia's mouth and trickling onto Suzanne's smooth cheek. Maya meanwhile moved her lips from Claudia to Suzanne and back again, licking, tickling, lapping, thrusting her tongue in and out of their openings.

"Enough," called Etheus, still sitting behind his massive desk. "All of you are to attend to our new guest . . ."

Etheus gestured with his right hand, and Eric placed Maya on a long leather sofa. Suzanne knelt on one side of her, taking the long nipple of one breast into her mouth, while Claudia sucked on the other. André placed his head between her sunburned legs and stroked her moist slit with his tongue, occasionally stopping to tickle the crack between her buttocks. Eric pressed his face to hers and inserted his thick tongue into her open mouth, thrusting it deeper and deeper into her wetness. Maya moaned again and again as the four eager tongues explored her naked body, Claudia moving from her breast to her golden-tufted armpit, André raising her legs and inserting his tongue in her tight asshole, Suzanne licking her belly and deep navel, then sucking on her stiff clitoris, Eric licking her ears and throat, finally squeezing her breasts together and taking both nipples into his mouth at the same time The fat cameraman walked endlessly around the couch, filming the scene from every conceivable angle.

Eric then lifted Maya from the couch, pulled her to his chest, pried open her thighs, and lifted her onto his large pale penis. Holding her by the buttocks, he lifted her up and down on his sturdy pole, enjoying the deep moans that issued from her throat. André aproached from behind and lodged the head of his penis in Maya's tight bottom, easing the long shaft in, inch by inch. Claudia, at a signal from Etheus, knelt behind Eric and thrust her tongue between his legs, licking his heavy blond-haired testicles, and simultaneously tickling the rim of his asshole with the tip of her nose. Suzanne knelt behind André and performed similarly, holding him by the ankles and running her tongue up and down the crack of his rump. The cameraman paused to load his camera, sweat drenching his thick black moustache and running over his thick upper lip, then resumed filming, taking an occasional close-up of Maya's ecstatic face. Faster and faster, Eric jerked Maya up and down on his throbbing penis, each jerk forcing her buttocks to squeeze André's long organ harder and harder, pulling it deeper into her tight bottom. Faster and faster, Suzanne and Claudia swirled their tongues inside the men, until Eric, his teeth clenched tightly, drenched Maya's pussy with his hot semen. Maya's frenzied writhing brought on André's orgasm, the rhythmic contractions of her buttocks squeezing his long penis dry.

Eric and André collapsed in nearby easy-chairs, Suzanne kneeling before one and then the other, licking their swollen organs clean. At Etheus' direction, Claudia helped Maya to the leather sofa, then stood at Etheus' side. Again, he toppled her over his knee and inserted his fingers in her vagina and asshole. With his free hand, he pressed a small orange button on the control panel before him, continuing to probe Claudia's depths, and waited for a small light to flash at the bottom of the control panel. He then spoke into the small microphone.

"Bring the beast to my study," he said, and sat back in his chair, kneading Claudia's plump white buttocks with his strong hands.

Within seconds, there was a double knock at the door and the gray-faced man who had earlier admitted Johnny and Phil entered the room, a huge German Shepherd at his side. The dog bounded to Etheus' side upon seeing him, and Etheus dismissed the gray-faced man with a wave of his hand.

Rising from his chair for the first time, Etheus led the huge dog to the sofa on which Maya lay. He pressed the dog's face to Maya's sopping, semen-covered bush, and smiled as the dog sniffed and licked it. He then held Maya's thighs apart, and the dog looked up at him, his gigantic penis rising flat against his furry belly. Etheus nodded, and the dog proceeded to work his organ into the girl, clutching her tightly with his forelegs. It took the dog ten minutes to work all of his hairy penis into Maya's hole. Suzanne, watching the dog, began tuggling violently on the head of Eric's penis, and Eric responded by thrusting two of his fingers deep into Suzanne's tight bottom

The dog pounded wildly away at Maya's straining hole, his tongue hanging from his mouth, his forelegs pressing into her hips. Maya groaned with pleasure as the dog's hairy penis plunged deeper and deeper into her belly, his large testicles banging against her dripping thighs. Suddenly, the dog accelerated his movements, his eyes rolled back in his head, and he filled Maya with his hot semen until it overflowed the lips of her vagina.

The dog fell across Maya's belly, utterly spent. After a few minutes, the dog tried to extricate himself from Maya, but his penis had grown so swollen within her that he was unable to withdraw it. At a command from Etheus, Claudia approached the sofa and held Maya down by the hips. Etheus grabbed the dog by its muscular shoulders and wrenched it free of Maya's pussy. Eric smiled as Maya's semen-filled hole emitted a loud gurgling sound. He got quickly to his feet, large penis twitching in the air, and started to mount her, but Etheus waved him away with a small motion of his strong fingers.

Etheus stared down at Maya's sweaty, sunburned body, his green eyes blazing, droplets of perspiration forming at the top of his broad forehead. Every muscle in her young body was tensed with pleasure. A strange half-smile played across her parted lips. Her eyes seemed pools of sperm.

Claudia and Eric took seats beside Suzanne and André as the gray-faced man led the panting dog quietly from the room. Etheus knelt at Maya's side and traced the curve of her nostril with his forefinger, then rose, and divested himself slowly of his clothing until he stood naked but for his gold chain and red stone. His body was massive, shaved clean of hair. His broad chest glistened with sweat. The veins pulsed in his neck and wrists as he placed himself between Maya's hot thighs. His penis was of an incredible size, the head of it almost the size of a light bulb. His erection was so powerful that his organ stood almost flat against his stomach, reaching slightly more than half-way to his chest.

He entered her slowly, holding her legs in the air by the ankles, feeling the curls of her pubic hair scratch against his smooth belly, the moist hairs around her hole tickling his huge shaft.

Suzanne mounted André, reaching behind herself to squeeze his hairy testicles. Claudia, her black hair tangled and damp with semen, knelt behind her and licked the crack of her soft bottom down to the lips of her moist hole. Eric positioned himself behind Claudia, spread her firm cheeks, and entered her asshole after lubricating his organ in her foamy vagina.

Etheus pushed Maya's legs back until her small bare feet were over her head. His hips resting against the backs of her thighs, he slid his tremendous organ into her until his belly pressed tightly against hers, causing her to moan as pleasure mixed with pain within her and an intense tingling sensation filled her entire body. Harder and harder, he rode her, her body shaking with orgasm after orgasm, his bunched-up foreskin tickling the contracting walls of her hole. Sweat pouring from his forehead, Etheus poured his love into Maya, his buttocks heaving rapidly in the air. Maya groaned, writhing on the cold leather couch, as cupfuls of Etheus' burning semen filled her hole to the mouth and overflowed down her smooth-muscled thighs.

Etheus withdrew his foam-covered penis from Maya's still-contracting hole. The massive organ stood straight up in the air. It seemed to have grown another two inches while inside Maya's pussy. Without so much as a pause, Etheus ordered Maya to crouch on her knees, approached her from behind, and slid the bulbous head of his penis past the rosy rim of her rear orifice. A scream escaped Maya's lips as he thrust four or five inches of his ivory shaft into her tight bottom, forcing the pink walls of her hole wide apart. The scream turned to a low groan as he jerked forward, thrusting himself deep into her innards and beginning a slow churning motion, massaging the depths of her hole with the velvety head of his massive organ.

Suzanne and Eric sat on the floor, their eyes glued to Etheus and Maya, and masturbated each other furiously. André possessed Claudia from behind, both of them holding their heads erect to watch Etheus pound into Maya's bottom

With a sudden groan, Etheus buried his penis in Maya's quivering hole and drenched her intestines with spurt after spurt of hot fluid which dripped from her distended hole down the crack of her rump and onto the sun-darkened backs of her thighs.

Again and again, Etheus possessed her, using her mouth, her vagina, her asshole, filling her with cupful after cupful of semen, this time taking her from behind, then pulling her on top of him, sucking on the large breasts which dangled in his face, placing her on her knees, on her back, against the wall. Again and again, he thrust his sturdy shaft deep within her while his disciples watched and the cameraman filmed, until finally, her lithe young body went limp and she fell into a deep sleep, her hand falling across her sopping bush, a smile playing across her slightly parted lips.

As the first rays of dawn slipped through the room's wine-colored curtains, Etheus dismissed his disciples, ordering them to bring Maya to a room where she might rest. Alone in the room, the strong odors of the evening's activity still lingering in the air about him, Etheus got slowly to his feet and began to dress himself, his massive organ still standing flat against his hard belly.

III

Slowly, Maya awoke from her sleep, sunlight flooding the room in which she lay. There was a strange, salty taste in her mouth, and a curious whirring sound coming from somewhere nearby. It seemed to Maya that she had been having strange dreams.

Suddenly, the room was plunged into semi-darkness. Maya looked up and gasped at the sight of a tall man pulling closed the room's heavy curtains. The man was dressed in a black robe and wore a gold chain with a large red stone about his neck. His green eyes blazed even in the darkness of the room.

"Who are you?" Maya gasped, her voice edging toward hysteria as confusing memories filled her brain, but just as the words escaped her lips, her attention was drawn to a large movie screen, on which flashed images ... yes ... of herself.

Maya stared in disbelief as she watched herself suck greedily on the penis of a naked blond-haired man, gasped as she noticed a second penis enter her writhing body from behind.

"No," she sobbed, "no," as she saw semen dripping from her mouth, saw herself lift it to her mouth and swallow it, an ecstatic smile on her face.

She turned to the black-robed man, tears streaming down her blushing cheeks. The man smiled at her, fingering the red stone that he wore about his neck. He gestured toward the screen with his free hand and whispered, "Watch . . ."

Maya turned helplessly back to the flickering images on the screen, saw herself being licked by a tall girl lying beneath her. Again, she turned to the black-robed man as the image faded from the screen, and again, he called her attention to the screen with a wave of his hand. Maya watched two women licking and sucking on the penis of a thin, dark-haired man, then burst into tears once against as the camera panned backwards to reveal her own naked body, her face pressed to the crotch of one of the women, her tongue thrust deep in the woman's contracting vagina. Waves of horror seized her as she watched herself move from the first woman to the second, licking each of them furiously.

"No, no, no," she moaned, as the camera panned backward once again, revealing the blond-haired man sitting behind Maya, his toe buried in her crotch.

Frozen moments passed as Maya watched herself being squeezed, licked, lifted in the air and impaled on rigid organs. Vague memories flooded her reeling brain, strange words, poignant sensations of pleasure and pain. She had been on the beach . . . and then . . .

"What's happened to me?" Maya begged of the black-robed man. "What have you done?"

Calmly, the man fingered the red stone that hung around his neck, indicating the movie screen with a small gesture of the hand.

Maya screamed as she watched a huge German Shepherd climb upon her screen image and slide his huge hairy penis into her foam-covered orifice.

"Oh, God no," she sobbed, seeing her face fill the movie screen. "God, God no." She saw her eyes roll back in her head, a mad smile fall across her lips. She buried her face in her hands.

"Watch," the black-robed man said. "You will learn . . ."

"Why have you done this to me?" Maya screamed. "Why?"

"In a matter of moments," the black-robed man said, "I will explain myself to you. For now, watch. See yourself."

Again, Maya turned to the screen. She saw a man, his back to her, tugging at the shoulders of the dog, pulling him free of her vagina. Slowly, the angle of the camera changed, until the man's face came into view. It was the man who now sat calmly at her side, fingering the red stone that dangled from his neck. Maya watched him divest himself of his dark clothing, stared fascinated at the huge organ that stood flat against his belly. A strange feeling of anticipation filled her as she watched the man's magnificent naked body walk across the screen, watched him lodge his gigantic penis within her.

"You," she whispered breathlessly as dim memories returned to her, memories of a strange, god-like man, who had filled her both with fear and admiration.

Her eyes wide, Maya watched her sweating, naked body writhe against the man's, watched herself thrusting her pelvis forward to meet his heavy lunges. She gasped as she saw the man's thick semen spill from the sides of her hole, saw him lead her to the floor and enter the tight channel of her rear orifice.

Continually, revulsion vied with attraction within her, as she watched the man possess her time and again, filling her with semen. A tickling curiosity grew in her mind as she noticed that the man's penis, even after five or six ejaculations, never lost its hardness. It was almost with disappointment that she watched the image of herself go limp with exhaustion as the film drew to its conclusion.

The black-robed man rose slowly to his feet, turned off the whirring projector, and threw open the heavy curtains. Again, terror seized Maya as she realized that she was naked, sitting in a strange room with a strange man, a man who had abducted her and forced her to participate in the most unholy of rituals.

"Who are you?" she said, her voice quavering with mounting fear.

"I am Etheus," the man said.

Yes, yes: she remembered the name.

"Even now, the dew of my love is dry on your body."

Maya looked down at her nakedness. Flakes of dried semen covered her thighs, belly, bosom and mouth.

"I, and only I," Etheus said, "am responsible for your abduction."

"Why have you done this? What are you going to do to me?" Maya shouted, her voice edging toward hysteria once again.

"Soon," Etheus said, "you will be free to go ... in a sense. I should like only to explain myself."

Abruptly, an idea entered Maya's head, and she began to gaze distractedly about the room. It was a tastefully furnished room, the walls done in pink, the ceiling in white. The man called Etheus sat in a wine-colored armchair situated next to the bed. At one end of the room, a large mirror hung from the wall, and at the opposite wall was a narrow white door.

Maya bolted for the door, but Etheus' words halted her in her tracks.

"Soon, you will be free to go," he said. "Can you not contain yourself but a few moments more?"

Maya faced him, droplets of sweat pouring down her cheeks, her breasts heaving excitedly.

"What have you done to me? What have you done to me?" she screamed. "You're mad. You're a madman ..."

"I have brought you truth," Etheus said. "You have seen the truth." He gestured toward the blank movie screen.

"Truth?" Maya screamed, "Truth? You've raped me, humiliated me ... When I ... just think ... of ... that ... that *dog* ... *I want to die!*"

"You felt pleasure," Etheus said, leaning forward, his large head resting on his hand.

"You're mad," Maya sobbed.

"You have seen the proof," Etheus said. "Can you deny that you felt pleasure?"

Maya didn't answer.

"Can you deny it?" Etheus said, his voice low.

Again, Maya was silent.

"Then hear me," Etheus said. "Hear me, and perhaps you will understand." He sat back in the wine-colored armchair, fingering the red stone that hung about his neck. "From my youth," he began, "I have been afflicted with a most peculiar ... abnormality ... not so much a malfunction as a super-function. The condition is known popularly as satyriasis. I am informed by a certain Dr. Shroeder that my case is an historic one. Look ..."

Etheus parted his black robe and Maya gasped at the sight of his huge organ, fully erected, standing flat against his belly, tied in place about his midsection with a thin silken cord. Etheus closed the robe.

"Perhaps now," he said, "you can understand the necessity of the dog ... the animal that brought you such vast pleasure ... that made you ... wish to die?" His green eyes blazed as he questioned the very depths of her being. "I am forced," he continued, "to the use of certain rather bizarre methods in order to consummate the act of love without causing great harm to my chosen partner ..." His aspect became grim. "There is ... a death on my soul," he said, his voice scarcely more than a whisper. "I am forced ... *forced* to the use of these methods. But ... on with my story ..."

Again, he paused briefly, his eyes turned inward, then continued.

"My parents," he said, "were caused great embarrassment by my condition. They were exceedingly wealthy people, and they decided that it would be best for all concerned to send me abroad. This they did, giving me a liberal allowance and occasionally writing brief letters, inquiring of my ... abnormality." He paused to indicate the gigantic penis, hidden in the folds of his robe. "I travelled all around the world, creating myths and legends wherever I went. I was sought after by both men and women, wherever I went. And then, as I have said, I killed a woman. I was drunk, maddened by liquor. As I filled her with my hot fluid, I took her dying gasps for gasps of pleasure. Perhaps ... they were ... I don't know. When I disengaged myself, she lay dead, pierced by my great organ, a pool of blood widening between her legs. I fled to this country, secluded myself as you can see. I spent futile months seeking a cure, while all the time, my house filled with disciples, men and women who had sought me from all the far corners of the globe, who had spent years searching for the man named Etheus. And I sought them. Yes. My need had to be filled..."

Maya stared wide-eyed at the man. Was he mad? Could his story be true? Time and again, the image of his fantastic penis entered her mind. His words began to have a hypnotic effect on her.

"And so, my house filled with men and women, some driven by necessity, some by inclination. My parents died shortly after I entered this country, leaving me a very wealthy man. I abandoned my futile search in favor of various precautions, one of which you have already experienced. I accepted my fate, even revelled in it ... but ... in time, I grew bored. I spent my days and nights in endless lovemaking. Always, my partners had first to be ... loosened ... made ready ... by the efforts of others, sometimes, by the efforts of my faithful pet ... sometimes, by other means. Consequently, long orgies became the order of the day, and eventually, as I have said, I became bored. Bored at watching endless foreplay, endless sexual activity, bored at the sight of naked bodies and sexual organs, bored at the very smell of love. My life had become purposeless, repetitive. I sought meaning ..." He paused, staring out the room's small window at the surrounding woods. "It was then," he said in a soft voice, "that I hit upon my present course. I ventured into the outside world, a vain attempt at alleviating my boredom. I was astounded at what I saw: narrowness, provincialism, blindness. I saw a foolish facade of respectability thrown around man's most natural desires and impulses. I determined, in whatever small way I could, to change this, and, as I had always been a lover of women, had always been a worshipper of woman's tender flesh, I focused my attention on that fair sex and devised a plan to liberate as many of their number as possible from their narrow preconceptions and prejudices. It has become my sole endeavor to bring to a state of purity those women that come into my hands. The sight of a woman writhing helplessly in the throes of new-found pleasure, the gleam in her eye as she discards her former life of sham and pretense, has become my only joy."

"This is what you want?" Maya interrupted him. "This is what you want for me? To rape me again and again, to humiliate me, until even my own degradation bores me?"

"Perhaps," Etheus said, "you will become bored. Yes, it is a possibility, although it lies in the distant future. There is much joyous exploration you have to look forward to before you become as saturated as I, who am forced to live in a state of continual excitement. And if you do, one day, become bored, then you will become even as I am now. You will draw your pleasure from the new-found joy of others. Like me, you will seek disciples, will become an instructor in the ways of the flesh. This is the way of the world . . ."

Etheus' defensiveness drew Maya back to her former indignation.

"You're nothing but a rapist," she shouted. "A kidnapper, a mad rapist . . ."

"Yes," Etheus said, quieting her with a small gesture of his left hand, "I have abducted you . . ."

"Oh," Maya sobbed, memories once again filling her head, "those men . . . those disgusting men . . ."

"Yes," Etheus said, "they are a low, ugly-minded breed, but they are necessary to my purpose. If it is any consolation to you, they are soon to be eliminated. I allow such men to serve me only five times apiece. I choose only the basest of men so that I need not trouble my conscience with the necessity of their elimination. I pay them well and have them eliminated. I consider this an act of service to the community in which they live. My purposes necessitate the employment of a great many men and women, many of whom receive other payment than money. Dr. Shroeder, for instance, enjoys a very peculiar perversion which I shall not name to you now, and Claudia, who is so helpful to me in preparing my pupils, enjoys the use of the whip. As I have said, these people are necessary to me, and thus I award them payment, on whatever their terms. Without their help, I would be quite incapable of fulfilling myself..."

Maya was overwhelmed with the strangeness of his tale. Again, she looked distractedly about the room, her eyes coming to rest on the narrow white door. She jumped from the bed, twisted the door's brass knob, and sank to her knees on the floor as she realized that the door was locked.

"Let me go," she pleaded, "Please let me go..."

"You will be free to leave very shortly," Etheus said. "I could not afford for you, nor those who have come before you, to disappear entirely from the society in which you have existed for so long. There would be questions, and with each successive disappearance, the questions would grow louder, more urgent. Men would search, and eventually, they would find me. Thus, I will allow you to leave, as I have allowed others, knowing that your return is assured."

"Return?" Maya shouted, tears streaming down her cheeks. "My return? I'll expose you for the madman that you are. I'll have you electrocuted..." At the sound of her own words, Maya felt a strange, burning sensation deep within herself, a twisting, painful feeling.

"As you must know," Etheus said, "I am too clever a man to allow that." As he spoke, he reached into the folds of his black robe and withdrew Maya's white purse. He opened the purse and withdrew two wrinkled slips of paper from it, glancing at them briefly. "Your name is Maya," Etheus said, staring at one of the cards. "A very pretty name. An unusual name. And this is your address."

He held the card up to Maya's face.

"And here, on the back, this is the address of your parents, address and telephone number . . ."

He showed Maya the words "Mom and Dad" written in her own handwriting and followed by an address and phone number.

"And this, I take it, is the address of someone very close to you."

He held the other slip of paper to her face.

"Your fiancé, perhaps. Peter, your fiancé?"

Maya tensed with anticipation as he returned the purse to her, keeping the wrinkled slips of paper in his hand.

"If for any reason you do not return here at a time which I will soon specify, the films which were made of last night's activity will be delivered to those people whom you hold most dear. As you must realize, you seem anything but a captive in those films. As for your threat of exposing me, suffice it to say that you would sooner be placed in a madhouse than believed, and that even if you were believed, only the most exhaustive search would stand even a chance of revealing this secluded place. Far simpler, Maya, for the authorities to brand you mad . . ."

Something in what Etheus had said didn't quite make sense to Maya, but her mind was too filled with the strangeness of his story to pinpoint it. She stared dazedly at her own bare feet.

"And now," Etheus said, "I must leave you. My needs have gone too long unsatisfied." He withdrew a small red card from the folds of his robe. "You will come to this place tomorrow night. Be there no later than eight o'clock. My man will meet you there and bring you to me. For now, please feel free to bathe and dress yourself at your leisure." He indicated a small bathroom that adjoined the room that they sat in. "A man will be here within the hour to take you to your home."

Etheus walked to the door, withdrew a small key from his pocket and fitted it in the keyhole. He turned, just before leaving the room, fingering the red stone that hung from his neck.

"I know that my story seems fantastic to you," he said in a soft voice. "I know that my methods may seem cruel to you. But in time, you will understand. Until tomorrow night . . ."

He turned abruptly and walked from the room, closing the white door after himself.

Maya sat at the edge of the bed in which she had slept and stared vacantly at the wall opposite her. Her mind reeled with thoughts, questions, images. Could the man's story be true? Certainly, it was fantastic, but no more fantastic than the giant organ which had been offered as proof. Continually, the image of Etheus' penis standing stiff against his belly entered Maya's head, lending credence to his bizarre tale. Could it be that she would return to this mad place? Would the strange man named Etheus actually deliver those hideous films to her parents, to Peter? Something was strange there: Etheus didn't seem the sort of man who could be motivated by a desire for revenge, and what else could be his motive?

As she realized that she was considering Etheus as something more than the mad rapist she had called him, Maya became angry with herself and dismissed her previous thoughts from her mind. He was quite mad, after all. He had raped her, humiliated her, forced her to make love to a huge dog. It was mad. The whole thing was mad. She was never to leave this lonely place. Etheus' words had only been a cruel hoax. She was a prisoner, a slave, to be used again and again by anyone that cared to have her.

Despite her growing doubts, Maya found herself entering the adjoining bathroom and running water for a bath. Within minutes, she was relaxing in a pink bathtub, washing the flakes of dried semen from her smooth skin. She could not help but admire the beauty of her naked body, the contrast of pale and sunburned flesh. Delicately, she traced the line her bikini had left across her hips, a smile playing at the corners of her mouth. She was reminded of a day long ago, a day when she had stared proudly at the reflection of her naked body in a mirror, just prior to taking a long walk in the woods.

Maya emerged from the hot tub and dried herself with a large red towel. She felt vibrant, alive, the muscles in her body tensed deliciously. She stared at herself in the mirror and was pleased with the tautness of her face and neck, the whiteness of her teeth, and brightness of her eyes. She felt like a jungle animal, like a panther. And yet, as this growing feeling of vitality coursed through her veins, she battled within herself to maintain her former sense of outrage and indignation.

Maya found her clothing folded neatly on a small dressing-table in the pink-walled room. She dressed hurriedly, conflict mounting within her, then sat down in the wine-colored armchair and looked out at the surrounding forest. On a small table to Maya's left was an ornately decorated humidor filled with imported cigarettes. She took one and lit it, inhaling deeply, then sat back in the armchair and tried to make sense of the bizarre situation in which she found herself.

As Maya snuffed out her cigarette in a red ceramic ashtray, there was a knock on the door and a short, stocky man, dressed in the uniform of a chauffeur, entered the room.

"I'm to take you home, Miss," he said. His face was expressionless. In one hand, he held a black silken handkerchief. "Do you have the card that the master gave you?"

Maya reached automatically for the pocket of her jeans. She felt the little red card and nodded to the chauffeur. Without a word, he led her from the room.

They walked through darkened hallways and down several flights of creaking stairs until they came to the vestibule. Here, the chauffeur straightened his dark cap and opened the front door with a great show of courtesy.

Outside, a black limousine gleamed against the dullness of the surrounding forest. The chauffeur held the door open for Maya, then placed the silken handkerchief over her eyes as she took her seat.

"Sorry about the blindfold, Miss," he said. "You'll be able to take it off in no time."

Maya leaned her head against the back of the seat and listened to the chauffeur start the car. Once again, words and images began to dance through her mind as the car began to move. An unceasing procession of questions without answers haunted her, frustrated her. Always, the procession came to a halt with the image of Etheus' impressive organ.

Within several minutes, the car stopped briefly, and Maya thought she heard the sound of a gate being opened, but then they were on their way again, and she didn't give it any thought. After what seemed to Maya slightly more than half an hour, the chauffeur told her that she could remove her blindfold. She did so, and was surprised to find that they were driving along residential streets. Maya had been sure that the house of Etheus lay deep in the country. But instead, she found herself staring at modest homes, at children playing on front lawns, at housewives talking over back fences. It was something of a shock to her: here she was, sitting in a car that was the property of a madman —a madman who had raped her, even more than raped her—just driving along a quiet street as if nothing had happened. She felt that she should scream for help. Yet, somehow, she didn't feel like screaming. Why was that? Yes ... the movies ... he would show the movies to her parents. That was it. Better to be quiet, to bide her time.

The chauffeur turned the car onto a main street and Maya stared out the window at bustling shopping centers filled with large, bright signs. As the car sped by, Maya caught a glimpse of a phrase written in small lettering at the bottom of one of the signs: LONG

ISLAND'S LARGEST CHAIN OF ... They passed too quickly for her to make out the rest.

"We're on Long Island, aren't we?" she asked the driver.

"I believe it says on the card where you're to come to. Isn't that right, Miss?"

Maya didn't answer. She hadn't actually looked at the card yet. Somehow, she was afraid to look at it.

The chauffeur turned onto a city-bound highway heavy with traffic. The ride became monotonous and Maya fell asleep, her head leaning against the back of the seat, her lips slightly parted. She dreamed that she was walking through the woods, when all of a sudden, all the trees burst into flame. Fire crackled through the woods, burning the dry leaves. Salamanders leaped crazily through the smoking grass, their orange backs aflame, their tiny eyes wild with pain. Maya was terrified. She whirled around and around, spinning faster and faster, desperately seeking some avenue of escape. Everywhere, there was flame. Then, as suddenly as it had begun, the fire was extinguished. The forest was completely charred, all the trees blackened by the fire. Maya seated herself in a pile of smoking leaves, stared dazedly at the ruined forest. Night fell. Again, Maya became afraid. Then, to her amazement, the trees began to glow. They glowed white at the root and red at the trunk and the branches were a strange, incandescent black. Slowly, the branches began to move, feeling for other branches, their tips crackling with energy. In her dream, Maya began to laugh. She raised her face to the miraculous trees, laughing madly, holding her pale hands to their glowing light. Then, a deep voice rumbled through the forest. Maya couldn't make out the words. What was the voice saying? Again, the deep rumble of the voice. Maya strained to make it out.

"I said, here we are, Miss. Miss . . ."

"Oh, yes. yes . . ."

"Here we are, Miss. You're home."

Maya stared out the window at the plate-glass entrance to her apartment building. She was startled at having arrived so soon. It seemed to her that she had only been asleep a few minutes.

"Yes," she said, opening the door. "Well ..." She didn't know what to say to the man. Vaguely, she recalled her previous impulse to scream. It would be proper to scream, she thought.

"I'll see you tomorrow night, Miss," the chauffeur said. "You just come to where the card says. I'll meet you there."

Maya was disturbed at the man's confidence. There seemed to be no question in his mind as to whether or not she would come.

"You're sure I'll be there, aren't you?" she said.

"All the others have come, Miss," the chauffeur said.

Maya caught his expressionless gaze in the rear-view mirror.

"Goodbye," she said.

"Until tomorrow night, Miss," the chauffeur said.

Maya stepped from the car and slammed the door. She watched the limousine travel slowly up the block and disappear into the midtown traffic. Then he turned and entered the aprtment building.

The red-faced doorman gave her a cheerful good-morning as he swung the door open for her. It took all of Maya's self-control to keep from laughing in his face. Strangely, she felt like a little girl with a secret. "I'll bet you don't know what happened to me last night," she thought as she walked past the doorman.

On her way up in the elevator, Maya actually burst out laughing. She laughed all the way to the sixth floor, forcing herself to stop as she walked down the green-and-white carpeted hallway to her door. A smile was still on her face as she turned the key in the lock and thrust the door open.

Maya heard footsteps in the apartment as she opened the door. She stood frozen in the doorway, her key still in the lock. Was it a burglar? Or some agent of Etheus' bent on murdering her? Wild thoughts filled her brain. The impulse to scream seized her once again. Then, to Maya's surprise, Peter stood facing her at the doorway to the apartment's small kitchen. His boyish face was taut with worry, his dark hair tousled as if he had been twisting it, as was his habit. His clothing—a pair of tight black slacks and a white, button-down shirt—were wrinkled and damp with sweat. His body looked even thinner than usual.

"Where have you been?" he said to her, his voice rising in anger. "Where were you?"

Maya couldn't think of an excuse. Oddly, Peter had barely entered her mind in the course of the strange events that had befallen her. It didn't even occur to her to tell him the truth.

"How did you get in here?" she said, stalling for time.

"Never mind how I got in here," he said. "Where the hell have you been?"

Droplets of perspiration dripped down the sides of Peter's thin face. Worry-lines formed on his forehead.

"Did you break in here?" Maya said, still unable to think of an excuse.

"The super let me in, O.K.?" Peter said. "Now, where in hell were you?"

"I went to visit my parents," Maya said. She let the apartment door close behind her.

"I called your parents," Peter said. "They said you weren't there..."

Maya searched her brain for an excuse.

"I told them to say I wasn't there," she said. "I was angry at you." She walked into the kitchen, put water on for coffee. "Do you want a cup of coffee?" she said. The familiar white walls of the kitchen gave her confidence.

"I don't believe you," Peter said after a pause.

"All right," Maya said. "Don't believe me."

"There was no reason for you to be angry," Peter said.

"No reason?" Maya said. "Don't you remember? You asked me to pose for those filthy pictures..."

Somewhere inside her, Maya felt disgusted at herself. She dismissed the feeling hastily. How could he ask her to pose for those pictures? And what business was it of his where she had been?

"You're so childish," Peter said. "Don't you understand that you're beautiful? I only want to take pictures of you because you're beautiful..."

"Do you want a cup of coffee?" Maya asked him again.

"O.K.," he said, after a pause.

Peter sat down at the kitchen table, twisting his hair into knots. He stared at Maya's tight buttocks as she pured two cups of coffee.

"You were really at your parents' house?" he said as Maya placed a cup of steaming coffee before him.

"Yes," Maya said. "I was angry at you. You knew I was angry. I wanted to be by myself for awhile."

Maya sat down opposite Peter and sipped her coffee. Peter did likewise, staring into Maya's green-blue eyes.

"Why did you tell them to tell me you weren't there?" Peter said.

"I told you," Maya said, her voice soft, almost edging toward laughter, "I was angry at you. I didn't want to talk to you."

"Why do you get so angry?" Peter said, still twisting his hair. "You're not a little girl anymore, you know?"

Again, Maya was seized with the impulse to laugh, but suddenly a strange object in the room caught her eye: a brown paper bag crumpled into a roughly rectangular shape rested on the kitchen counter.

"What's in the bag?" Maya said.

Peter started to look up, then stopped.

"Nothing," he said.

Maya stood up and started to walk toward the counter.

"What's in it?" she said.

"I said, nothing's in it," Peter said. His tone was grim.

Maya paused, then turned toward the bag once again.

77

"Don't look in the bag," Peter said. "It's something I don't want you to see . . ."

"All right," Maya said. "I don't want to pry."

She sat down at the table and drank the rest of her coffee. The contents of the bag obsessed her. She was determined to have a look at it. She stood up and ran her fingers through Peter's thick hair.

"I'm going to change my clothes, baby," she said. "Be with you in a minute . . ."

Maya walked through a blue-carpeted hallway to her bedroom. It was a small room, done in white and yellow, furnished with a single bed, a low dresser, and an antique vanity. Maya undressed, stuffing her green bikini in the bottom drawer of the dresser. She stared at herself in the mirror of the vanity, hands on her hips; she turned from side to side, staring at her naked body from various angles, enjoying the sight of her swelling curves, the tautness of her muscles. Despite the heat and humidity, her nipples were powerfully erected, the flesh hard and bumpy, the long tips pointed upwards. Maya felt her pussy throb and grow moist. She paced back and forth in the little room, rubbing the cheeks of her rump with both hands. She wanted to run from the room and grab Peter by his cute ivory prick, but something within her resisted the impulse. Still, she became hotter with each passing moment, until finally, she was mad with desire, unable to resist the needs of her flesh. She went to her closet and took a pink robe from its hanger, started to put it on, then cast it to the floor of the closet, and walked naked from the room, the image of Etheus' penis in her mind.

Peter stared dumbly at her as she entered the kitchen, her slim hips rotating as she walked.

"I've missed you, Peter," she said, thrusting her hot bush against his cheek. She spoke as one possessed, her voice like the softest velvet.

Peter groaned and grabbed her buttocks in his hands. She opened her legs, clasping him around the neck, and rubbed her slit against his lips until her clitoris stiffened and found its way into his mouth. Peter sucked it wildly, licked it with his tongue as he ran his fingers up and down the crack of her rump. Maya swayed back and forth, teasing him by withdrawing the pink clitoris from his mouth, making him dive for it.

"Good baby," she said to him. "Suck that pink little thing like a good baby . . . suck it nice . . . good baby . . ."

Maya bent toward him and buried his face in her smooth breasts.

"Suck the nice big titty," she said, guiding his lips to her stiff nipple. "Suck it, suck it, suck it . . ."

Peter sucked half of her breast into his mouth, pawing at the other with both hands. Maya panted with desire. She pulled him to his feet, unzipped his pants, reached inside and withdrew his plump, pretty penis. She squeezed it with both hands thrusting her tongue deep in his mouth as she did so. His penis stiffened in her hands, the head swelling with each squeeze. Maya pulled back the foreskin, and watched a small drop of clear liquid form at the tip. She got to her knees and took the head into her mouth, licking up the sticky fluid and swallowing it. Peter groaned and pushed her head way down on his twitching penis. Maya made strange, animal-like sounds as she took the penis deep into her throat, squeezing Peter's small testicles with both hands.

"Let's fuck," Peter said breathlessly, pulling his saliva-coated cock from her mouth.

"Hmm," Maya said, "you want to fuck?" She raised one finger to her lips, teasing him unmercifully. "I don't know if I want to," she said. "Let me see you naked first."

Peter tore off his clothing, stood naked before her, his prick rising in the air. Maya leaned against the kitchen counter, her eyes glued to his prick, one hand stroking her slit.

"Well," Maya said after a pause, "I tell you what.

I'll let you fuck me . . . if you'll lick my asshole first. Is it a deal?"

She bent before him, thrusting her buttocks high in the air, spreading the cheeks with both hands. Peter fell to his knees and licked her crack up and down, holding her by the hips. Maya spread her cheeks still wider, forced his lips to the rim of her asshole.

"Stick your tongue in there," she said. "Stick your tongue in . . ."

Peter inserted his tongue in the tight hole, feeling the sparse hairs that surrounded it tickle his nose and lips.

"Deeper," Maya moaned, "deeper, deeper . . "

Peter thrust his tongue as deep into her as it would go, swirled it around and around, moved it back and forth. Maya pulled away from him, panting, and lay down on the floor.

"Eat me," she said, spreading her legs and raising them high in the air. Her own words and actions were strange to her, but she was powerless to resist the force that burned within her.

Peter flung himself on top of her, his hard penis smacking against her cheek as he buried his tongue in her dripping hole. Maya pulled his penis into her mouth as she felt his tongue probe her moist depths, tickling the contracting walls of her hole. Inch by inch, she took the penis into her mouth until she had it all. The swollen head was lodged deep in her throat. Her lips rubbed against Peter's scratchy pubic hair. She bit it, chewed it, sucked it, licked it, all the while pushing her hot hole harder and harder against his face. Intoxicated with the feeling of having Peter's entire prick within her mouth, Maya reached forward and spread the cheeks of his little boy's rump, inserting just the tip of her middle finger into his tight asshole. She worked the finger deeper and deeper, felt his prick grow harder with each turn of her finger.

Peter tore himself from her.

"I want to fuck you," he said.

Maya's answer was automatic.

"Fuck me between the tits first," she said.

Peter squatted on Maya's chest. She squeezed his cock between her large breasts and felt his buttocks rub against her midsection as he jerked backwards and forwards, felt her own saliva lubricate the valley of her smooth mounds. As each thrust brought Peter's cock in contact with her face, Maya took the head into her mouth and gave it a quick lick before it was withdrawn. Finally, she grabbed his cock in her hands and forced him to a halt.

"Now you can fuck me in the cunt," she said.

She got to her feet, still holding him by the penis, and pulled him through the blue-carpeted hallway into the yellow-and-white bedroom, squeezing him as she walked. She started to lead him to the bed, then stopped and faced him, a smile forming on her lips.

"Would you like to fuck me from behind?" he said.

Peter groaned and closed his eyes in answer.

Maya walked to the open bedroom window. She stuck her head out the window and leaned her elbows on the windowsill, spreading her legs and exposing her golden-haired hole between the backs of her thighs.

"Put it in," she said to Peter, wiggling her tight little rump.

She stared out the window, looking down at the slow-moving traffic, the figures of men and women in the street. She felt the head of Peter's ivory cock slip easily into her hole, then inch after inch of the bone-hard shaft, until she had it all inside her. She felt Peter's small testicles bounce against the backs of her legs, felt his pubic hair scratch her upraised buttocks. She squeezed her pussy around his hard cock, trying to pull it even more deeply into her hole. Peter began thrusting in and out of her and Maya responded with a slow circular motion, raising herself on tiptoe to meet his violent thrusts.

A long-haired delivery boy saw Maya from the street and waved up at her, a broad smile on his face. Maya smiled back and made a small gesture of her hand, hoping that Peter wouldn't notice. Maya was seized with the impulse to laugh. If only the delivery boy knew what she was doing, she thought. If only Peter knew what had happened to her only hours ago. If only everybody knew...

"Harder, Peter, harder," she said, reaching between her legs to squeeze his hairy testicles.

Peter drove violently in and out of her, his belly making a smacking noise against her buttocks as their naked bodies collided. Maya felt herself nearing orgasm. She reached behind herself and grabbed Peter by the hips, pulling him in and out, in and out of her greedy hole. Then, as her climax approached, as she found herself wishing that she could go naked into the street, lie on the hood of a car and take on anyone that wanted her, Maya sensed that something wasn't right. A frenzied frustration gripped her as she realized that Peter's cock was going soft within her. She pulled him harder and harder to her grinding buttocks, made animal sounds in the throat, but it was to no avail. The penis grew smaller and smaller within her until finally it slipped out and lodged in the moist crack of her rump.

Peter stood silently behind her for a time, rubbing his foam-dripping penis in the crack of her ass. Then he stepped back as she turned to face him, her eyes begging him to somehow grow hard again. Maya stood in front of the open window, half-hoping that someone would see her and come up to her apartment and throw her on the floor and bring her to orgasm after orgasm. Not realizing what she was doing, she squeezed her thighs rhythmically around her hot vagina.

Peter threw himself on the bed, his thin legs pressed tightly together, and buried his face in the pillow. Maya stared at him for a while, not knowing what to do. Then she sat beside him on the bed rubbing her pussy with one hand and lightly tracing the curve of his buttocks with the other.

"Peter..." she said.

He didn't answer.

"What's the matter, Peter?" she said, her voice soft and loving.

Peter buried his face deeper in the pillow.

"Don't you like to fuck me?" she said. "Don't you like my cunt?"

She waited for Peter to answer, staring at his smooth back and squeezing his buttocks with both hands.

"I love your prick," she said. Then, after a pause: "Why don't you answer me?"

Maya spread the cheeks of Peter's ass and pressed her lips to his pink asshole. She tickled the rim with her tongue, then thrust her tongue inside him, lapping at the motionless walls of his hole. With one hand, she squeezed his balls and stroked his shrivelled penis.

"I love your asshole," she said, still licking, "and I love your prick, and I love your balls . . ."

"Leave me alone," Peter muttered. "Leave me alone . . ."

"I thought about everything," Maya said. "I thought about everything we always fight about . . . when I was with my parents . . . and I'm really sorry about everything. I mean, I was wrong . . . I was wrong all the time. I was stupid. I want to do whatever you want, Peter . . . whatever you want . . ."

"Leave me alone," Peter said.

Maya left the bed and sat on the floor, the woolly yellow carpet tickling her rump. She was raging hot, willing—eager—to do anything. She fingered herself, whipping herself to a froth, staring at Peter's little boy's buttocks. She had to have a cock inside her. She *had* to . . .

Maya got to her feet and left the room. She walked quickly into the kitchen, her breasts bouncing with each step, and opened the refrigerator door. She peered into the refrigerator, her flesh tingling with the coolness of the air, and . . . *yes,* thank God, it was there . . .

Maya withdrew a pressurized can of whipped-cream from the bottom shelf of the refrigerator and broke off the red plastic top. This would do it, she thought. This would give him a nice big hard-on to fuck her with.

She closed the refrigerator door and walked to the kitchen table. She shook the can for a few seconds, then braced her leg over the back of one of the kitchen chairs. On a mad impulse born of her frenzied desire, she tore open the kitchen curtains, hoping that someone in one of the buildings opposite hers would see her. She took the can in one hand, her forefinger pressed to the white plastic nozzle, and placed the end of the nozzle at the opening of her pussy. Her eyes closed, she pressed the nozzle, filling her hole with the cold whipped-cream. She squirted the squishy cream into her pussy until it overflowed and splattered on the white linoleum floor. Then she covered her slit and bush with it, even squirting a drop into her almond-shaped navel. Excited by her own mad actions, Maya filled her asshole with cream, finally squirting two drops onto her taut nipples and half-throwing the can back into the refrigerator.

She walked quickly back into the bedroom, enjoying the feeling of the cold whipped-cream as it squished inside her pussy and anus.

"Peter . . ." she said.

Peter didn't answer.

"Turn around, Peter," she said. "I have a little treat for you."

He didn't move.

Maya went to the bed, grabbed him by the shoulders and turned him over on his back. He started to shout at her, then saw the whipped cream dripping from her pussy, navel and nipples.

"Lick it up, baby," she said, squatting over him and thrusting her cream-covered bush in his face. Peter groaned as Maya reached backwards and grabbed his cock in her hand. As Peter lapped up the sweet whipped-cream, Maya felt his cock stiffen to its former size. Afraid that his erection might go away again, Maya slid down his belly, rubbing the half-eaten cream on his smooth skin, and pulled his hard staff into her cream-filled hole. Not wasting a minute, she began pumping up and down on his cock, moaning with ecstasy as she felt her orgasm begin. Whipped-cream flew in the air as her buttocks slapped against his thighs, her entire body jerking wildly with the force of her orgasm.

Still coming, Maya tore herself from Peter and bent forward on the floor, her buttocks raised in the air.

"Fuck me in the ass," she said breathlessly. "Fuck me in the ass, Peter, fuck me in the ass . . ."

Peter got on his knees behind her and forced the head of his cock into her creamy anus.

"Shove it all in," Maya panted. "Shove the whole thing in . . ."

With one tremendous thrust, Peter buried his cock deep inside her. Maya felt his hot semen mix with the cold whipped-cream as he twirled his prick around and around in her asshole.

"Oh, God," she said, "Oh, God," as she felt herself come again and again.

Finally, when she had squeezed every drop of fluid from Peter's shrivelling cock, Maya fell forward on the yellow carpet and buried her face in the crook of her arm. Totally spent now, she was at a loss to understand her strange behavior. How could she have acted as she had? Like a crazy, crazy whore. How could she have done those ugly things? Even *ask* to do them? Like a whore. She remembered the hot words that had escaped her lips, felt the remnants of the sticky cream inside her, and she burned with shame. Was she truly going mad?

Peter lay at her side, one hand stroking her cream-smeared buttocks. Breathing softly, he spread her cheeks and inserted his middle finger into her rosebud of an asshole. He scooped out some whipped-cream and licked it from his finger, then inserted his finger once again.

"Stop that," Maya said. "Don't do that."

"What's the matter?" Peter siad.

"Don't do that," Maya said.

Peter withdrew his cream-and-semen-covered finger and held it to Maya's lips.

"Have some whipped-cream," he said, laughing.

"Stop it, Peter," she said.

"What's wrong?"

"Nothing. Just don't do that . . ."

"O.K. But why not?"

Maya didn't want to talk to him. She didn't know what to say. She felt estranged from herself, was unable to choose between the two very distinct personalities that vied with each other within her. Her mood was in a constant state of flux, her intellect unable to place any reasonable interpretation on what was happening to her. Suddenly, she got to her feet.

"I'm going to have something to drink," she said to Peter. "Do you want anything?"

"No," Peter said. Then, as she turned to leave the room: "Maya . . ."

"I'll be back in a minute," Maya said without stopping.

She walked into the kitchen, drawing the curtains closed immediately as she remembered how she had displayed herself in front of the window. She went to the refrigerator and took out a container of orange juice, trying not to look at the messy can of whipped-cream that lay on its side on the bottom shelf of the refrigerator. She took a small red-and-white striped glass from the kitchen cabinet and poured some orange juice into it, then sat at the kitchen table and sipped the juice, trying to restore order to her mind. Her brain wandered hopelessly. She thought of Etheus and his disciples, of the confident chauffeur, of her own erratic behavior, of Peter's growing impotence . . . Suddenly, she remembered the brown package on the kitchen counter. She turned to make sure it was still there, then rose quietly to her feet, listening for sounds from the bedroom. She walked to the counter and took the package in her hands. It was heavy, hard. She couldn't imagine what was inside it. Very carefully, she opened the package and peeked inside it. The package contained a shiny revolver. Maya gasped and dropped it to the floor.

"Maya," Peter called from the bedroom. "What was that, Maya?"

"What are you doing with a gun?" Maya screamed, running into the bedroom. "What are you doing with a gun?"

"I told you not to open that package," Peter said, sitting up in bed and staring at her angrily.

"What are you doing with that gun?" Maya shouted again. "Tell me what that gun is for..."

"You weren't supposed to open that package," Peter said. "I told you not to open it..."

"Are you going to shoot somebody? That's what guns are for, Peter. Are you going to shoot somebody? Are you going to shoot me, Peter?"

"No," Peter said, his voice somewhat softer. He turned away from her and stared out the window at the slow-moving traffic.

"Peter," Maya leaded, "tell me what you're doing with the gun. I'm afraid, Peter..."

Peter remained silent, tapping his fingers lightly on the windowsill.

"Please tell me, Peter. I'm frightened..."

"Please don't ask me," Peter said.

"You wanted to kill me, didn't you?" Maya said, her voice quavering with fear. "Didn't you? Peter... I'm afraid of you..."

Peter sighed, his head bowed.

"I was... going to kill myself," he said.

"Kill yourself?" Maya shouted. "Why were you going to kill yourself? Are you crazy?"

Peter turned suddenly and faced her, his thin figure silhouetted by the afternoon sunlight that streamed in the window.

"I didn't know what to do," he said, his voice high and cracking. "I don't know what's the matter with me ... I don't know. Everytime I ... fuck you ... it gets ... soft. I don't know. It's been driving me crazy ... just crazy ... You went away .. you were gone. I didn't know what to do ... I bought the gun. I ... just don't know what's wrong with me. I just don't know ..."

Maya stared at him for a few seconds, her arms limp at her sides, her mouth open. She watched tears well up in his large eyes and roll quickly down his smooth cheeks. She went to him and wrapped her slender arms around his back and waist and squeezed him with all of her strength.

"I love you, Peter," she said. "Don't you know that I love you?"

Peter sobbed against her shoulder for a few seconds, then pulled away and stared out the window again. Maya put her arm around his shoulder, then gently rubbed his back.

"Don't ever think about that," she said. "About killing yourself."

"I don't know," he said after a pause. "I just don't know ..."

"Just don't ever think about killing yourself. I love you, Peter. I don't want you to kill yourself. Promise me you won't think about it anymore ..."

Peter turned and faced her, his body relaxing somewhat.

"Promise me," Maya said.

"I promise," Peter said.

He left the room and disappeared down the blue-carpeted hallway. Maya followed him and found him in the kitchen pulling on his black slacks.

"Are you leaving?" Maya said.

"Yes," he answered, his voice very soft.

"Don't go," Maya said.

"I want to be by myself. I want to think about things."

Maya didn't want him to go, but she felt that it would be selfish of her to stop him. She watched him button his white shirt and tuck it into his pants.

"I'll come back tomorrow night after work," Peter said, pulling on his cordovan loafers.

Something clicked in Maya's brain: Tomorrow night. Etheus.

"O.K.?" Peter said. "Tomorrow night?"

Maya couldn't think of an excuse. Even as she racked her brain for an answer, she told herself that she was mad for even thinking of going back to Etheus' isolated house.

"Fine," she said, pretending to herself that she would definitely be at home, but inwardly putting her decision off until later, rationalizing that she could always call Peter at work.

She walked Peter to the door, hiding behind it as he opened it, afraid that someone in the hall might see her naked. She kissed him goodbye and closed the door after him, watching him through the little door-viewer until he disapeared into the elevator. Then she walked into the kitchen and poured another glass of orange juice, sipping it slowly as she stared at the brown package on the floor. She finished the orange juice and left the room, leaving the package where it had fallen.

Maya walked into the living-room of her apartment and seated herself on a blue vinyl sofa. She took a fashion magazine from the coffee table and thumbed rapidly through its pages, casting it down only seconds after picking it up. She stood up and paced nervously through the apartment, her mind flitting from image to image, from idea to idea: She would tell Peter the whole terrible story. No. She would leave Peter and go someplace where no one knew her. No. She would call the police. No, no, no. Etheus. She saw the picture of Etheus.

Maya walked into her bedroom and stared at her reflection in the mirror of the vanity. Whipped-cream dripped from her breasts and thighs. Her long hair was damp and tangled. Her body smelled of sweat and semen and vaginal foam and whipped cream.

She went into the bathroom and ran water for a bath. The shaggy orange bathroom mat felt good on her naked feet. The wisps of steam rising in the white-and-black tiled bathroom relaxed her, filled her with a sensation of warmth and security. She left the bathroom and walked lazily through the apartment, tidying whatever odds and ends she could find, then returned to the bathroom and lowered herself into the hot tub. She lay perfectly still in the tub, her legs bent, her head thrown back, her full lips slightly parted. She listened to the slow dripping of the water, the evening sounds of traffic in the street.

Slowly, she began to soap herself, first her feet and legs, then her belly and breasts. As she rubbed the slippery soap over the pink lips of her vagina, she felt an involuntary tremor run through her body. She ignored it, and continued soaping herself, as wave after wave of warm pleasure washed over her body. Maya wrenched her hand from her thighs. What was wrong with her? After all, she was only trying to clean herself. She lay still in the tub, determined not to give in to the strong compulsion to stroke herself. Yet, after a time, she found herself powerless to resist, and her hand moved, almost of its own accord, to her throbbing sex. She stroked it wildly, trying, in her mind, to capture all the impressions of her afternoon with Peter. She saw his mouth pressed to the lips of her vagina, his hands roaming over her naked body. As the movements of her hand became more and more frenzied, the bath water splashed up and down around her, streams of it spilling over the sides of the tub. Then, abruptly, she tore her hand from her hot sex and stood up in the tub. This time, she would not give in. She would not.

She stepped out of the tub and dried herself with a white towel, rubbing it roughly against her body in an effort to focus her attention on pain rather than pleasure. She let the water run out of the tub, hung the towel on its black rack, and left the room.

She entered her bedroom and sat at the edge of her bed, staring vacantly out the small window. It was dark outside. In the apartment buildings across the street Maya could see families sitting down to dinner, sitting in their living-rooms and watching television. How strange it was to see people going about their business, doing the common things that occupied them every day of their lives. Maya spent a long time staring out the window, her mind a blank, her hands resting placidly on her muscular thighs. Eventually, a powerful exhaustion possessed her, and she stood up, turned off the light, and got into bed.

As she lay in bed, Maya found herself absentmindedly stroking her belly and thighs, remembering scenes from the movies that Etheus had shown her. She saw herself crouched behind a dark-haired woman, licking the crack of her shapely rump. She saw a blond-haired man lifting her up and down on his long penis while another man entered her from behind.

With an effort, Maya turned over on her stomach and buried her head in the pillow. Within a few minutes, she was asleep.

IV

Maya's sleep was restless, troubled by strange dreams. She felt herself falling through space, her white dress flying over her head. She wore no underpants, and as she tumbled head-over-heels through the air, she felt a hot breeze waft over her golden bush from somewhere far below. Even as she fell, she felt a burning shame at her exposure. With her left hand, she groped for some object with which to stop her fall, while with her right, she sought desperately to pull her dress down over her thighs. Her left hand slid along a slippery, porous wall of some kind, a wall that moved when she touched it, then snapped back into place when she withdrew her hand. Her efforts with regard to her dress were similarly disappointing. She found herself gripping her plump vagina time and again, her hand unable to find the wispy fabric of her white dress, and she burned with an even greater shame.

After what seemed hours of falling, Maya found herself sinking into an odd spongy substance which stretched with her falling body, then snapped back to its original shape, throwing Maya several feet into the air. As she bounced up and down on the spongy substance, Maya felt a sensation of warmth course through her. She was reminded of a trampoline she had once bounced on as a child. Then, as she came to a gradual halt, Maya became filled with revulsion. The substance beneath her oozed a thick, slippery fluid. Her bare bottom was sticky with it. The odor of pus and stanched blood was heavy in the air. Maya felt that she was sitting on a huge wound of some sort, on a festering sore. With a sudden, involuntary jerk of her entire body, Maya retched. Streams of a hot, red liquid poured from her lips. Had she been drinking wine? Maya couldn't remember.

"Ruined," Maya whispered, looking down at her stained dress, still choking on her vomit. "Ruined, and can't be cleaned." Then, oddly, she began to laugh, her head thrown back, her whole body shaking with her laughter. "An ugly dress," she gasped between bursts of laughter. "It was an ugly dress . . ."

Then, a foreign voice surrounded Maya. The voice had no texture. It was like liquid.

"Dressed in red," the voice said. "Dressed in red when we met."

Maya peered into the darkness. Was it Etheus? Was it Etheus that spoke? A dim, green light glowed at an indeterminable distance. Slowly, the figure of a man came into view, his body illuminated by the small green light. At first, the man seemed huge, his body cloaked in black, but as Maya stared at him, it occurred to her that he might be smaller than he seemed . . . and . . . yes . . . he seemed naked from the waist up. Somehow, Maya felt that he might be a very young man. Or, was he naked? Was he naked, and very slender, his body hairless? Was it Etheus that she saw? Or the simple, dark-haired boy she had met long ago in the woods? Or . . . was it Peter? How was she to know who it was? How could she know what to do?

Slowly, the man stepped backward, beckoning to Maya with his long forefinger. Abruptly, a thought occurred to her: She would go to the man and . . . yes . . . she would look at his penis. It was the only way she could know. If the penis was completely erected, tied about the man's waist by a thin black cord, it would be Etheus. If it was long and thick, bulging along the man's thigh, it would be the simple boy from the country. And, if small and limp, she would know it was Peter.

Maya got to her feet and approached the man as he inched slowly away from the green light. It seemed hours before she reached him, her bare feet sinking deep into the porous substance beneath her, sticking to its slippery secretion. Finally, she stood facing the man. Once again, she tried to pull her dress over her thighs, but found that the bottom of the dress had disappeared altogether. From navel to toes, Maya was naked. She felt ashamed of her impulse to examine the man's penis. Blushing, she stared up at his face. He seemed to be wearing a black hood of some sort. Only his eyes were visible, his pupils reflecting the dim green light that glowed somewhere behind Maya's back. She couldn't remember having passed the green light, although it was certain that she had done so.

"Yes," the man said as Maya stared up at him. "Yes, you will see something there." He nodded toward his groin.

Maya hesitated for a few seconds, then reached toward the man's genitals. Her fingers found a cold, metal zipper, and she pulled on it, her entire body tingling with anticipation. As she yanked the zipper open, she thrust her hand inside, but she felt only coarse pubic hair. She pulled the zipper further and reached inside. Again, only coarse hair, scratching her slender fingers. Further and further, she opened the zipper, more and more desperately she groped for the warm flesh of the man's penis. Still, she felt only hair. The zipper seemed yards long, then longer and longer still as Maya found herself once again suspended in space, the cold metal zipper—grown huge now—the only thing keeping her from falling to her death. She groped frantically for the meaty penis, convinced that it was the only thing that might save her from certain death. She touched only hair, hair and more hair, and when she pulled at it, clumps of it came out in her hands, tickling her face as it fell through the air. Faster and faster, Maya plunged downward, pulling the cold metal tab of the zipper with her, until finally, after what seemed a distance of a mile or more, the zipper reached its end. Maya lost her hold and fell several yards to a soft, muddy place.

Her legs and rump half buried in mud, Maya looked desperately about, seeking some avenue of escape. Just ahead of her, to her utter amazement, she saw two gigantic feet planted in the thick mud, the unbelievable length of zipper curled between them. Swinging her gaze upward from the feet, Maya beheld two huge, muscular legs rising into the darkness, a pillar-like phallus dangling between them. The rest of the man's body was hidden in the darkness. Or ... were those black clouds that surrounded the torso and head?

Maya became frantically confused. What could account for this giant that stood before her? Had she shrunk to so tiny a size that what was only a man seemed to her a giant? Or, had the man actually grown to such astounding proportions? Who was out of size here? Or had they both been transformed?

Above her, Maya saw the huge penis rise slowly into the air. It made a soft, swooshing sound as it rose, like a mute bird. A huge droplet of clear liquid formed at the tip of the penis, shimmering in the air above Maya's tiny body. Slowly, the liquid began to fall. Maya jumped to her feet, trying desperately to escape the gigantic droplet, but again and again she slipped in the squishy mud until her entire body was covered with it. The droplet fell, bathing Maya in warm, sticky fluid, cleansing her of the mud. A tingling sensation ran through Maya's body. The smell of jasmine rose from her oil-dripping body. She reached her arms upward in a vain attempt to squeeze the gigantic phallus that twitched in the air above her, and as she did so, bucketfuls of semen spurted from the penis and formed a deep pool around Maya. She found herself treading water to stay afloat, her arms moving with difficulty through the thick, hot liquid. The semen was a shimmering white color, a pearl-like color, or was it . . . yes . . . it *was* liquid pearl. She was floating in liquid pearl.

"Pearl," Maya said, her voice high with pleasure.

"Dew," a deep voice from far above her answered.

"Pearl," Maya said, somewhat annoyed at the voice.

Abruptly, the pool turned a deep reddish color.

"Blood," Maya gasped, her eyes closing. "Oh, blood . . ."

Again, the voice: "Wine . . . wine . . ."

"Oh, blood," said Maya. "Blood . . ."

The pool turned a deep black. Maya couldn't gauge its depth, couldn't detect its substance. She raised her head to the huge figure of the man.

"What is this that covers me?" she said, her voice quavering with fear.

As if in answer, explosions of light suddenly filled the sky, forcing Maya to lower her eyes. When she was able to raise her head once again, Maya found herself staring at the backs of the man's legs. Slowly, the man walked into the distance, each of his footsteps causing waves to rise in Maya's black pool. He walked further and further into the distance until he seemed to be the exact size of Maya. His entire body was visible now. He was entirely naked, his body flushed and sweaty as if greatly excited. With a small gasp, Maya noticed a shiny gray revolver thrust into the man's anus. With a slow, painful gesture, the man reached behind himself and withdrew the shiny revolver. A tiny droplet of blood formed at the rim of his anus and dripped down the back of his thigh.

"Blood," the man said without turning. He continued walking until he disappeared into the surrounding blackness.

Maya turned around and around, seeking the dim green light she had seen before. The light was gone; there was only blackness. The blackness swirled around Maya, enveloping her entirely. It became impossible for Maya to distinguish the blackness of her pool from the blackness of the air, and finally, the outlines of her body merged with the blackness until she felt herself become a part of it, felt herself disappear.

Maya's sleep became numb, empty of sensation, empty of dreams.

"Hurry, hurry. It's late . . . ."

Maya sat bolt upright in bed, her hand to her chest, her breasts heaving.

"Yes," she said. "Yes, I'm sorry."

Then she shook her head and looked quickly about the room. The room was empty; there was no one there. Maya cupped her head in her hands. Could it be that she was hearing voices now? Was she going mad? No, it must only have been a dream, a nightmare of some sort.

Maya stood up and stretched, feeling the muscles tauten in her arms and legs. She yawned, and a ringlet of golden hair fell across her eye. She brushed it away and stared vacantly down at the bed she had slept in. The sheets were crumpled, damp with perspiration. The pillow had fallen to the floor. Maya yawned a second time and walked to the window, throwing open the curtains. Outside, the sun was orange as it set behind the skyscrapers in the distance. Afternoon shadows stretched across the city. Well-dressed men and women walked briskly up and down the streets, their arms swinging at their sides.

Maya stared at a green metal alarm clock that stood on her vanity. It was five-thirty. Maya picked up the clock, held it to her ear. Yes . . . it was working, ticking away. It was five-thirty. She would have to hurry. There was little time. She had only until eight o'clock.

Maya hurried to her closet and put on a yellow terry robe. She couldn't find the belt to the robe—she had no time to look for it—and she walked from the room with the robe open, its edges brushing against her naked hips.

She entered the kitchen and made a cup of instant coffee, drinking it hurriedly, burning her tongue with each sip. She took a package of filtered cigarettes from the kitchen drawer, opened it, and lit one of the cigarettes, inhaling deeply, exhaling through her flared nostrils. With a slight start, she noticed the brown package that lay on the kitchen floor. The thought of the gun stirred some vague memory within her, but she was in too much of a hurry to attempt to pinpoint it. There was no time. She would have to leave within an hour, an hour and a half at most. There was simply no time.

Maya rushed into the bedroom, cigarette dangling from her full lips. The edges of her terry-cloth robe brushed against the sides of her breasts as she walked. Inside the white-and-yellow bedroom, Maya threw open her closet door and rummaged through her clothing for something to wear. Suddenly, she stopped, one hand on the waist of a white silk dress. What in God's name was she doing? What sort of madness was it that compelled her to prepare herself for a return to the house of Etheus? And to think: she hadn't even questioned the compulsion.

Maya sat down on the edge of her bed. She lit a second cigarette with the glowing tip of the first, then put out the first in a pink enamel ashtray that rested on a small mahogany night-table. No, she thought, she wouldn't return to the isolated house. But ... the films. Etheus would send the films to her parents, or would he? It didn't make any sense. She didn't know what to do.

Maya stood up and paced around the room, the edges of her open robe caressing her naked hips and thighs. Droplets of sweat trickled from her golden-haired armpits. She was hopelessly confused, but even in the midst of her confusion, she found herself worrying about the lateness of the hour.

Then, abruptly, Maya's flow of thought was interrupted by the insistent ringing of the telephone. It had to be Peter. He always called at this time.

Maya ran into the kitchen, her bare feet making a soft sound against the hallway's blue carpet. She reached for the phone, then stopped, her arm poised in mid-air. What could she say to Peter? She hadn't had time to think of an excuse, didn't even know whether an excuse was necessary or not. She would wait. Peter would call again. She would speak to him then, after she had reached a decision. The phone rang ten times, then stopped.

Maya walked into the bathroom. She dropped her yellow robe to the black-and-white tiled floor and turned on the shower, absent-mindedly rubbing her buttocks as she adjusted the hot and cold faucets. She had decided to prepare herself in any event. She would make her decision later, but she had to be ready in case she decided to go. There was so little time.

Maya took a quick shower, then dried herself with a red-and-white striped towel. She walked into her bedroom and brushed her long golden-brown hair, staring at her reflection in the mirror that stood atop her vanity. She opened the top drawer of the vanity and withdrew a light beige lipstick and a flat, circular container of eye-shadow. She started to apply the lipstick, forcing her lips into a pout, when a small, whisper of a voice tickled at her brain.

"You should be naked," the voice said.

Maya threw the make-up back into the vanity drawer. Better to be natural, she thought. Then, impulsively, she seized a small vial of perfume from the top of the vanity. She placed a drop of perfume under each armpit, and then, without understanding her own action, she stood up, braced one leg on the seat of her chair, and placed a tiny drop of the perfume at the top of her pink slit.

Maya glanced at the clock. Six-thirty. No time. She would have to leave by seven at the very latest. At the very latest. *If* . . . yes *if* she decided to leave.

She opened the top drawer of her dresser and rummaged among her underclothes. She chose a pair of sheer white underpants and a matching, non-restrictive bra. She pulled the panties over her smooth, sun-bronzed legs and stood back to admire herself in the mirror. Her golden bush was clearly visible through the sheer fabric of the panties. Then, as she hooked the brassiere behind her back, fastening it at the third row of hooks to allow her full breasts the greatest possible freedom, small lines of worry crossed her smooth forehead. What in God's name was she doing? Was it possible that she was trying to make herself as attractive as possible ... for the mad Etheus? For the man who had raped her, threatened her?

In a moment of frustration, Maya wrenched the panties down to her ankles, then stopped, as abruptly as she had begun, and pulled them back up to her hips. After all, she hadn't made a decision. Quite possible that she would spend the night with Peter, and, if that were to be the case, there was certainly no harm in her looking her best ... her most alluring. Peter needed that ..."

Again, Maya rummaged through the top drawer of her dresser. She chose a pair of textured pink stockings and a narrow white garter belt. She fastened the garter belt snugly about her muscular belly, then sat on the edge of the bed to slip on the stockings. As she smoothed the second stocking around her sloping calf, she caught a glimpse of herself in the mirror atop her vanity. For a brief second, she was reminded of the cover of some magazine she had seen displayed at a newstand. What sort of magazine had it been? A fashion magazine probably ... or ... had it been one of those sick men's magazines? No ... a fashion magazine, or perhaps a movie magazine. Or, perhaps she was totally mistaken. Perhaps the thought had just come out of nowhere.

Maya turned from the mirror and walked to her closet. She poked about in her clothing, finally pulling two dresses from her closet and throwing them across her unmade bed. The first dress was the white silk she had considered earlier. It was a somewhat simple affair, buttoning down the front in six pearly buttons. The top was tight fitting and low-cut, graced with a huge collar and bloused sleeves, the skirt short—thigh-length—and flared. The second dress was a pale green A-line, tighter at the buttocks and somewhat more chic owing to its suppressed waist and the single pleat that graced its back. It clashed rather interestingly with Maya's pink textured stockings. Actually, Maya would have preferred her black-and-red houndstooth dress to either of those that she had chosen, but the black-and-red houndstooth clashed terribly with the pink stockings she wore, and for some reason, it never entered her mind to change the stockings.

Maya put on the white silk dress and studied herself in the mirror, admiring the deep cleavage between the suntanned tops of her breasts. The pink of her stockings and white of the dress went well with her long strands of golden-brown hair. Yet, something about the dress displeased her. It was too simple, too plain. Maya took the dress off and tried on the green A-line. It fit beautifully around her buttocks, accentuating their plumpness and the depth of the crack between them. But the flatness of the top concealed the pertness of her breasts, and, perhaps the contrast of pale green and hot pink was a bit too ... fancy. Again, Maya thought of the red-and-black houndstooth. She glanced at the clock. It was almost seven. No time to change her stockings. No time. She would be late.

Maya felt a droplet of perspiration trickle from her armpit and roll down her side. She pulled off the green A-line, lit a cigarette, and tried on the white dress again. No, no ... too simple, too plain. And didn't it show a bit too much of thigh? Maya puffed nervously on her cigarette, inhaling deeply and exhaling through her nostrils. Then, the phone rang. Maya stood stock-still. The phone rang a second time.

Impulsively, Maya ran to her closet and pulled a pair of white patent leather pumps from a green shoebox. She pulled them on and buckled as the phone rang three, four times.

The card ... the red card ... Where was the red card?

The phone rang a fifth time. Maya threw open the drawers of her dresser. The phone rang a sixth time.

The jeans ... the pocket of the jeans ...

A seventh ring. Maya found the jeans in the middle drawer of her dresser. She searched first in the left pocket. No. Eight, nine rings. The right pocket. The tenth ring. She found the card. The phone stopped ringing.

Once, when Maya had had a fight with Peter—so emotional a fight that she had refused to answer the phone for the entire day—he had called her once every half-hour, always letting the phone ring ten times. How, she wondered, had he come by such a habit?

Maya took her white purse from the top of the vanity and stuffed it, with her cigarettes, into a pink patent leather bag. Without another thought, she left the apartment, the image of Etheus' incredible penis in her mind.

Outside, the red-faced doorman hailed a cab for Maya, his heavy jowls shaking as he waddled into the evening traffic. A yellow cab stopped in front of the apartment building and the doorman threw open the door with a flourish.

"Going somewhere special tonight?" he said, his thick lips twisted into a wet smile.

Involuntarily, Maya giggled, then absent-mindedly tipped the doorman a dollar bill and stepped into the cab.

"Where to, lady?" the cab-driver said. He was a thin man with a taut, angular face, long dark hair, and a bushy moustache.

Maya pulled the red card from her patent leather pocket-book and read him the address.

"That's pretty far out, lady," the driver said. He stroked his moustache very thoughtfully. "I don't know if I want to go out that far. Wouldn't get a fare on the way back ..."

"I'll tip you half the fare," Maya said, her voice flat, toneless.

"Well . . ." the driver said, still stroking his moustache.

"I have to be there by eight," Maya said, taking a cigarette from her pocket-book and lighting it. "Let's get going."

The driver stared at her for a second, his eyes narrow in the rear-view mirror, then stepped on the accelerator and headed for the Long Island Expressway.

For a time, Maya was nervous, angry with herself. What in the name of God had made her decide to return to the house of Etheus? Had she even decided, for that matter? What was wrong with her? What was she doing? But then ... yes ... it all became clear to her: she simply couldn't have taken a chance on Etheus showing the films. No, she couldn't have taken that chance. There had been no decision to make. She had been powerless, and so she had gone.

Having come to this conclusion, Maya found herself relaxing gradually with the motion of the taxi. The driver turned on the radio and soft chamber music filled the cab, interrupted at regular intervals by the ticking of the meter. Maya opened the window, leaned her head on the leatherette back of the seat, and enjoyed the steady breeze that blew strands of her golden-brown hair soothingly over her forehead.

With a slight start, Maya noticed the driver's large brown eyes peering at her from the rear-view mirror. She narrowed her eyes to slits, hoping that the driver would think she had closed them altogether, and watched, fascinated, as the driver's eyes darted from the road to the rear-view mirror. Somehow, it filled her with a wicked sensation. Once, when she thought that he was looking at her, she reached her hand into the top of her dress and pretended to adjust her brassiere. Then, a little while later, she reached under her white silk dress and made a show of adjusting her panties. Her eyes still narrowed to slits, she heard the loud blaring of a car-horn to her right and felt the taxi veer sharply to the left. Maya sat up, opened her eyes, and watched tree after leafy tree pass by the window. The shadow of a smile played across her full lips.

After what seemed to Maya approximately an hour, the taxi-driver turned off the expressway and followed a winding road past a number of small, isolated ranch-type homes. Eventually, he turned right onto a straight, poorly-paved road and sped over bump after bump, causing Maya to bounce uncomfortably in the backseat. Finally, a small, white wooden structure came into view.

"That's it straight ahead," the driver said.

A flashing red neon sign in front of the structure read: BLAKE'S SEAFOOD RESTAURANT. Even at a distance, Maya could make out the shiny outlines of Etheus' black limousine parked at the building's side.

"Only reason I knew how to find the place, I took somebody out here once before," the driver said.

Maya was startled for a second.

"You got a date with somebody out here or something?" the driver said. He halted the taxi several yards from the black limousine. Maya felt herself tense slightly at the sight of the stocky, bull-necked chauffeur.

"I said, you got a date or something out here? You meeting somebody?"

Maya remained silent for a few seconds. Then, without actually willing her words, she said, "Do you think I'm pretty?"

The driver turned full around, his arm resting on the back of the seat, his neck twisted uncomfortably. Maya stared back at him and smiled.

"You'd like to fuck me, wouldn't you?" she said.

The driver's mouth fell open. Before he could respond, Maya pressed some bills into his hand, tipping him half the fare as she had promised, and stepped quickly from the cab.

Etheus' chauffeur stepped brusquely from the limousine as Maya left the cab. He opened the door for her, then closed it after her, standing rigidly at attention, a slight scowl on his face.

"You're rather late, Miss," he said as he resumed his place in the front seat. "You were to be here at eight . . ."

Maya was stunned, then outraged at the nerve of the man.

"Why didn't you leave without me?" Maya said, her tone heavy with sarcasm.

"Because I knew you'd be here, Miss," the chauffeur said simply.

He sat motionlessly for a time, his eyes focused steadily on the rear-view mirror. Then, as the taxi-cab drove, swiftly up the road, he turned to Maya, withdrawing a black silken handkerchief from the breast-pocket of his uniform.

"Please lean forward, Miss," he said, holding the handkerchief in both hands.

Maya stared at him without moving, her eyes glowing with anger.

"Please, Miss," the chauffeur said impatiently. "We're late as it is. The master will be terribly displeased."

With a great show of annoyance, Maya leaned forward. The chauffeur tied the handkerchief securely over her eyes.

"Now, please sit back in your seat, Miss," he said. "I'll be driving in a bit of a hurry . . ."

He started the car and Maya felt herself being jerked backwards against the seat as the car sped forth. For a few seconds, Maya held her breath, frightened at the speed of the limousine, but she quickly lost all sensation of motion as her thoughts came to center on the madness of her situation. Was it possible that she was returning to the madhouse in which she had been imprisoned and abused? What insanity had possessed her, forced her to return? But . . . far to late to do anything about it. What was done, was . . . But . . . yes . . . she would confront this Etheus, this madman who fancied he could do as he pleased. She would confront him, scream her anger in his face. She would show him for the weakling—the coward—that he was. And then

... yes ... she would leave ... leave of her own free will, and have him thrown in prison ... that was where he and his kind belonged ...

Yet, even as Maya pictured Etheus being thrown behind bars, the image of his god-like face caused her flesh to tingle, the harshness of her thoughts caused a painful, twisting sensation in her chest.

Without warning, the car veered sharply to the left. Maya heard a soft, scraping sound from the sides of the limousine. The ride became slow, bumpy.

"Are we almost there?" Maya asked. She sounded terribly timid to herself, her voice high and cracking. She could sense the presence of Etheus' isolated house.

"Does it make a difference, Miss?" the chauffeur said.

Maya didn't answer. She was overwhelmed by alternating sensations of fear and anticipation.

The car came to a gradual halt and Maya heard the unmistakable creaking of an iron gate being opened. She listened for footsteps, but couldn't detect any over the hum of the limousine's engine. Then, slowly, the car moved forth again. Maya edged toward panic. Suddenly, she wanted to scream. She resisted the impulse, folding her hands tightly in her lap to keep them from shaking. Strangely, the cool feeling of the silk comforted her, gave her courage enough to remain in control of herself. Slowly, slowly, the car moved forward, rolling over bump after bump after bump.

Finally, as Maya's anxiety edged dangerously toward hysteria, the limousine came to a halt. The chauffeur turned off the ignition.

"You can remove the blindfold now, Miss," he said.

Maya tore the black handkerchief from her face and looked nervously about. Her eyes came to rest on a huge oak door that stood atop a steep stone stairway. The door was illuminated by a small light bulb encased in a rectangular green glass fixture.

The chauffeur stepped from the limousine and held the door open for Maya.

"Hurry, Miss, Hurry," he said. "We're terribly late ..."

Continually, Maya's legs threatened to buckle beneath her as she followed her chauffeur up the steep stone stairway. A powerful dizziness overcame her when she reached the small stone landing at the entrance to the house. She gripped a gnarled wooden handrail as the chauffeur knocked heavily on the huge oak door. After two knocks, the door was swung open by a thin, gray-faced man wearing the uniform of a butler. Dimly, Maya recalled him.

"Come in," the gray-faced man said. "You're late." He spoke in a low monotone.

The chauffeur, cap in hand, led Maya into the dimly-lit vestibule.

"All right," the gray-faced man said to him. "You may go. But you must try to be more prompt in the future..."

The chauffeur left through the door he had come in. The gray-faced man turned from Maya and walked to the far wall where he slid a section of wood panelling along rollers concealed in the wall, revealing a shiny metal plate dotted with multicolored lights and silvery switches. He raised his hand to one of the switches—it stood in the center of the shiny metal plate—but stopped without touching it and slid the wood panelling back into place.

"No time..." he muttered under his breath.

He turned to a large door that stood at the left of the vestibule, and flung it open to reveal a long, dim passageway. He raised his hand to the door's molding and knocked twice, loudly and insistently. In a matter of seconds, two black-garbed men appeared at the far end of the hall and walked briskly toward the vestibule. The gray-faced butler spoke to the first of the two, a tall, powerfully-built Negro with skin the color of cocoa.

"Take her to Etheus immediately," the butler said. "You will find him in his study." The Negro, and his partner, a gigantic Latin, nodded in unison. Maya stared at the men, their faces... and their bodies...

stirred vague recollections in her whirling brain. Ten ... she remembered the number ten ...

The Negro took Maya by the arm and led her from the vestibule, closing the door behind them. "You come this way, darling," he said, winking at the Latin. He spoke with a heavy Jamaican accent. "You just come with us ..."

They walked down the dimly-lit corridor and up a darkened flight of stairs that creaked beneath them as they walked. The Negro paused half-way to the landing and slid his arm around Maya's waist. She tried to slip away from him, but he held her tightly, his fingers pressing into her smooth belly.

"Stop it," Maya said, her voice a desperate whisper.

"You don't like it, darling?" the Negro said.

"Stop it," Maya hissed, trying to squirm away from the man.

"Darling," the Negro said. "What's the matter with you? They didn't give you your medicine tonight? A couple of days ago, you was licking out my sweet asshole. You was sucking my big dick ... You don't remember that, darling?"

"Leave me alone," Maya said. "Leave me alone ..." She turned to face the huge Jamaican and noticed two livid marks across his throat.

"Come on," the Latin said to his partner, "We got to hurry ..."

"O.K., O.K.," the Jamaican said. "I just wanted to see if she remembered, all right?"

"O.K.," the Latin said. "Come on. We got to hurry ..."

His arm still around her waist, the Jamaican led Maya down another dimly-lit hallway and up a steep, darkened staircase.

"Maybe we see you later," he said to her, rubbing his hip against hers and dropping his hand to her rump.

"Stop it," Maya pleaded, still trying to resist his strong grip.

"Come on," the Latin said, "Leave her alone. We'll get her later..."

"O.K.," the Jamaican said, dropping his hand to his side. "I just wanted her to know, O.K.? I just wanted her to know we got some big dick for her, O.K.?"

"Come on," the Latin said.

They turned to the left and walked down a narrow hallway lit by a brass-encased candle that hung from the ceiling by a heavy chain. At the end of the hallway was a large wooden door. The Jamaican knocked twice on the door, the sound of the knock echoing hollowly through the narrow hallway. From inside the room came the sound of hurried footsteps and hushed whispers. Somewhere, a door was closed. Then, after a slight pause, came a deep, calm voice: the voice of Etheus.

"Come in," the voice said.

The Jamaican threw the door open and led Maya into the room, the Latin following behind them. Maya gave a slight start as she found herself staring at a group of gigantic photographs that hung from each of the room's four wine-colored walls, depicting young, smooth-skinned couples in various phases of lovemaking. Her shock gave way to an overwhelming feeling of anxiety as her eyes came to rest on the majestic, black-robed figure of Etheus. He sat on a long leather couch in the center of the room, one hand resting gracefully on a thick armrest, the other extended to his throat, the thumb and forefinger toying with the red stone that hung about his long neck. Droplets of sweat dripped from his high forehead.

Maya stepped hesitantly forward until she stood a few yards from Etheus, her hands trembling at her sides. Automatically, her eyes sought the huge bulge beneath his robe, extending from his groin to a point more than half-way up his stomach.

"You may go," Etheus said to the two men who stood uneasily behind Maya, their dark eyes averted. Then, as they walked quickly from the room: "And remind Gorgas that I am to be signalled before any ... interruption. He must not forget this in the future."

The men nodded vigorously and left the room, closing the heavy door after themselves. Etheus turned his attention to Maya. Without speaking, he indicated a large, leather-upholstered armchair, motioning for Maya to sit down. Maya hesitated, and Etheus whispered, "Please," and Maya finally complied, brushing a few strands of golden-brown hair from her forehead.

For a long time, Etheus merely stared at her, his face expressionless, his green eyes gleaming strangely. Finally, he spoke.

"So," he said, "you have returned."

Maya glared at him, indignation rising within her.

"You left me no choice," she said, fists clenched in her lap.

"No choice," Etheus whispered to himself, his eyes turned inward. Then: "You are very beautiful. You are ... magnificent." His large green eyes swept over Maya's pink-and-white clad body, came to rest on her anger-contorted face. "I am glad you wore no makeup. Your face is so beautiful ..."

He fell silent for a time and stared intensely at Maya, all the while stroking the red stone that hung from his neck on a heavy gold chain. Maya glowered back at him, her outrage growing stronger with each passing second.

"You feel that I have been cruel?" Etheus said. "You feel that I have not given you a choice?"

"You forced me to return here," Maya shouted suddenly, gesticulating wildly with her hands. "You threatened me ..."

"Forced you?" Etheus said. "Threatened you?"

"Don't pretend you don't know what I'm talking about," Maya shouted. "You know what I'm talking about. You said you'd send those disgusting films to my parents, to my fiancé. You forced me to come here. What else could I do? Those disgusting films ..."

"Ah," Etheus said, his voice calm and low. "So you

returned to prevent me from sending those films to your loved ones. Is that it?"

"Yes," Maya screamed, bursting into tears. "You made me come back. I had to come back . . ."

"You believed that I would show those films to your parents? To your fiancé?" Etheus said. He leaned slightly forward as he spoke.

"Yes, yes, yes," Maya sobbed, hot tears rolling down her cheeks. "I knew you would. You said you would . . ."

"You believed that? Tell me the truth," Etheus said.

"Yes," Maya sobbed. "You told me you would ... You told me . . ."

Etheus sat back, crossed his powerful legs. His eyes narrowed to slits.

"What reason could I have for showing those films?" he said. "What would be my motive?"

"You told me you would," Maya said, sniffling, trying to gain control of herself.

"What would be my motive?" Etheus asked again. He stroked his massive jaw with the back of his hand. Maya didn't answer. "Tell me, what would be my motive?" Etheus said.

"I don't know, I don't know," Maya screamed suddenly. "You're crazy ... You want to make me suffer ...You want to hurt me again and again and again . . ."

"Hurt you?" Etheus said. "Have I hurt you?"

"You raped me!" Maya screamed. "You humiliated me. You forced me to make love to an animal . . ."

"You felt pain? You suffered at my hands?" said Etheus.

"Yes!"

"You lie!" Etheus shouted, suddenly rising to his full height. *"You* saw the films. You felt only pleasure. Your entire body shook with pleasure . . . and love . . ."

"No, no," Maya moaned, burying her face in her hands. "You raped me ... You threatened me . . ."

"Ah, yes . . ." Etheus said, his voice lowered almost to a whisper. "I threatened you . . ."

"Yes!" Maya screamed. "You threatened me . . . you threatened me . . . you . . " She sobbed uncontrollably, her entire body trembling, tears streaming from her eyes.

"I . . . threatened you," Etheus said, his tone grim, reflective. Then: "Maya . . . I merely offered you an excuse. You accepted . . . calling my offer a threat . . ."

"Excuse?" Maya gasped. "An excuse? What are you talking about? You're crazy . . . You don't make any sense . . ." Mucous began to drip from her nose and she wiped at it angrily with the back of her hand.

"An excuse," Etheus said, his voice filled with the most profound tolerance. "An excuse for your return to my house . . . for your return to ecstasy. You see, you needed an excuse . . . needed one very badly . . ."

"Needed?" Maya said, her arms braced defiantly on the arms of her leather chair. "*I* needed? You *kidnapped* me . . ."

Etheus paced up and down before Maya. As he paced, he toyed absently-mindedly with the red stone.

"At first," Etheus said, "a drug was necessary." Abruptly, his tone changed. "You speak of madness," he said angrily. "This is truly madness: that a drug was necessary . . . necessary to restore the womanhood that is your birthright." He lowered his voice, as if checking himself, and continued, Maya following him with her reddened eyes as he paced to and fro like a caged tiger. "And then," he said, "an excuse took the place of the drug. Yes . . . the excuse was another drug actually . . . one which you were able to administer to yourself once it was prepared for you. And you administered it . . . faithfully. Your presence here is proof of that. You administered it—nourished your excuse—though you knew it to be a drug, an excuse—what you will—because you wanted, somewhere deep inside you, to claim your birthright . . ."

"You think I *wanted* to come back here?" Maya said. "You think I *wanted* that? You must be totally out of your *mind* . . ."

"Can you honestly believe," Etheus said, "that you

did not wish to return here? At very least, you wished it more than that the films ... of your great joy ... should be shown to those you hold dear. Does that make sense to you? If I was truly mad, as you have claimed so often and so vehemently, how could you dare to return here? How could you guess what fiendish end I might have prepared for you? Perhaps ... yes .... perhaps I intended to bleed you ... slowly ... to watch the droplets of blood escape your quivering body as I stroked this incredible organ." He paused to indicate the gigantic bulge beneath his robe. "Perhaps I intended to find my own selfish ecstasy, as the last breath of life escaped your bloodless lips. How could you have returned here, beautiful Maya, thinking me mad, unless ... you are as mad as I?" He paused again and faced her, his green eyes gleaming, one thin eyebrow arched, then continued pacing back and forth, his bare feet making a soft, scraping sound against the wine-colored carpet as he walked. Maya watched him, her eyes drying, her resistance wilting, anger and admiration vying within her. Occasionally, her mind would wander, her eyes come to rest on one or another photograph of a naked couple.

"You knew full well," Etheus said, "that the films of your great passion would not be shown, as you know that I am not mad ... at least, not in the sense that you have called me so. I do nothing without purpose ... *nothing*. You have seen this for yourself. And what purpose could I have claimed for placing those beautiful films in the hands of men not able to enjoy them? The films, the films ... how you moaned at the sight of yourself. Oh, how you moaned. But ... somewhere ... somewhere deep within you, did you not feel a secret thrill? Did you not feel some sensation of warmth run through your body?" He faced Maya, his green eyes burning into hers, his left hand feverishly fingering the red stone that hung around his neck. Maya did not answer him.

"Yes," Etheus said, *"there* was purpose. To make you see ... to make you see your beauty. *There* was purpose. To tantalize you with your own beauty ... and ... to furnish you with the excuse you so desperately needed. Do you still think me mad?"

Again, Maya did not respond. She tried to look away from Etheus' blazing green eyes, found herself staring at the throbbing bulge beneath his robe.

"Perhaps," Etheus continued, "I am mad. Perhaps I am. But my madness is of a different sort than you have implied. It is the madness of truth." He paused, then murmured so softly that Maya could barely hear him. "Or ... the absence of truth . ." Then, resuming his former tone: "Each man that walks the face of this spinning planet—this dot on the face of a dot—senses the truth, feels it, lives with it, every moment of every day that he breathes. The truth! It pricks man even in his sleep, even as he snores upon his sour-smelling mattress." Etheus paced thoughtfully, his head bowed, his eyes turned inward. "There is a word," he said, "which I have often heard men use, and each time I hear it, it causes a tempest to rage within me ... a tempest. Mistake. This is the word. Mistake. *Man does not make mistakes!* No, never. All the time, he senses the truth, feels it tickle the back of his neck, tighten around his throat, and, if he chooses to ignore it, men call this a mistake. A mistake! Men know their paths before they choose them, know what lies at the end of each road they consider, but, often, one chooses his path because he is filled with fear at the sight of its better." Again, he lapsed into a low murmur, seeming to speak to himself more than Maya. "Fear ... death ..." he said. And again, he turned back to Maya who stared at him, seemingly hypnotized. "And some," he said, "more than sense the truth. They glimpse it ... glimpse the truth of the truth ... glimpse its force ... and beauty. You," he said to Maya, "have glimpsed the truth ... and so you have returned to me. That is good ... but there is better still. For, you see, some men come to possess the truth. Yes. I possess the truth. And it possesses me ..." Etheus stopped pacing and sank down on his dark leather sofa, his eyes closed, one hand to his forehead.

Maya was shocked at the silence that filled the dimly-lit wine-colored room. She became conscious of the perspiration that drenched the underarms of her white silk dress, conscious of the position of rapt attention that her body had taken. The flared skirt of her dress was bunched almost at her waist, exposing the voluptuous contrast of white garter strap and sun-darkened skin. Long strands of golden brown hair fell across her forehead. Her slender, long-fingered hands rested tranquilly on the arms of her leather easy-chair.

Maya waited long moments for Etheus to break the silence but he remained motionless, one hand resting on his forehead, his eyes closed, his soft, regular breathing the only sound in the room. Maya felt that she must make a move of some sort. Etheus, she was sure, was awaiting some signal from her, some sign by which he could plan his next move. She sat uncomfortably on her leather chair, her stomach tightening, her brain whirling, waiting for a coherent thought to come to her. Her eyes darted uncertainly from one to another of the huge photographs that hung from the wine-colored walls of the room. Here, she saw a pale-bodied dark-haired girl bend forward, spreading the cheeks of her tight rump to facilitate the entrance of her partner's pole-like organ; there, a light-skinned Negro girl knelt at the feet of a lithe European boy and sucked his ivory penis, her delicate hands tickling his small hairless testicles. Somehow, the effect of the photographs, combined with that of Etheus' long speech, produced a strange irritation within Maya, a feeling of smallness and ineptitude which made still more urgent her impulse to respond. Everywhere, she saw the larger-than-life-size photographs, and in their center, the graceful figure of Etheus, his eyes still closed, the whiteness of his bare feet emphasized by the dark-wine color of the carpet. With incredible rapidity, Maya's eyes darted about the room, focusing on photograph after photograph until she saw only a blur of soft flesh. Desperately, she sought words, substance, her long fingers drumming incessantly on the arm of her leather chair, the feeling of smallness growing within her with the passing of each silent second.

Then: "You threatened me," she said.

"You knew full well," said Etheus without so much as opening his eyes.

"I didn't know," Maya said. "You threatened me . . ."

"You knew full well," Etheus said. He remained motionless.

"You threatened me," Maya said. "You're a madman . . . a *madman*." Her voice rose steadily as she sucked conviction from the sound of her words. "You're a madman . . . sick, twisted, evil . . . You *threatened* me . . ." Then, sensing a final opportunity to deflate the relaxed and confident Etheus, she said: "I want to leave. I'm going to leave. You can't stop me . . ." She rose to her feet, straightening the skirt of her silken dress and brushing a strand of golden-brown hair from her sun-darkened forehead. She stood defiantly before Etheus, her hands on her hips, a striking study in pink and white. Her breasts heaved proudly, their tops visible over the white V-neckline of her dress.

Etheus opened his eyes and stared up at her. Was it a look of growing frustration on his smooth-featured face? One of sadness? Yes . . . she had won . . . she had won . . .

"You are free to go," Etheus said quietly, gesturing toward the room's oak door.

Maya stood dumbstruck, staring vacantly at Etheus, not knowing what to do. Etheus' green eyes glowed coldly into hers. She turned, took a step toward the door, and then stopped, her back to Etheus, weight resting on one foot, her head bowed, arms limp at her sides.

"Do you admit?" Etheus said after a pause.

Maya's response was almost inaudible. "I admit," she said, her back still to Etheus, her head bowed.

Etheus rose majestically to his feet, his hand returning automatically to the red stone that hung about his neck, his black robe flapping soundlessly against his bare calves as he approached Maya and placed his cool hand upon her lowered shoulder.

"In time, you will forget," he said, "the world of sickness . . . of weakness . . . In time, you will forget . . ."

Maya felt herself caught in the knots of an invisible bond created by her admission. She had struggled with every last ounce of her strength, but Etheus had triumphed over her as perhaps she had known he must, and his triumph had been rightful, inescapable. He had shattered her every pose and left her bare of defenses, and now she would be subject to his will, bound by her admission, from which an endless spiral of events would grow . . .

Etheus stood before her, something that might almost be called a smile turning the corners of his mouth. Impulsively, Maya threw her arms around his broad back and clutched him with all the strength left in her slender arms. Her face buried in his chest, the lobe of her ear pressing against the cold red stone that hung about his neck, she felt his massive penis press fiercely against her belly, its huge head lodged between her silk-covered breasts, forcing wide the valley between them. Maya was at a loss to understand her sudden gesture, could not tell if she was begging Etheus for mercy, or declaring her love for him. She knew only that she didn't want to let go of him, whether for fear of what lay ahead, or out of delight in his closeness.

"What now?" she whispered finally, her parted lips pressed to Etheus' black-robed chest.

Gently, Etheus pulled her arms from his body and stepped several paces back from her. "Now," he said, "you must become one of my disciples . . . You must be initiated into my society . . . You are prepared to do that?"

"Yes," whispered Maya after a brief pause, her eyes wide, doe-like, seeking some sign of tenderness from the strange man who stood before her.

"Excellent," said Etheus, moving gracefully toward his mahogany desk. "Remove your clothing, Maya. It is important that you be naked..."

Maya removed her silk dress without a second's hesitation, glad to be rid of its sweaty coldness, then kicked her pumps from her feet and peeled stockings, garter belt, and panties from her body with one smooth motion. Finally, she arched her back to undo the hooks of her brassiere, letting the flimsy undergarment slip down her slender, sun-darkened arms. She stood naked before Etheus, her body tingling under his strong gaze, the wine-colored carpet warm under her bare feet. She felt almost a part of the spacious study, as if she were one of the photographs that lined its dark walls. She paced restlessly around, sweat drying on her brown-and-white body, her golden bush tickled by a slight draft that seemed to enter the room from somewhere behind Etheus' desk.

Etheus sat on the edge of his desk. With one hand he flicked a yellow switch set into the center of the silvery metal plate that rested on the desk-top. Within seconds, a tiny yellow light began to flash on and off and a thin, metallic voice crackled through the room.

"At your service," the voice said.

"Is everything ready?" said Etheus.

"Everything," said the voice.

"I will bring the girl myself," said Etheus. "I will meet you at the usual place..." He flicked a second switch on the silvery plate and the flashing yellow light disappeared.

Maya was doing an impromptu dance, her hands on the tops of her buttocks, her head thrown slightly back.

"You are happy?" Etheus said, hands on his black-robed hips. His eyes followed her bouncing breasts.

"I'm a little nervous," Maya said, trying to smile.

"You mustn't be nervous," Etheus said. "The initiation is very... beautiful..."

"I believe you," Maya said. "I'm just a little nervous..."

"Come," said Etheus, "the hour grows late..."

V

He led Maya to the room's oak door and opened it, its brass knob making a rusty sound as he turned it. He motioned for Maya to precede him into the hallway, then took a thick red candle from a small wooden table that stood to the side of the doorway and lit it with a long match that he withdrew from the pocket of his robe.

"I will lead the way," Etheus said, closing the door behind himself and walking several steps ahead of Maya into the darkened hallway, candle held at the height of his shoulder. As they walked away from the study, Maya thought she heard a sound, as if of a door being opened and closed somewhere within the room, but she couldn't be sure, her mind filled with anticipation as it was. Had there been a door in the wine-colored study?

Etheus walked several yards in front of her, the thick red candle tilting slightly as he walked, hot red wax dripping to the thinly-carpeted floor. The hall was completely black but for the few square feet of dim candle-light. Maya could not see herself in the blackness. Only Etheus' head and shoulders were visible to her, and from the waist down, he too disappeared into darkness. Occasionally, Etheus would unexpectedly turn a corner in the darkned hallway, his seemingly disembodied torso disappearing altogether from view, plunging Maya into total blackness for a period of several seconds at a time. Otherwise, he walked steadily, his manner stately, ceremonial, his footsteps echoing hollowly through the twisting hallway. Oddly, Maya felt that other men and women walked with her in the hallway, silent, hidden in the darkness. She felt as if she were part of a strange dream-procession.

Carefully, Maya followed Etheus down a narrow flight of stairs. The red candle bobbed as they walked, throwing strange shadows on the dust-streaked walls of the stairway. Once, as Etheus turned a corner to descend a second flight of stairs, Maya caught a glimpse of her own shadow, thrown briefly on the wall. The legs of the shadow were short and thin, the trunk elongated, the head huge and oblong. The shadow frightened Maya—it seemed to her the shadow of some huge insect—but it disappeared as quickly as it had come, leaving Maya enshrouded in darkness once again.

"Are we almost there?" Maya said, reaching the landing on which Etheus stood.

"Almost," whispered Etheus. He led her down a narrow hallway to a small wooden door. It reminded Maya of the door to her parents' house in Vermont, so crudely was it made.

Etheus doused the red candle and stood for a second in perfect darkness, then threw open the little door and led Maya out of the house.

"The woods ..." Maya said breathlessly as she felt a damp breeze waft over her naked body. Somehow, she had not expected to be taken outside. Anticipation melted and flowed from her body as she felt the damp earth squish between her bare toes, felt dew-covered blades of grass tickle her ankles. The sounds of the night filled her ears, bringing memory after bitter-sweet memory to her mind. The dissonant chirping of crickets surrounded her, punctuated at odd intervals by the distant screeching of an owl, by the low, flapping sound of a bat. Maya wanted to stretch herself in the tall grass and spend the night in the wild bosom of nature.

Fascinated, Etheus watched her as she paused, her body completely limp, fluid-like, to listen to the sounds of the forest. She seemed like a child, her slender arms stretched at her sides, her head thrown slightly backward, strands of hair falling over her bare shoulders. Her body seemed to have lost its bronzed darkness, seemed, in the moonlight, to be composed of beams of pure, ethereal whiteness. She seemed, somehow, more than naked.

"Come," Etheus said after a time. "The others are waiting..."

He led her down a narrow pathway in the woods, stumbling occasionally, seeming less accustomed to the forest than was Maya. Maya walked very slowly, delighting in the touch of moist leaves and dry branches. Overhead, the leaves of the trees rustled softly, disturbed by even the slightest breeze. In the moonlight, the leaves seemed to be edged with bright silver, their tiny veins so beautifully etched as to be the painstaking work of some superbly-skilled craftsman.

Ahead of her, Maya could make out a clearing in the moonlit foliage. Slowly, Etheus walked toward it, his black robe catching on small thorns, trailing over the moist earth of the forest. Maya wondered why Etheus bothered with the black robe. Somehow, it seemed terribly out of place in the depth of the forest.

Etheus paused at the edge of the clearing and Maya found herself peering at the moon-whitened, expressionless faces of a number of men and women gathered about a rectangular stone platform. There were about twenty people in all, standing at regular distances from one another, each of them dressed in a flowing black garment similar to the robe worn by Etheus. They were quite beautiful, these silent, somber, black garbed men and women, but for all their ceremonial beauty, it seemed to Maya that there was something perhaps pretentious about them. They seemed so out of place in the wildness of the surroundings.

"Come," Etheus said to Maya. He took her by the hand and led her—a bit too insistently perhaps—to the rectangular stone platform that stood in the center of the circle formed by the white-faced men and women.

"This woman," Etheus said, pulling Maya to the center of the platform, "comes before you in her nakedness..."

How like a preacher he sounded, his voice deep and sonorous as he addressed the assembled group. And why, Maya wondered, did he find it necessary to point out her nakedness?

"She wishes," Etheus continued, "to renounce her former timidity. She wishes to become one of us..."

How pompous he sounded, standing on his manmade platform amidst the chaos of the forest. Maya was almost tempted to laugh at his pious solemnity. Yet, he had forced the truth from her, had made her see the truth...

"She stands naked before you..." Etheus went on. "She admits her guilt..."

Again, the mention of her nudity. Yet, Maya was utterly comfortable without her clothing. She stood perfectly relaxed in the center of the stone platform, her legs slightly parted, her arms resting lightly at her sides. She stared over the heads of the assembled group, peering deep into the blackness of the forest. Far in the distance, an owl screeched. Maya imagined the owl swooping down on a small gray mouse, his talons tearing into the little creature's brittle neck.

"She wishes to become one of you," Etheus was saying, his huge arms waving in the air. "Will you accept her?"

"Yes," came the chant of the assembled disciples.

"Then let the initiation begin," said Etheus.

Maya became annoyed at her inability to fully accept the ceremoniousness of the occasion. She looked out at the shining, somber faces of the assembled men and women and felt that she should more than mirror their seriousness. They seemed so filled with purpose, these silent, black-garbed people who stood motionless around her, so very disciplined and attentive. Could it be that she was less than they, that she could only heed the voice of the breeze?

"Lie down," Etheus said to her, a trifle impatiently, as if embarrassed for her ineptitutde. "Lie down on the platform..."

Maya complied, stretching herself slowly at Etheus' feet, her buttocks flattening beneath her, the coldness of the smooth stones causing her to arch her back.

Etheus stepped from the platform and disappeared from view. The group of men and women tightened about the platform, their garments rustling slightly as they moved. Maya could not distinguish their black robes from the blackness of the forest and it seemed to her that she was surrounded by a group of hovering white ghost-faces. As Maya stared at them, the faces became sexless. Then, gradually, all the faces became alike, until finally they seemed not to be faces at all, but old, white masks fashioned at the hand of some monomaniacal genius.

Out of the corner of her eye, Maya saw a torch being lit at the edge of the clearing. Red and yellow flames leaped high in the air, casting flickering shadows across Maya's naked belly and legs. Then, above the crackle of the fire, Maya could hear the sound of many footsteps on the forest's floor. The mask-like faces about Maya turned expectantly in the direction of the torchlight, their wide eyes reflecting in miniature the bright flames of the torch.

From the edge of the clearing came the sound of rustling leaves. Suddenly, two leafy bushes were parted, and a man stepped effortlessly into the clearing, his naked body gleaming orange in the torchlight. He was tall and pale, his sinuous body hairless but for a small dark patch over his plump penis. Maya watched him as he walked toward her, smooth muscles bunching in his thighs, then lay back and looked up at the stars that filled the blackness of the sky. She hadn't seen the stars so clearly for several years now, since she had left her parents' house in Vermont. In the city, there seemed always to be a haze cast over the heavens so that there were hardly ever more than a dozen or so stars visible at a time, and even those that did shine through the haze seemed distant and dim, as if dots painted on shoddy blue canvas. But here, the sky was black—pure black—and the stars—thousands upon thousands of them—literally filled the sky, most of them swirling in endless, brilliant clusters, others standing apart, shining with a brilliance unmatched even by the crescent moon. As she lay on her back, the stars became Maya's only reality. So elusive was their light, that they seemed both distant and near to her; she felt both microscopic and gigantic in comparison to them.

Nimbly, the tall man mounted the platform and stood above Maya, his legs astride her knees. He stared down at her as would an actor, his eyes filled with a ritual fire. Maya looked up at him, her soul laid bare in her liquid eyes. She wished only that he would smile at her.

The man parted Maya's legs and squatted between them, his heavy penis rising in seemingly measured beats as he massaged the insides of her open thighs. Then, holding her by the backs of her thighs, he lifted her legs high in the air, simultaneously lowering his solemn face until it was flush with her curly pubic triangle. His nose pressed against her meaty clitoris, he began lapping at the smooth lining of her vagina, circling the tender hole again and again with the tip of his tongue. Briefly, he thrust his tongue within her, just wetting the walls of her hole with his saliva. Then, abruptly, he withdrew his tongue and returned to his squatting position. It seemed to Maya that the man had only licked her until he felt that she had been properly moistened. It made her feel very odd, as if she was not a living, breathing woman, but only a dull abstraction of one, a ghost of one.

Still holding her by the backs of the thighs, the man inched forward until the upthrust head of his pale organ came into contact with the moistened lips of Maya's vagina. Maya was surprised at the coldness of the tall man's organ. It reminded her of a fish fresh caught from an icy stream. The man's hands seemed equally cold as they slid along the backs of her thighs until they were cupping her firm buttocks. Then, without looking down at her, the man thrust forward and buried himself in Maya's warm pussy, a lock of dark hair falling across his pale forehead as he did so. Maya gave a small cry as the man entered her, and for a second, the forest's crickets ceased their chirping. There was a scurrying sound, as of some small animal seeking shelter, and then the crickets resumed their song.

Gracefully, the man leaned forward and placed his head between Maya's large breasts. For a moment, Maya thought that he was going to kiss them, to suck on their pointed nipples, but as he placed his weight on his elbows and commenced an automatic, churning motion within her, she realized that he was only responding to the dictates of some calculated form.

Despite the ritual rigidity of the initiation, Maya felt desire rise within her. The eyes of the assembled men and women, passionless as they were, excited her. To make love to a stranger under the eyes of strangers produced a feeling of abandonment within her such as Maya had never know. She thrust her pelvis upward to meet the man's calm, even strokes, threw her arms around his back and squeezed his smooth sides, but despite her efforts, the man remained cold, automatic, utterly detached. As Maya found herself spiralling toward orgasm, she reached downward and squeezed the man's tight buttocks, her little finger searching for his hole. The man immediately brought his buttocks tightly together, as if trying to bar Maya entrance to his anus. Even as Maya scratched wildly at his strong back, her body writhing with climax after climax, the man remained aloof, the tempo of his thrusts unchanged. Suddenly, Maya felt the man ejaculate within her. She was astonished at the unexpectedness of it. The man had given no warning whatsoever, though now, peering curiously at him, Maya could see that his eyes had gone slightly out of focus. His orgasm completed, the man pulled his penis from Maya's foamy hole without so much as a pause, got to his feet, and walked gracefully from the platform.

As the pale man disappeared into the forest, a second man appeared. He too was naked, but broader, more powerful than the first. Swiftly, he mounted the platform, his body framed in orange torchlight. He bent over Maya's supple body and without speaking a word to her, pushed and pulled at her arms and legs until she was propped on her hands and knees. Maya found herself staring at the moon-whitened face of one of the black-garbed onlookers as the man positioned himself behind her and pulled open her thighs, parting the lips of her pussy with his fingers. In her mind, Maya begged the man to indulge in even the most perfunctory preliminary: just a kiss on the back of the neck or a light pat on the bottom would do beautifully. But no. The man plunged violently into her, his heavy testicles thudding against the insides of her thighs, the throbbing head of his penis distending the tender walls of her pussy. Once within her, the man moved very little. Rather, he grabbed her firmly by the hips and pushed her back and forth on his long pole, his dense pubic hair scratching the insides of her cheeks with each backward motion of her body. The movement that the second man forced her to was more forceful than that of the first man, but despite its violence, it was utterly regular and precise.

Wishing desperately to establish some closeness with the powerful man who moved her effortlessly up and down on his penis, Maya threw her weight on one outstretched hand and extended the other between her legs to squeeze the man's hairy testicles. Instantly, the man moved backwards and held himself motionless, just the tip of his penis tickling Maya's lips. He stood frozen until Maya withdrew her hand, then grabbed her by the hips and commenced his former motion.

Again, Maya upbraided herself for not being able to accept the mood of solenmity which surrounded her.

She found herself questioning her very essence: was it possible that she was simply too shallow a person to feel the depth of this mood? Earlier, when Etheus had forced the truth from her, she had felt something deep ... but that had been different ... a feeling of weightlessness ...

Even as Maya tried to force herself into solemnity, her thoughts became frivolous. She stared at the smooth-faced disciple—was it man or woman?—who stood directly before her and delighted in his voyeuristic attention. She literally fixated on the simple fact of his voyeurism, mad phrases running rapidly through her mind, passionately addressed to the motionless disciple.

"You're watching me fuck," she said to him in her mind. "Do you like to watch me fuck? Like the way my pussy looks with a fat cock inside it? Would you like to fuck me?" Then, as an orgasm surged through her body, her pussy sucking on the penis of her silent stud: "Like to ... watch me? Like to ... watch me? Watch me ... watch me ... watch me ... watch me ... watch me ..."

The man behind Maya ejaculated seconds after her orgasm began. Maya felt his hot sperm shoot into her just as her own climax reached its peak. Then, as she squeezed her pussy around his hard shaft—a gesture of affection to which Peter had always responded with a wet kiss on the ear—the man pulled himself violently from her, turned, and disappeared into the forest's blackness.

Maya stood perfectly motionless, afraid of being pushed into position by the next man to take her, her legs spread wide, her buttocks thrust upward. A damp breeze caressed her sweating body, tickling her dripping bush and the sparse hairs that adorned the rim of her anus. She closed her eyes and let her head fall forward, silky strands of hair swirling in wispy ringlets against the top of the stone platform. In the distance, she thought she heard a door open and close, but she couldn't be certain. It might only have been the low flapping of a bat or the clatter of one black branch against another.

As Maya held her crouching pose on the platform, listening for the approach of the next passionless stud (and beginning to wonder if perhaps the initiation was over), she felt something tickle the ltttle finger of her left hand. She opened her eyes and stared down at a large daddy long-legs who crawled with a fluid grace from her left hand to her right. She watched, fascinated, as the insect propelled himself to the edge of the platform, his threadlike legs moving with incredible precision, and disappeared over the side. Immediately, Maya found herself saddened at the insect's departure. There had been something happy about him, something free and easy.

Behind her, Maya heard the slap of bare feet against stone. She turned and gave a slight start at the sight of the muscular Jamaican who had earlier led her through the musty halls of Etheus' house. His cocoa-colored body was even more impressive naked than it had been in the tight-fitting black garment that he had worn in the house. From where he stood, Maya saw him bathed half in moonlight, half in the leaping flame of the torch. His fat penis was completely erected. It pointed upward toward the stars.

With a great deal of silent directing, the Jamaican stretched Maya on her side. It seemed to Maya that the man was annoyed at not being able to speak. He guided her impatiently, his hands wandering unnecessarily over her breasts and belly, and once he raised his hand as if to smack her bottom, but seemed to check himself at the last second. When he had positioned her to his satisfaction, the Jamaican placed himself beside her, his mouth to her vagina, penis to her mouth. He pulled her legs roughly apart, slipping his arms behind her and cupping the smooth halves of her bottom, then forced the velvety head of his organ to her lips.

"I told you you was gonna get dick," he whispered just before plunging his penis in her mouth and burying his face in her pussy. He said it as softly as possible, as if afraid that someone might hear him, and coughed immediately afterward to cover the sound.

Maya realized that the Jamaican's words were cruelly intended, but his slight infraction of the rules of the ritual—even if motivated by his cruelty—greatly endeared him to her. She grabbed his muscular buttocks in her hands and squeezed them passionately, the tips of her fingers slipping into his moist crack. She took his fat penis all the way into her throat, her lips touching his heavy scrotum, her tongue caressing the sides of his bone-hard shaft.

The Jamaican stifled a groan and lapped wildly at the squeezing walls of Maya's hole, his long fingers stretching the moist lips of her pussy to their limit. Then, as Maya's middle finger slipped slowly into his asshole, the Jamaican thrust frenziedly forward, his penis jerking back and forth in the tight channel of her throat, his balls falling heavily against her cheek. With a loud groan, he filled Maya's throat with thick, salty semen as his swirling tongue moved in time to the jerking of her middle finger, bringing her to a thunderous climax and leaving her, finally, limp and exhausted.

The Jamaican lay still for a moment, the head of his brown penis still lodged in Maya's mouth. Maya caressed him with her tongue, licking the last drops of fluid from the tip of his organ, hoping that he would stay with her for a while. Then, as she slid her hands along the Jamaican's smooth flanks, someone in the audience coughed, and the Jamaican, with an obvious show of reluctance, got to his feet and disappeared into the forest.

Maya lay still on her side, her head resting on one outstretched arm, her toes curled tightly inward. Her legs remained open, bent at the knee, saliva glistening on her thighs. Overhead, dark clouds obscured the crescent moon, blanketed the thick clusters of stars. From far in the distance came the low rumble of thunder. The crickets ceased their chirping. Lazily, Maya ran her forefinger over the cold stones of the platform. She hoped that it would rain.

After the Jamaican's performance, the ritual of the initiation became more complex, more elaborate. Two and three men at a time mounted the stone platform and possessed Maya, their faces only vague, torchlit blurs to the exhausted girl. Continually, they bent her body into more and more elaborate positions, stuffing her pussy, mouth, and anus with their stiff organs. Always, they were expressionless and rigid, their movements always regular and precise. Always, they waited for Maya's involuntary and barely-felt climax before filling her with their thick fluid.

As penis after penis pumped into her, Maya found herself thinking of the country boy who had made love to her in the woods. She remembered the sweet smell of the sweat that had trickled down his cheeks, the softness of his voice, the sight of his bare back as he had disappeared into the forest at dusk, faded denims crumpled under his arm. She wondered what had become of him, wondered if he remembered her tender love-making.

Maya was stretched on her side, sandwiched between two hard-muscled men who thrust mechanically in and out of her vagina and anus. She felt like a mindless puppet jerking crazily on a double string. She felt utterly detached from the orgasm that rocked her body, hardly noticed the flow of hot liquid within her, a seeming consequence of her climax.

Then, as three more men climbed onto the platform, throbbing organs held stiffly in their hands, the sky went suddenly pink with lightning and ear-shattering thunder cracked through the forest. Maya rolled over on her back, arms and legs outstretched, as tiny droplets of rain began to trickle from the sky.

The men stood awkwardly on the platform, confusion wrinkling their smooth-featured faces as the rain fell harder and harder, droplets of it splattering against the platform's cold stone. At the edge of the clearing, the flame of the torch sizzled and died, white wisps of smoke winding upward through the falling raindrops. At some unseen signal—from Etheus, perhaps—the disciples ran clumsily into the forest, their black robes pulled over their heads, their bare feet squishing in the mud. Rain dripping freely down their naked bodies, the men on the platform also turned and ran, their stiffly-erected organs slapping at their hips. They seemed to Maya like ducklings as they ran.

When the clearing was empty, Maya threw her head back and parted her lips to taste the falling raindrops. Her muscles were so exquisitely tensed that her body seemed that of a gymnast as she lay upon the slippery stones of the platform, her back forming a perfect arch, her bare throat thrust forward. She writhed with the sting of each slashing raindrop, her head twisting from side to side, rain-slicked strands of sun-bleached hair pasted to her forehead.

Bolt after bolt of zig-zagging lightning shot through the sky, casting the forest in hot, electrical pink, then fading to reveal the blackness of the night, no longer enlivened by the pinpoint brightness of the stars. Leaves rustled wildly on the trees, an occasional branch whooshing through space and thudding wetly to the forest's muddy floor. As Maya luxuriated in the storm, she wondered if the forest's creatures had all fallen silent, or if the sound of the splashing raindrops had drowned out their small voices. Years ago, as a little girl, she had pondered the same question. Then, as now, she had not found an answer.

As abruptly as it had begun, the rain stopped. Clouds passed lazily across the crescent moon for a few moments, then disappeared altogether, leaving the sky clear and starry. The only sound in the forest was the tiny patter of raindrops as they fell from leaf to shimmering leaf. Maya lay perfectly still as the last droplets of rain trickled down her naked sides and splashed lightly against the flat stones of the platform. Slowly, she raised her hand to her mouth and licked a raindrop from her little finger. Above her, the tops of the trees seemed covered with clear ice. It was as if the forest was frozen, or made of some fine glass that reflected the light of the unseen stars. Maya fancied that beams of starlight bathed her naked body.

In the wake of the storm, the forest became cold. Reluctantly, Maya sat up and held her arms about her shivering shoulders. Her eyes narrowed, she peered into the blackness of the forest, trying to determine the direction of Etheus' house. A tiny gasp escaped her lips as her eyes came to rest on the thin figure of a man who stood quietly at the edge of the clearing. The man wore a crumpled tan raincoat and a pair of dark trousers. His hair, slicked down by the rain, was brushed forward over the top of his forehead. He was soaked with rain, droplets of it still falling down the sides of his dark, angular face. In one hand, he held a yellow woolen jacket.

Maya got quickly to her feet and stared apprehensively at the man, water trickling freely from her rain-soaked bush.

"Are you ready to go?" the man said.

"Who are you?" Maya said. He didn't look like one of the disciples. His physique was much slighter than theirs, and his eyes were too . . . sly . . .

"I'm to take you back to the house," the man said. "All the others are gone . . ." With the hand that held the yellow jacket, he gestured sweepingly at the empty clearing.

"Who are you?" Maya said again.

"I'm . . . me," the man said, a quick smile lighting his face. "I'm to take you back. The others are gone . . ."

Maya stepped cautiously from the platform and inched toward the man, one hand unconsciously moving to cover her wet mound.

"Do you live in Etheus' house?" Maya said. She was sure she had never seen the man.

"Sometimes," he said. "I live there sometimes." Then, still smiling, holding the yellow jacket before him: "It's cold out. Why don't you put on this jacket?"

Maya hesitated, then reached forward and took the jacket, resisting the man's attempt to place it on her shoulders.

"Follow me," the man said. "It's not far . . ."

Hands in the pockets of his raincoat, the man led Maya slowly through the woods, humming an unidentifiable melody as he walked. The man reminded Maya of someone she knew, but she couldn't quite place the familiarity. She followed him at a distance of about two yards, yellow jacket pulled tightly around her chest, its damp hem sticking to her thighs.

"It's beautiful after the rain," the man said, pushing back a slippery black branch and holding it for Maya to pass.

"Yes," Maya said testily, remembering the feigned warmth of the man who had drugged and kidnapped her two days before.

"I like the rain too," the man said. "The rain is beautiful."

A small frog hopped from his perch on a fallen branch and disappeared into the woods. Maya listened for the sound of a stream, but heard only the steady chirping of the crickets.

"Yes, the rain is beautiful," Maya said.

"But," the man said, "the others don't like the rain. It . . . I don't know . . . They don't like it . . ." A raindrop spilled from the tip of a moon-silvered leaf and dripped down the back of the man's slender neck.

"But you like the rain," Maya said. "You aren't one of the—"

"I stand in the rain," the man said, "and wait for naked girls who lie on the stone altar and taste the raindrops . . ."

"Tell me the truth," Maya said. "Who are you?"

"I am telling the truth," the man said. "I brought you a jacket, didn't I? That was nice of me . . ." He turned his head and stared at her over his shoulder, a mischievous smile on his lips. "And you look very pretty in the jacket, very pretty . . ."

"You say you don't live in the house? You don't live with the others?"

"Sometimes I do," the man said, "but I try to keep my distance . . ."

"Why is that?" Maya said.

"I'll tell you that another time," the man said. "Here we are..."

He parted the branches of two leafy bushes and indicated the stone-and-wood front of Etheus' house.

"I didn't come this way," Maya said. "I came from the back..."

"Ah," the man said. "But you see, I never travel the beaten path..." He paused a second, staring at the house, then turned again to Maya. "That sounds like a joke, doesn't it?" he said. "That I never travel the beaten path, I mean..."

"Is it supposed to be a joke?" Maya said.

"I don't know," the man said. "I never know when I'm joking..."

Maya peered closely at the man, as if by studying his face she could come to an understanding of his strangeness. He seemed constantly to be smiling, his face lined with tiny wrinkles at the corners of his mouth and eyes. Perhaps, Maya thought, it was the permanent expression of his face.

"Well," the man said, "I really must be going. If you just walk up those steep stairs over there, and open that large wooden door, you'll meet a thin old shadow of a man who will be more than willing to take you to a warm room and wish you a very good night. But, you see, if you mention me to him, if you ask him about the queer, smiling fellow who stands out in the rain with a yellow jacket for anyone he should chance to meet, he will assure you, most emphatically, that he doesn't know who in the world I might be."

"But he does know?" Maya said. "He knows who you are?"

"I don't know," the man said, turning from her, a wicked smile on his face, and walked briskly into the woods.

"Wait," Maya said. "Where are you going?"

"I don't know," the man said, disappearing into the woods.

"I have your jacket!" Maya shouted into the blackness.

"Keep it," came the faint reply. "It's a present..."

Maya stood still for a mminute, listening to the sound of the man's receding footsteps until they blended with the soft night-sounds of the forest and finally disappeared. Then, taking long strides, she walked toward the house, wiping her muddied feet on the carefully-tended grass of the front lawn. She climbed the stairs to the house two at a time, buttoning the yellow jacket as she approached the heavy wooden door. The door was opened before Maya had a chance to touch the latch, and she found herself staring at the wraith-like figure of the gray-faced butler.

"Come in, Miss," the butler said.

Maya entered the dim vestibule, the floor's mosaic tiling icy cold against the soles of her feet.

"There was a man out there," Maya said immediately. "A thin man wearing a tan raincoat. Do you know who he might be?"

"A man?" the butler said, his large eyes cold and vague.

"Yes," Maya said. "He gave me this jacket."

"I'm sure I don't know who it could be, Miss," the butler said. "Shall I take you to your room?"

"He was a little taller than I am ... He was wearing a tan raincoat ..." Abruptly, Maya ceased her description. "Yes," she said, "Take me to my room."

"Follow me, Miss ..." the butler said as he lit a candle and held open one of the vestibule's doors for Maya.

Maya followed the butler through twisting corridors and up creaking flights of stairs, her eyes fixed on the orange-yellow point of the candle's flame. Having been so recently in the rain-freshened forest, Maya became uncomfortable at the stuffiness of the hallways. Her nose was constantly tickled by rising sneezes that receded, for some reason, before materializing.

"Here we are, Miss," the butler said finally, turning a rusty iron knob and throwing open a tall wooden door that creaked loudly on its hinge. He reached into the room and flicked a switch that turned on two wrought-iron lamps that projected from the far wall, then motioned Maya into the room.

"The bath is to the left, Miss," he said, gesturing to a narrow pink door, "And you'll find your clothing in the closet. Will you be needing anything else, Miss?"

Maya said no and the butler left the room, closing the door quietly behind himself. Maya listened at the door until the sound of the butler's footsteps disappeared, then turned and paced around the room, casting her yellow jacket over the back of a beige armchair.

The room was large and high-ceilinged, its walls painted a neutral mocha shade, the molding's plaster chipped in places. Between the wall's wrought-iron lamps stood a wide fireplace, its empty mantle covered with a thin layer of dust. A large, four-poster bed projected length-wise from the opposite wall, a predominantly blue Persian rug surrounding it. The rest of the floor was bare, its wood recently polished. Maya warmed her feet on the Persian rug for a time, its intricate patterns of blue, green, and gold fascinating her, then found her attention drawn to a gigantic portrait that hung on the wall to her right.

The portrait was full-length, depicting a tall, hollow-cheeked man standing erect before a dull green background, one hand resting on the back of an elegant, satin-upholstered chair. The man was dressed in a military uniform of what seemed to Maya to be the nineteenth or perhaps early twentieth century. The uniform was of a deep blue, the jacket short and tight with a double row of shiny brass buttons. Across the chest was a shining white band which criss-crossed a thicker band of gold braid. The uniform's high collar and pointed cuffs were of the same spotless white as the chestband, and a second band of gold braid hung around the shoulder. The man's boots were black and shiny, the bottoms of his white-striped trousers tucked neatly into their rounded tops. The man was bareheaded, his honey-colored hair combed forward over his high forehead. He seemed somehow uncomfortable in the uniform, as if glad to have dispensed with the shiny helmet that rested on the chair beside him. Maya had the feeling that the man had not wanted the portrait painted. It occurred to her that he had only agreed to the sitting after imposing some ridiculous condition on whoever had insisted on it—his wife, perhaps. She could see the hollow-cheeked man adamantly refusing to wear his medals. Somehow, Maya was certain that he had been decorated many times.

Maya drew close to the portrait and stared up at the man's pale face. His eyes were of an indeterminate color—now blue, now hazel, now gray—and focussed on what seemed to Maya some distant object to his right. Or were they actually focussed? Were they not, in fact, rather vague, turned inward in hazy reflection? Was this the fault of the painter, Maya wondered, that the portrait was so ... uncertain? Was that a tiny twinkle in the eye, or a deadly gleam? And the lips! Certainly, they were thin, bloodless (or was that only the effect of shadow?), but what was their expression, their pose? Now, they seemed turned with an adolescent smile, now, twisted in pain.

Maya stepped back and studied the painting from a distance of several feet. Still, she was unable to categorize the expression of its subject. He seemed the possessor of some great secret, which both amused and tortured him. Maya studied the painting inch by inch, searching for some hidden clue to the man's soul, but found that the man—or had it been the painter?—had been careful not to betray himself.

Gradually, Maya's gaze became more and more vacant and soon she found herself yawning. She dismissed the portrait, deciding that it was utterly inscrutable, and walked across the polished wooden floor to the adjoining bathroom. She opened the door and flicked a plastic wall-switch, standing in the doorway while the overhead fluorescent lighting flickered on.

The bathroom was a stark, hospital-like white, its tub, toilet, and sink old-fashioned and clumsy-looking, its tiling chipped and cracked. Maya entered the room and stared at herself in the dust-streaked mirror that stood over the sink. Her face seemed thinner and more taut than usual, her eyes larger and more intense. Her cheeks were flushed although the rest of her face had grown quite pale, despite her recent exposure to the sun.

Maya thought of taking a bath—she could feel thick semen still clinging to the walls of her anus and vagina—but the barrenness of the small bathroom made the prospect rather unappetizing. Instead, she ran the cold water and washed only her hands, then dried her hands and rain-dampened hair with a starchy, rough-surfaced towel. Her hair became wild with the vigorous drying she gave it and she looked in the bathroom's metal medicine cabinet for a comb or brush but found it completely empty, its shelves covered with dust. She made a half-hearted attempt at combing her hair with her long fingers, then left the bathroom, turning off the light.

She sat on the edge of the four-poster bed for a time, gray woolen blanket itching her soft bottom. She stared down at the blue Persian rug until she became lost in its intricate, weaving patterns, then stood up and turned off the light after first throwing open the room's heavy drapes. She got into bed and pulled the woolen blanket over her, vaguely annoyed that there was only a single sheet on the bed, and tried to go to sleep.

The light of the moon shone directly in her face and after a short time, Maya turned over on her stomach, the woolen blanket scratching against her side as she turned. It had always been difficult for Maya to sleep on her stomach; her large breasts made it almost impossible for her to find a comfortable position. Sometimes, when she rolled over in her sleep, her breasts ached in the morning from having been squashed under her all night. Now, Maya found it impossible to come to terms with her breasts, and she turned over on her back again, the rough wool of the blanket pressing painfully against her nipples, moonlight seeping through her eyelids. In desperation, Maya flung off the blanket and covered her eyes with her forearm, and after more than an hour of wakefulness, she began to drift gradually toward sleep.

Dimly, Maya heard the sound of footsteps. At first, she thought she had been dreaming, and she searched her sleep-hazed mind for the face of some slow-stepping dream-vision. But no, the footsteps were real. Lightly, with great stealth, they approached the door to Maya's bedroom, then ceased.

Immediately, Maya thought of screaming, then grew disgusted with herself for the commonness of her impulse. She remembered how, in the forest, she had scoffed, in her mind, at Etheus' fiery speech. Now, she felt duty-bound to accept the presence of danger outside her door in stoic silence. Maya raised her forearm from her eyes and peered through narrowed eyelids at the slowly-opening door. For a brief second, she thought of the strange, smiling man she had met in the woods, then closed her eyes so as to seem asleep.

Slowly, the door was closed. All was silent. Had it been only a mistake? Had someone entered the wrong room, looked about in bewilderment for a few seconds, then left upon the discovery of the error? No. Slowly, lightly, footsteps creaked across the wooden floor, drawing ever-closer to Maya's bed. Very gradually, the mattress was depressed at its edge with the weight of the silent intruder. There was a slight motion, a tiny rustling of the sheet, and Maya felt warm breath on her knee, fingertips on her ankle.

For long minutes, the intruder remained motionless, then, with a deep breath, slid a warm hand slowly up Maya's leg. Maya's leg jerked involuntarily as the intruder touched her thigh.

"Are you awake?" It was a girl's voice, soft and high.

Maya twisted and stuttered for a few seconds, trying

to convince the girl that she had been asleep, then sat bolt upright in bed as if greatly startled. As she sat up, her knee grazed the girl's hip.

"Who are you?" Maya said. "What do you want?"

"My name is Suzanne," the girl said. "I was with you the other night when you were all doped up, and tonight, I was watching you in the forest. I was one of the people in the black robes that were standing around that big stone thing you were on . . ."

"Why are you here?" Maya said. "What do you want?"

The girl turned away and stared into the darkness of the room. In the moonlight, her profile was extremely striking. But for her red hair and pug nose, she seemed almost like an Egyptian painting, her eyes large and almond-shaped, her lips thin and straight.

"I was lonely," the girl said. "I get lonely sometimes. I wanted to sleep with you. Everyone else locks their door here at night . . ."

Maya stared at the girl without speaking, wondering what it was like to make love to a woman. She had dreamed of it once, but the dream-woman had been only half a woman. Midpoint in the dream, she had become very flat-chested and her dark hair had grown very short, and when Maya had reached for the woman's vagina, it had become a plump, hanging thing, not quite a penis, but nothing like a vagina. Maya also remembered the films of herself—she had seen herself making love to . . . two women? three?—but her actual memory of the evening was terribly vague, almost sexless. She remembered only tongues and holes and endless dripping secretions, everything passing before her in a long, sensuous blur.

"Haven't you ever been lonely?" the girl said.

"Yes," Maya said, remembering the thousands of nights she had spent alone in the bedroom of her parents' little house in Vermont. "I used to be lonely."

She wondered if perhaps the girl only wanted to talk. The idea of sitting up all night and talking to the redheaded girl appealed greatly to Maya. She had never actually had any sort of a girl friend, but only a few school acquaintances who lived miles away from her parents' house in the country, plain-faced girls who talked seldom and only of themselves.

"You come from the country, don't you?" the girl named Suzanne asked.

"How could you tell?" Maya said, staring into the girl's large almond eyes.

"Just something about you," the girl said. "Something clear, I think. There's something very clear about you."

"How do you mean?" Maya said, wanting to understand the girl.

"Oh, I don't know," the girl said. "Just the way you are is very clear. Just . . . clear . . . I'm not good at saying what I mean. I just get these feelings about people." The girl was silent for a time, her head slightly lowered, one hand grazing Myra's calf. Then she looked up, a ringlet of red hair falling like a comma over her eye. "Can I get into bed with you?" she said.

Maya didn't answer but moved slightly to the left of the bed to make room for the girl. The girl stood up and pulled the long nightgown that she wore over her head, then dropped it on the Persian rug. Her body was very long and lissome, her neck slender, her breasts small and firm, her buttocks very round and tight, like two perfect halves of a cantaloupe.

"My hair is dyed, you know," Suzanne said, pointing with one hand to her elaborately-coiffured red hair, with the other to her dark, curly bush. "It's a big disappointment to some people," she went on, "so sometimes I dye my pussy too, but I don't like to. It gives me a rash sometimes. Once I shaved it, but it itched like hell for a month. I walked around scratching it all the time . . ."

Suzanne got into bed beside Maya and laid one hand on her shoulder. Without any warning, she bent forward and planted a wet kiss on Maya's navel, sliding her mouth down a few inches until Maya's silky bush grazed her cheek.

"You're very pretty, you know," Suzanne said, resting her head on Maya's belly and running the tip of her forefinger over Maya's stiffly-erected nipple. "Do you mind for me to touch you?"

"No," Maya whispered, her eyes closed.

"I'd love to make you come," the girl said.

Maya didn't say anything and the girl slid down the bed until her head was at Maya's feet. She stroked the soles of Maya's feet for a time, then bent forward, strands of her red hair falling over Maya's ankles, and took Maya's little toe into her mouth. She sucked it for a while, tickling its plump bottom with the tip of her tongue, then licked the spaces between Maya's toes with long, slow strokes, finally taking Maya's big toe into her mouth and moving her lips up and down on it.

"I love to suck on toes," the girl said, lifting her head for a moment as she tickled Maya's feet with her fingers. "Toes were made to be sucked on. Here ..." She pushed one of her long-toed, gracefully arched feet in Maya's face and went back to her sucking.

Maya took the girl's foot in both her hands and licked it, hesitantly at first, then with greater and greater passion, until finally she took three of the girl's slender toes into her mouth and sucked them as if they were covered with honey.

The girl sat up in bed and rested her hand on Maya's thigh.

"Would you like for us to eat each other?" she said. "Do you think you could come like that?"

Maya didn't answer the girl, after waiting several seconds, stretched herself across the bed and pushed her vagina toward Maya's lips, her flat belly pressing against Maya's large breasts, one long nipple slipping into her deep navel. Suzanne parted Maya's silk-haired lips with her fingers and tickled the double cleft of buttocks and pussy with her tongue. Then, as she felt Maya's mouth fall lightly on her stiffening clitoris, she slipped her tongue slowly into Maya's smooth-walled hole. Maya's pussy made a soft sound as the girl's tongue explored it, as of two sections of an orange being pulled gently apart, and Maya took Suzanne's meaty clitoris into her mouth, swirling it around and around with her long tongue.

"You're all sticky in there," Suzanne said, raising her head for a minute, tickling Maya's slit with her fingers. "I like the way it tastes..."

She lowered her head again and lapped at Maya's hole, squeezing Maya's clitoris with one hand, and exploring her grinding buttocks with the other. Slowly, Suzanne's hand sought the deep cleft of Maya's bottom, slender fingers circling the ridged rim of her anus. Then, as Maya's tongue hesitantly entered her darkhaired pussy, Suzanne wriggled her rump, grabbed one of Maya's hands, and guided it to her own rear aperture, forcing Maya's middle finger knuckle-deep in the squeezing hole. Suzanne wetted the tip of her forefinger in Maya's dripping vagina and thrust it slowly into Maya's rosy-rimmed anus, allowing Maya's rhythmic contractions to pull it more and more deeply in.

The girls licked and fingered each other for several more minutes, their motions growing progressively more rapid and deliberate, their stifled breathing waxing hotter and heavier. Suddenly, Maya moaned and squeezed her legs tightly around Suzanne's neck, the bedsprings creaking with the violence of her movements. As she circled closer and closer to orgasm, she pulled the lips of Suzanne's pussy wide apart and thrust her tongue so deeply into her that her jaw ached. Her entire head shaking in animal frenzy, her tongue slapping from side to side in Suzanne's hole, she forced the red-haired girl to orgasm as her own body heaved with wave after wave of hot release. For several minutes both girls jerked and writhed on the foam-dampened mattress, their breath coming in sharp gasps, their hands roaming wildly over each other's naked bodes. Then, gradually, they slowed to a halt and rolled over on their backs, panting and sighing and holding hands. The redheaded girl was the first to speak.

"Are you tired?" she said.

"No," Maya said. "I feel very lazy but I'm not tired."

"Good," said Suzanne. "Neither am I. Would you like to talk?"

"All right. What would you like to talk about?"

"Anything you like," Suzanne said. "Sometimes I can talk for hours..."

"What do you do for a living?" Maya said. "You look like a model... or maybe a dancer..."

"I don't do anything," Suzanne said. "I just stay here... you know. I don't need any money."

"What did you do before you came here?" Maya said, stroking Suzanne's hip and staring vacantly at the beams of moonlight that sliced through the room.

"I don't think I ever did anything," Suzanne said. "I don't remember doing anything, but I hardly remember anything anyway. I remember that I had a very nice mother and father, but I can't remember what they looked like. I think my father was bald. They're probably both dead now anyway."

"You've been here a long time then?" Maya asked, puzzled at the girl's seemingly customary vagueness.

"I think I have, yes," Suzanne said. "I don't know how many months or years or anything like that, but I think it's been quite a while. They broke my little cherry here, you know. Oh, I was so, so sad. I cried for a whole day. So, I was probably pretty young, I guess. But I remember that before I came here, everybody was always after me to go out with boys—I never liked boys too much—so maybe I wasn't so young after all. I don't know..."

"How did you come here?" Maya said. "Were you kidnapped?"

"Kidnapped?" Suzanne said. "I don't know. They just... I was just here, that's all. I hardly remember anything anymore. It's not good to remember all these things... silly old things. It just confuses you..." Suzanne was silent for a time, her fingers buried in the moist crook of Maya's leg. Then, suddenly, she raised her head, a child's smile on her lps. "You know what I do sometimes?" she said.

"What?" Maya said, raising her head, then lowering it on Suzanne's pale thighs.

"Sometimes," Suzanne said, "I go into this little room downstairs. I don't think anybody knows about it because it's very dusty and empty. All there is in the whole room is this old purple chair. It's made out of ... you know ... velvet ... purple velvet. It's so *soft* and *pretty*. So sometimes I go in there—in the mornings usually—and I just sit in the purple chair ... and pretend I'm Etheus." She touched Maya's knee excitedly. "Yes," she said. "I pretend I'm him, and I act very solemn and wise and ..."

Suzanne fell silent for a time, then turned herself around on the bed and laid her head on Maya's stomach. "Do you ever do things like that?" she said, tickling the smooth undersides of Maya's breasts. "Do you ever ... you know ... pretend you're somebody else or pretend you're a king or something?"

"No," Maya said. "I don't think so. I used to when I was little. I used to pretend I was an orphan girl, and when I got a little older, I remember I once pretended I was a spy ..."

"You don't pretend anymore?" Suzanne asked.

"No," Maya said softly. "Not for a long time now ..."

"You have such big breasts," Suzanne said, weighing one of them in both her hands. "They make mine look like little midgets or something."

"You have very beautiful breasts," Maya said to her. "They're much nicer than mine. Mine are too big."

"What do you do now?" Suzanne said. "I mean, now that you don't pretend ..."

"I'm a model."

"I don't know anything about that," Suzanne said. "Tell me about being a model. What do you do?"

"Well, I just put on clothes ... dresses mostly ... and wear them in front of people to see if they want to buy them."

"That's funny," Suzanne said. "I mean, couldn't you just show them the clothes and ask if they want to buy them?"

"Well," Maya said. "They like to see them on somebody..."

"And you have to run back and forth putting on all these clothes? You must have to hurry..."

"You do have to hurry," Maya said. "But there are other models too. I don't have to do it all by myself."

"Oh," Suzanne said with a tone of great understanding. "How many other models are there?"

"Oh," Maya said, "fifteen or twenty. Sometimes more."

"Do you make love to all of them?" Suzanne said.

"No," Maya said, more surprised then taken aback. "I don't make love to any of them..."

"Really?" said Suzanne.

"Really," Maya said. "You're the first girl that I ever made love to."

"No," Suzanne said, laughing.

"Really," Maya said.

"I can't believe that," Suzanne said.

"It's true," Maya said.

Suzanne started to say something, then stopped, curled herself into Maya's side, and lay still, her breathing slow and regular. Maya laid her head on the girl's supple flanks and stared ahead at the huge portrait that hung on the room's far wall. She tried to remember if the painting had had a name-plate, decided that she would check it in the morning. Gradually, exhaustion dragged her nearer and nearer to sleep. She closed her eyes and thought of the forest after the rain.

VI

Maya awoke at noon, bright sunlight streaming into the room, making the brass posters of the bed gleam golden. Suzanne was gone though her long nightgown still lay on the Persian rug beside the bed. More asleep than awake, Maya got out of bed and walked, as if in a trance, to the huge portrait that had held her fascinated the night before. Her eyelids all but closed, she searched the bottom of the portrait's wormwood frame for a name-plate, but as she had expected, found none. She looked up at the portrait, focussed groggily on its subject's averted eyes, then suddenly turned and searched the room to see what had so amused or horrified him. She laughed as she came sharply to her senses, jarred by the idiocy of her sleepy misconception, then stumbled back into bed and pulled the rough woolen blanket over her bare shoulders.

Maya lay on her back and stared up at the mocha-colored ceiling. She wanted to get back to the city—Peter's suspicions must be unbearable—but she didn't know if it was permissible for her to leave her bedroom without being called for. She didn't want to seem foolish to anyone, to make a pest of herself. She fantasied herself leaving the room and being halted in the corridor by the gray-faced butler: "Miss! What do you think you are doing? Are you mad?"

Maya turned over on her side, closed her eyes, and drifted into restless sleep. She had a nightmare in which both her father and mother lay in a narrow hospital bed surrounded by a railing composed of thick bars of glass. One of them was dying—she was unclear as to which one it was (or was it both of them?)—and two fat doctors stood at the side of the bed, leaning over the glass railing, one of them examining her father with a huge magnifying glass, the other peering at her mother through a long telescope. Then Maya was in the dream (had she come to visit, or purely by accident?) and the doctor who was examining her mother handed her his microscope and bid her look through it. As the microscope came slowly into focus, Maya saw the face of her mother more and more clearly. The face was all smashed and purple, the lips twisted in agony, blood pouring from the eyes, ears, nose, and mouth. Maya's hands were trembling uncontrollably when she woke from the dream. She decided not to go back to sleep.

Maya sat on the edge of her bed and stared at the tiny bits of dust that seemed to hang suspended in the bright rays of sunlight that flooded the room. Bored, she blew on the particles and watched them swirl in the light, rising and falling, until they returned to their normal, almost-motionless course.

Maya stood up and paced lazily around the room, enjoying the squeaking sound her bare feet made on the highly-polished floor. She hummed fragments of songs to herself, finally singing part of the first verse to *Button Up Your Overcoat* which her mother had taught her when she was a little girl.

"... Take ... good ... care-of-yourself ..."

Then she stopped singing and walked into the white-tiled bathroom. She ran the cold water and washed her face and her hands, laughing at the sight of her hopelessly tangled hair in the mirror, then ran the hot water and washed some of the dried foam from the closed slit of her vagina. She decided against taking a bath—the tiled floor was terribly cold and there was only the one scratchy towel—and left the room, patting her long strands of hair as much into place as possible. She continued pacing around the bedroom for several minutes more, staring blankly at the nameless portrait or the intricate design of the Persian rug, then pulled on the long flannel nightgown that Suzanne had left behind, and stole quietly into the hallway.

She wandered almost on tiptoe through the thinly carpeted corridors of the house, surprised at the ill state of repair everything was in. The carpet was worn through in places, dried old strips of wood visible through its frayed edges. Dirty chips of plaster had fallen from the ceiling which itself had turned an indeterminate color with age. The wooden panelling that lined the musty-smelling hallway was scratched and dry, little pieces of finish peeling from its surface. Both cracked molding and creaking floor were covered with a soft layer of dust which, in the case of the floor, was interrupted by the imprints of many bare feet, some seeming recent, some ancient, ghost-like. The stuffiness of the hallway made Maya sweat beneath her flannel nightgown.

Maya paused in the hallway, trying to figure the direction of Etheus' study. Then, guided only by intuition, she walked up and down long corridors and creaking flights of stairs until she came to the large wooden door that she remembered from the night before. Hesitantly, she knocked.

No answer.

She knocked again, then opened the door a crack and peered inside. The room was empty.

Maya entered and closed the door behind her, taking the room in with a glance. Something about it seemed different, vaguely disturbing. Maya wondered if it was simply the absence of Etheus that made the room seem so ... barren ... so one-dimensional. Somehow, the huge photographs that hung from the walls, the perfectly-arranged leather-upholstered furniture, even the matching wine color of wall and thick carpet, made the room seem oddly evanescent, like a temporary exhibit in a museum or a brief show in a fashionable art gallery. The room seemed to await the arrival of four or five burly, gray-clothed men who would busily dismantle its props, load them on a van, and drive quickly into the distance, leaving the room utterly empty but for a few discarded scraps of paper, a forgotten package of cigarettes, and perhaps a hand-crushed can of beer. Then, within a day or so, two or three painters would arrive to paint the room white, transistor radio blaring tinnily in the corner while they painted. And finally, a dark-suited man with a craggy face and long hair streaked with gray would enter the room, his shiny Italian shoes creaking as he walked, and tack a sign on one of the walls announcing the date of the new exhibit or stating a telephone number that anyone interested in the hire of the room should call.

Maya sank down into one of the cold leather chairs, a look of depression on her face, and stared out a large window that faced the front lawn. Outside, it was turning gray and windy, leaves rustling wildly on the trees, dark branches clacking violently against one another. Maya remembered sitting at her bedroom window in Vermont during a hurricane that had uprooted trees and torn half the shingles off the roof of the house. She had not seen nature unleash itself so furiously since leaving the country.

Maya took a cigarette from a humidor that rested on a small end-table beside her chair. She lit it with a tarnished silver cigarette lighter, then dropped it to the floor as the door slammed shut behind her.

"What are you doing here?"

Etheus stood at the door, one hand still resting on the brass knob, his face contorted with anger.

"I'm sorry," Maya stuttered, "I just . . . I don't know . . ."

"What are you doing here?" Etheus said again, stepping slightly forward, large hands on his hips. His eyes were somewhat bloodshot. "Why aren't you in your room?" he said.

"I didn't know it was wrong for me to come here. I was ... bored ... I had nothing to do ..."

"You were bored," Etheus said, one eyebrow arched. "And you just decided to wander through the house? You decided you could go where you pleased?"

"I didn't know it would upset you," Maya said. "You see—"

"I'm not upset!" Etheus cut her off. "I am angry ..."

"I'm really sorry," Maya said. "I just didn't know ... Do you want me to leave now?"

Etheus was silent for a time, his pulse throbbing at the side of his thick neck. He seemed to be thinking, his eyeballs moving occasionally from side to side as if trying to focus on some elusive object, his left hand toying compulsively with the red stone that hung about his neck.

"No ... Don't go," he said after several minutes of contemplative silence. "It's just as well that you're here. Once you're settled down here, you'll learn the rules ..."

"Settled down?" Maya said. She bent forward and picked up her cigarette which had singed the woolen fibers of the rug.

"You will be staying with us, won't you? It would be foolish for you to spend all your time commuting."

Maya hadn't thought of moving in. It made her feel queer to think of it.

"Yes, I guess so," Maya said. She felt that she should have anticipated this. It seemed such an obvious part of the bargain.

Etheus stared out the window for a moment, a look of annoyance on his face, then pulled the heavy curtains closed and walked to his desk. In the dimness of the room, the red stone that hung from his neck gleamed more brightly than it had in the light of day. He sat back in his chair for a moment, his eyes closed as if with fatigue or slight pain, then leaned forward, elbows propped on the top of the desk, and rested his square chin on his elegantly-clasped hands.

"How long will it take you," he said, "to take leave of your people?"

Again, Maya was surprised. Things were happening too quickly. She felt cramped, unable to breathe.

"I don't know," she said.

"Several days?" Etheus said.

"At least a week," Maya said quickly. "Maybe longer. I don't know . . ."

"We'll say a week then," Etheus said rather declaratively. "And then you will return . . ."

"All right," Maya said. She couldn't see herself living in the city any longer anyway. Her problems with Peter were really getting insurmountable. Perhaps it would be best, after all, for her to live in the old house with Etheus, to live in isolation from the nervous city people who had always made her so uncomfortable. Curiously, she felt both that it suited her, and that it was a fitting punishment of sorts for her errors of the past. And, somehow, she felt duty-bound to accept Etheus' wishes. He had been right, and she wrong. It was her duty to accept . . .

"Take care," Etheus was saying, "that your disappearance is in no way unusual, that your departure is perfectly explained beforehand. We have . . . enough troubles here . . ." As he spoke his last sentence, he stared vaguely down at his desk-top. It was as if he hadn't know what he was saying.

"What troubles?" Maya said.

"What?" Etheus said, looking up from his desk with a puzzled look on his face.

"What troubles do you have here?" Maya said.

"I have no troubles," he said. "I was just . . . I have no troubles."

"You just said—"

"Never mind what I said. Don't question me. It isn't for you to question me."

Again, he fell silent, hands bridged over his forehead, thumbs pressing into his temples. He seemed to be in pain.

"So," he said, looking up, "You will return in a

week. You need not bring any of your things ... Life here is very ... unostentatious. We live very simply."

Maya crossed her legs, hem of her flannel nightgown slipping to her thigh. She leaned forward and lit another cigarette, silver cigarette lighter cold on her slender fingers.

"I don't like this habit, this smoking," Etheus said. "Please put out your cigarette ..."

"Why do you keep them here?" Maya said, pointing to the humidor.

"Don't question me!" Etheus shouted. "I'm tired of your questions." He stroked his forehead as if troubled with a headache. "Go to your room," he said without looking up. "The chauffeur will come for you presently ... You have the red card that you were given?"

"Yes," Maya said very softly.

"My car will meet you at the address printed on that card one week from tonight. Be there no later than eight o'clock ... Now go ..."

Maya stood up and walked to the door, hurt by the coldness of Etheus' dismissal. She hesitated at the door, framing an apology in her mind, but was interrupted by an impatient gesture of Etheus' before she had a chance to speak.

"Go ... go ..." he said, waving his arm angrily in the air.

Maya found her way back to the mocha-colored bedroom, pulled her clothing from the closet, and dressed hurriedly, chain-smoking the cigarettes that she had packed in her pocketbook the day before. Her panties were slightly soiled and she left them in a dusty corner of the closet, throwing her brassiere in after them for no special reason. It made her feel sexy to walk around the large bedroom with no underwear beneath her dress save garter belt and stockings, and the feeling of sexiness assuaged her nervousness enough so that she could sit down in the room's single armchair and stare out the window at the crisply-cut grass on the front lawn.

Outside, it was exactly as before, a flat, gray, windy

day. Dimly, Maya remembered that it had been sunny when she had awakened, but then later ... Maya enjoyed the sight of the wind-vexed forest. It made her feel alive.

After a short time, there came a knock on the door and the chauffeur entered the room, his round face more cheerful than usual.

"Ready to go, Miss?" he said, holding his cap in his hand.

Maya nodded and followed him through the house to the front door. Just before they reached the vestibule, they passed the tall Jamaican in the hallway and Maya smiled at him, remembering the intimacies of the night before. The Jamaican ignored her and continued down the hall, his head held perfectly erect, his eyes cold.

Outside, the chauffeur held open the door of the limousine for Maya, cap still held in his hand. Just before Maya got into the car, a gust of wind blew her flared skirt up in the air, revealing her garter-strapped buttocks to the chauffeur. He smiled briefly and got into the front seat.

"That's all right, Miss," he said, staring at her in the rear-view mirror. "You're not the first and you won't be the last ..."

He started the car and drove slowly down a narrow dirt road until he came to a wrought-iron gate adjoined by a guardhouse painted in gaudy stripes of white and black. The guardhouse looked to Maya like something from a childhood dream though the man who emerged from it to open the gate looked a good deal more sinister.

Just before the car turned out on the main road, Maya thought that she heard soft laughter coming from the edge of the forest. She stuck her head out the window and looked in all directions but couldn't see anyone.

"What were you looking for, Miss?" the driver said when she had sat back in her seat.

"Didn't you hear laughter?" Maya said.

"Can't say that I did, Miss," he said. "Probably just the wind . . ."

Maya closed her eyes and thought of the smiling man. She tried for a long time to remember what he had said to her in the forest after the rain, but only remembered something about a joke, something that sounded like a joke or something like that. Yes, it had probably been the smiling man's laughter that she had heard just now. He had probably been laughing at one of his jokes, standing in the forest and laughing at a joke he had told himself.

Maya dismissed the whole thing. It was just too confusing . . . and besides, she understood it all perfectly anyway.

"You can let me off here," Maya said to the chauffeur.

The limousine was caught in crosstown traffic and it made Maya anxious to sit in the almost motionless car. Besides, she felt like taking a walk. The ride had seemed much longer than before, perhaps because she had not worn the customary blindfold.

"You're sure, Miss?" the chauffeur asked, a note of disappointment in his voice.

"Yes," Maya said. "I think I'll take a walk . . ."

"All right, Miss," the chauffeur said, opening his door.

"No, don't bother," Maya said, stepping out of the car. "I can manage . . ."

"All right, Miss," the chauffeur said somewhat gruffly. "See you a week from tonight then. Don't be late . . ."

"I won't," Maya said, slamming the door behind herself.

She walked east to Third Avenue, then walked uptown, stopping frequently to look in the windows of the little antique stores. She stopped at one window to look at a graceful statuette of a man kneeling beside two little babies. It moved her more than anything else in the window though it was surrounded by a number of larger, more elaborate pieces. She considered pricing it but decided that it would just be a waste of time, and continued up the avenue

The warm summer air blowing on her uncovered crotch made her feel very wicked, and every time someone stopped to stare at her, she found herself wishing that a sudden gust of wind would blow her dress up over her hips for just the tiniest little second. She bounced slightly as she walked, enjoying the slight jiggling of her breasts against the thin silk top of her dress and the whistled admiration that followed her up the street. Yet, she felt uncomfortable. There was something . . . ugly . . . about the people that followed her with their eyes, something very unnatural about them. They didn't excite her. Rather, she excited herself with their help. They even . . . frightened her, these people with their big eyes and loud whistles.

Suddenly, Maya hailed a cab and rode the two blocks east to her apartment. At the entrance to the building, the red-faced doorman told her that "her young man" had waited half the night in the lobby for her to come home.

"Staying with a sick girl friend, were you?" the doorman said, a ghastly leer on his face.

Maya walked to the elevator without answering him, both angered and amused by his childishness. Upstairs, she turned the key slowly in her door, half-expecting Peter to leap out of the kitchen and strangle her. She stepped inside, holding the door open behind her and shouted, "Is anybody here?" There was no answer and she shut the door quickly behind herself and double-locked it.

She took off her dress, stockings and garter belt immediately, letting them drop to the floor of the dining area, and walked into the kitchen for something to eat. She put water on for coffee and chewed on a cold slab of meatloaf while waiting for it to boil, then fixed scrambled eggs and toast and orange juice. The kitchen window faced an old office building and Maya stared at the dark-suited men and overdressed women scurrying from office to office while she ate her breakfast, wondering if they could see her sitting naked in the kitchen.

After breakfast, Maya dumped her dishes in the sink, ran some hot water over them and walked into the bathroom to fill the tub for a bath. At the last moment, she decided against taking a bath, let the water out of the tub and took a quick cold shower, soaping herself vigorously. Then she dried herself and combed her tangled hair as best she could, finally putting on a pair of bellbottom jeans and a lime-green sleeveless cotton top.

After dressing herself and drinking another cup of coffee, Maya began to feel wonderfully vibrant and healthy. She went into the living room and turned on the radio and danced to a loud rock tune that she had heard once or twice before. She enjoyed dancing alone in her apartment with no one watching her and now she danced particularly wildly, so that droplets of perspiration rolled from her armpits and stained the sides of her lime blouse. Still moving in time to the music, she pulled the blouse over her head and danced naked from the waist up, her heavy breasts jiggling crazily with each jerk of her torso. She fancied herself a topless go-go girl dancing in a crowded night-club atop a tall platform, multicolored lights flashing in the background, bathing her breasts in green and blue and yellow.

Then suddenly Maya stopped dancing and stood motionless in the center of the living room, her forehead lined with worry. Somehow, in the midst of her dancing, Etheus had entered her mind. It was as if he had entered the room or called on the telephone. Maya felt his dark presence, and felt ashamed of her levity before it. She pulled on her green top and sat woodenly on the floor, the pulsing music of the radio saddening her so that she finally turned it off. Of course, Etheus had never specifically prohibited her lightheartedness, but somehow it was an unspoken part of the ... agreement. It was part of his manner, part of his tone. Maya couldn't imagine him dancing, though the thought of it made her giggle.

The ringing of the phone interrupted Maya's reflections and she picked up the extension in the bedroom, flopping down on the bed and kicking her legs in the air.

"Hello," she said in a childish voice, wiggling her toes as she stared up at the ceiling.

"Maya?" Peter's voice said.

"Hello, Peter," Maya said, cooing slightly.

"What are you, drunk?" Peter said.

"No," Maya said, laughing. "Why do you say that?"

"You sound funny," Peter said. "You're not drunk?"

"I said *no,* Peter," Maya said.

"Listen, Maya, where the hell were you last night?"

"I went out . . ."

"Where?"

"None of your business," Maya pouted, her eyes darting quickly back and forth, one hand tucked into the waistband of her bellbottoms.

"What do you mean, none of my business? Where the hell were you?"

"Don't shout at me, Peter. I told you, it's none of your business where I was." She kept staring sideways at the receiver, as if checking it for a reaction of some kind.

Peter mumbled something, paused, then mumbled something else.

"What did you say? Peter? What did you say? I can't hear you . . ."

"Nothing, nothing. I wasn't talking to you. Listen, I have to get off the phone . . ."

"Okay, bye . . ."

"Hold it, Maya, will you hold on? I'm coming over later . . ."

"Don't come over, Peter. I'm tired. I'm going to sleep."

"Listen, Maya, don't play games with me. I'm coming over later and if you don't answer the door, I'll break it the hell down..."

"Oh, Peter, don't be so—"

"Never mind don't be so blah-blah-blah. I'll be over in a little while and you better be there. I gotta have a talk with you. Okay?"

"We'll see, Peter," she said.

Peter started to say something but Maya hung up the phone and lay on the bed smiling to herself for a few minutes. Then she stood up, took off her clothes and perfumed her pussy, breasts and armpits, then put away her silk dress, stockings, bellbottoms and sleeveless top. She considered answering the door naked when Peter arrived, but decided against it and put on her shortest miniskirt, a tight-fitting pink affair with two large patch pockets in the rear and a double row of ornamental buttons down the front. She considered putting on underwear and a blouse but decided in favor of the miniskirt's provocative simplicity. She felt primitive wearing just the skirt, like the high-priestess of some mysterious jungle cult.

Pretending that she was a cat, Maya prowled into the living room and turned on the television set. She switched from soap opera to soap opera, finally settling for a cartoon show about a boy with bushy hair and very big eyes whose legs turned into small rockets that enabled him to fly. The big-eyed boy did battle with a number of talking dinosaurs who were under the control of a skinny little scientist who wanted to destroy the earth. At the end of the show the boy beat all the dinosaurs and dumped the skinny scientist in a vat of glue or something and the show went off the air.

The news came on and Maya got up and changed the channel. She hated to see the films from Vietnam with all the loud noises and frightened little people running madly around and crying. It made her think that the world was coming to an end. She turned on a movie about a fifty-foot-tall man who was running around with just a little loin-cloth and overturning cars and busses and trains. He was kind of fat and bald and he looked like he didn't know what he was doing.

After about an hour—a pretty blonde woman was shouting up at the fifty-foot bald man, begging him not to kill anybody else—the doorbell rang and Maya adjusted her miniskirt so that its waistband came just under her navel, its hem an inch or two past her bush, mussed her hair a little bit and answered the door.

Peter stood scowling in the doorway, his finger poised above the buzzer. He wore a crisply-pressed light gray suit and a light blue Oxford shirt. The pants of the suit fit him very snugly and the jacket was subtly suppressed at the waist, double-vented in back. His shirt was unbuttoned at the throat, the knot of his blue silk tie pulled away from his neck. His thin face was flushed, as if he had been running or walking very quickly, and Maya thought she could smell whiskey on his breath.

"What are you doing?" Peter said, throwing a quick glance over his shoulder. "You want somebody to see you?"

Maya stepped out into the hallway, holding the door open with one hand.

"I don't care if anybody sees me," she said.

"Will you get inside?" Peter said, pushing the door open and half-forcing her inside.

"Don't shove me, Peter . . ."

"What do you mean, don't shove you? You're running round naked in the hall . . ."

"I thought you liked me naked," Maya said, twirling around in a circle and raising her pink skirt over her buttocks. "Don't you like me naked, Peter?"

"Where were you last night?" Peter said, sticking his hands clumsily in his pockets.

"Tell me if you like me naked . . ."

"I like you naked. Where were you last night?"

"I was in the forest. A whole bunch of men fucked me on top of this big stone thing. About ten of them, maybe more. They fucked me all night long . . ."

"Where were you, Maya?" Peter said. "I waited for you all night."

"I got fucked by a whole bunch of men in the forest..."

"Maya.."

"They did it to me every way you could imagine... in my mouth... everything."

"Maya...."

"You wouldn't have believed it, Peter... They had such big things... like this..." She raised her hands in the air and spread them about a foot apart. "Even bigger..."

Peter grabbed her by the wrist and stared angrily down at her grinning face.

"Where were you?" he said.

"Don't you want to fuck me, Peter?" she said, pouting, tickling his neck with her free hand. "I feel like fucking you..."

"You're getting me angry, Maya. Tell me where you were."

"Oh," she said in a little girl's voice, "I was out in the forest... and there were all these lovely naked men..."

"I'm not kidding around with you Maya. Tell me where you were..."

"Don't you want to fuck, Peter? Look..." She raised her skirt over her hips and stroked her curly triangle with two fingers. "Isn't it pretty?" she said, still talking like a child.

Peter raised his hand, held it poised in the air for just a split-second, then smacked her resoundingly across the face. She stumbled backwards until she hit the wall, then collapsed to the floor, blood trickling from her nose. Immediately she burst into tears.

"I'm sorry," Peter gasped, running forward to help her.

"Leave me alone," Maya sobbed. "Just leave me alone..."

"I'm sorry, Maya, I'm sorry... Please..." He knelt beside her and dabbed at her nose with his handkerchief.

"Leave me alone, Peter. Go away..." She pushed

his hands from her face and wiped at the blood with her forearm. "I didn't want to fuck you anyway . . . I don't want to fuck you . . ." Sniffling, she gained control of herself for a short time, then burst into tears once again. "You're always asking me questions," she moaned, her naked breasts heaving. "Always questions . . . All you ever do is ask me questions . . . *I'm tired of your questions!* Who do you think you are? My father? Do you think you're my father? You're not my father! So just stop asking me all these *questions* . . ."

She sobbed uncontrollably for several minutes, her face turning a deep red, tears streaming from her eyes, dripping to her chest and belly. Peter watched her without speaking, his eyes wide, his lips slightly parted. He seemed almost to be smiling.

Even in the midst of her sobbing, Maya felt ashamed of herself, though she could not quite pinpoint the source of her shame. She felt at a loss to understand any of her words or actions since Peter had entered the apartment. She wanted desperately to hurt him— though she didn't know why—but felt that with each new attempt, she left herself all the more vulnerable to him, so that with each new attack, her infantile rage found itself increased.

Maya straightened, controlling herself once again, and looked into Peter's face. He seemed to be staring at a small teardrop that trickled slowly between her breasts.

"Why don't you leave, Peter?" she said coldly. "You make me sick."

"I want to stay until you feel better," he said very calmly.

"I don't want you to stay," she said. "Go home . . ."

"No," Peter said.

"Go *home*," Maya shouted. "I don't want you here . . ."

"Yes you do."

"Will you please leave?"

"No."

Maya faced him silently for a few seconds, her tightly-clenched fists trembling at her sides.

"I wish you were dead!" she screamed suddenly, doubling over and weeping hysterically. *"I wish you were dead!"*

Peter leaned closer, took her shaking breasts in his hands and fondled them softly.

"Shhh," he said as if trying to soothe her. "Shhh . . . shhh. . ."

Suddenly, Maya raised her head, a vicious smile across her tear-streaked face.

"Leave me alone, faggot," she said.

Peter stared at her, his hands still on her breasts, a puzzled look on his face, freezing his half-smile idiotically.

"I said, leave me alone, faggot," Maya said.

"Don't say that, Maya," Peter said.

"Why not?" Maya said, grinning at him, mucous dripping from her nose.

"Don't say it, Maya," he said.

"You're a faggot, Peter," Maya said, very matter-of-factly. "I should know, shouldn't I?"

"I'm warning you, Maya . . ."

"Don't warn me, faggot. You're a little faggot. . ."

"Don't call me that, Maya. Please don't call me that . . ."

"Faggot," she said. "Faggot . . . Little faggot . . . Faggot . . ."

Peter hauled back and smashed her across the face, his whole frail body behind the blow. Maya threw back her head and laughed, gasping for breath, her entire body shaking.

"You stupid little faggot, you," she screamed. "You're such a stupid little faggot!"

"Shut your mouth, Maya . . ."

"Faggot . . ."

He smacked her again, knocking her over on her back. She laughed more and more loudly, screaming, "Faggot! Faggot!" whenever she could catch her breath. He hit her three more times, each blow harder than the former, then fell across her bare chest, tears flowing freely from his eyes.

"Please don't call me that, Maya," he begged. "Please don't call me that..."

There was a long silence, broken only by Maya's heavy breathing. Peter lay motionless on top of her, his head pressed to hers, his eyes shut tightly.

"You know what you are, Peter?" she whispered in his ear.

He raised himself on his arms and looked down at her, his eyes begging her for mercy.

"You're a cocksucker," she said and she spat in his face.

Peter held his rigid pose for a full minute, spit dripping slowly down his cheek.

"You know what I'm going to do to you?" he said after a long pause, his words very crisp and precise. "I'm going to fuck you till you can't walk anymore... and then I'm going to split your fucking head apart..."

He jumped to his feet, grabbed Maya by the arm and dragged her into the kitchen. He threw her down on the linoleum floor, then turned, a look of annoyance on his face and pulled the kitchen curtains closed.

"Don't you want everybody to watch?" Maya cooed, pulling her skirt up over her belly.

Peter kicked her in the side and pulled off his pants and shorts. Maya laughed at the sight of him fully dressed but for his pants.

"You look like somebody in a dirty movie," she said. "Except your little dickie isn't big enough..."

He squatted over her face, his small testicles hanging over her chin, and pressed the head of his shriveled penis to her lips.

"Suck it," he said gruffly.

Maya burst out laughing.

"I don't want to suck it," she said. "It's too small."

Peter smacked her and forced her mouth open with both hands.

"I'll bite it," Maya warned just before he slipped it in.

He dangled it in her mouth, shaking it with his hand and reaching behind himself to give Maya's pussy a rough massage. Suddenly she sank her teeth into the limp shaft of his penis and he jumped back, groaning with pain. He grabbed the lips of her vagina and twisted them until she screamed, then smacked her twice across the face and forced his penis back into her bleeding mouth. She sucked it obediently for about five minutes, sighing with boredom and staring blankly up at a small fly that walked around in a small circle on the ceiling.

Peter's organ achieved a partial stiffness in her mouth, but would not come to a full erection despite Maya's bored sucking and his own insistent squirming.

"Woh ih geh a-ie harrer?" she said, pulling the whole of it into her mouth and tickling Peter's tight testicles with her forefinger.

He pulled it out of her mouth and squeezed it in his hand.

"I could fit your balls in there too," Maya said, lifting Peter's suit jacket and shirt and tickling his sweaty rump. Then, measuring his penis with her eyes: "Your balls and three more of those..."

Peter stared down at her, still squeezing his half-erect penis, sweat trickling down the sides of his face.

"Don't be so worried, baby," Maya said softly. "If you can't get it in, you can always go find somebody to let you suck on his cock..."

Peter made a tremendous effort to control himself, then smashed her across the face. He got to his feet, blue silk tie slapping against his penis and grabbed Maya by the knees, but before he could apply any pressure, Maya spread her legs wide apart and opened the golden-haired lips of her pussy with both hands. Peter breathed convulsively as Maya raised her legs high in the air and wiggled her pink-slitted pussy in his face, her little finger lightly circling its moist hole.

Peter threw himself on top of her, bracing himself on one skinny arm, and tried to force his flaccid penis into her.

"Put it right in ... there ..." Maya said, trying to guide his organ into her. "Right in ... the ... little ... hole "

The head slipped in and Maya squeezed it tightly, trying to suck in the shaft, but as soon as Peter moved forward it slipped out the side and flopped against her thigh.

Peter squatted between Maya's legs, squeezing his penis with both hands, but the more he squeezed the more it shriveled. Maya laughed hysterically, fingering her hole and rubbing her clitoris, enjoying Peter's utter impotence to the fullest.

Peter backed himself into the corner and watched Maya masturbate, his face ugly with pain and sadness.

"Do ... you want me to ... eat you ... or something . . ." he said very softly. ". . . Make you . . . come?"

"I'm doing fine," Maya said, tilting her head to smile at him. "Don't you like to watch?"

Peter stood up slowly and pulled on his pants. He stared dumbly at the wall for a few seconds, then turned to Maya, tears welling in his eyes.

"I ..."

"You're a faggot, Peter," Maya said.

Peter closed his eyes for a second, his mouth falling shut, then turned and walked out of the room.

Maya lay still for several minutes after the apartment door clicked quietly closed, then rolled over on her stomach, her elbow grazing a brown package that lay beside her on the floor. Very slowly her tears came, dripping to the cold linoleum floor as her body shook from head to foot. She cried silently, biting her lip to keep from screaming, praying feverishly that she would die. Then, still sobbing, she fell asleep, her face pressed into a shimmering pool of mucous, blood and tears.

Hours later, in the dead of night, Maya awoke suddenly, brown paper package clutched to her breast. She stared at it stupidly for a moment, overhead light hurting her eyes, then started to moan as if in labor, rocking back and forth on the floor, her head bent to her chest, her eyes rolled upward. Then, mechanically, she got to her feet, holding the package in front of her with both hands, and walked out of the apartment to the little incinerator room in the hallway. Her eyes closed, she dumped the package into the dark metal chute and listened to the clang of package against chute until all was silent. She stood for a minute, smelling the dank garbage smell that rose up out of the chute, then unzipped her skirt, pulled it down her legs and stuffed it into the incinerator's rectangular opening. Then she left the incinerator room and walked naked back to her apartment.

Inside, Maya turned out all the lights in the apartment and paced slowly back and forth in the bedroom, listening to the distant sound of jazz playing on a neighbor's radio. Later, when the music disappeared, she stretched herself on her bed and fell quickly to sleep.

VII

Loud ringing, like steel clattering against thick ice.

"She's not here ..." Maya mumbled in her sleep. "Why don't you leave her alone?"

Lingering vibrations of the church bell, ringing ... ringing ... Who was it died?

"I'm too tired ... too tired ..." Maya muttered, burying her face in the pillow, sweat-dampened hair sticking to the back of her neck.

Ringing through the frost night air, icicles falling from the trees, cut by the vibrations. High ringing rising like a wave, calling ... calling men to arms. Who was the silent enemy?

Tinnier and tinnier, shrill like a baby's cry. Was the battle over so soon? Were all the people dead? People ... in the steeple ... open it up ... and ...

Maya sat up in bed, brushed the hair from her eyes, yawned and answered the phone.

"Hello? Hello?" the voice said. "Hello?"

It was a funny voice, thick and dumb like a voice from a cartoon.

"Hello," Maya said. "Who is this?"

"Who is *this*? Who are *you*?"

"What number are you calling?" Maya said, growing annoyed.

"Is this Maya?" the voice said. "Am I talking to Maya? Where's Maya?"

"This is Maya," Maya said. "Who's speaking?"

"Who's *speaking?* This is Mr. P., Maya..."

"Oh," she said, "Mr. P. How are you?"

"How am I? What do you mean, how am I? Where the hell have you been?"

"I'm sorry, Mr. P. I couldn't make it..."

"Couldn't make it? What do you think I'm running here, a health club or something? You just take two days off without telling anybody?"

"I'm sorry, Mr. P.—"

"Don't give me this *I'm Sorry*... What's the matter with you, Maya? You can't give us a call even? I should tell the buyers you're sorry?"

"I'm sorry, Mr. P.—"

"The hell with it! When are you coming in? We need you here... We got a lot of new stuff, you know, for your look. Mr. Aronson says you gotta come in today..."

Maya looked down at the pastel-yellow carpet, her hand curled tightly around the telephone receiver.

"Maya? You there?"

"Yes..."

"When are you coming in? Aronson says he's got three dresses that were made for you, you know what I mean?" His voice became low, confidential: "I mean ... these other girls here ... bags of bones, you know what I mean? I mean, that's what people want? All right, that's what they get. But we need somebody with a shape for some of this stuff, you see what I mean?" Then louder: "So, when can you come in? Couple of hours?"

"I'm not coming in. I'm ... going to Europe. I have to pack..."

"You're not coming in? Maya, what's the matter with you? Did I ... you know ... hurt your feelings? I mean, I was a little angry before..."

"I'm going to Europe, Mr. P. I'll be busy all this week..."

"Busy? Maya, give me a break. You didn't give me any notice or anything..."

"I'm sorry..."

"Look, Maya, just work till the end of the week, till we break somebody in..."

"I'm sorry..."

"What do you think, you can just walk out on people like that? You got no responsibility?"

"I'm really sorry..."

"So come in for the rest of the week....."

"I can't."

"Maya..."

"I'm sorry, I can't."

"Awright, Maya, but I just wanna tell you something. I just wanna tell you that you just screwed yourself but up the *ass!* You won't get another job in this city as long as you *live!* You won't get a job modeling *hot-dogs!* You ugly *bitch, you!* You won't get a job modeling *Tampax!* You think you can just walk out on people? I'll show you who you can walk out on..."

Maya lay back in bed, phone pressed to her ear, and stroked herself gently as Mr. P. screamed at her.

"Are you still there, you bitch? 'Cause I got something else to say to you..."

A mad gleam in her eye, Maya held the receiver in both hands and rubbed it up and down against her sleep-moist pussy, laughing at the tinny sound of Mr. P.'s voice as it blended with the wet gurgling of her warm vagina.

"Are you there? Are you there?" Mr. P. was screaming. His voice sounded like that of a midget with a bad cold. "Ah, go fuck yourself..." he said, and the phone went dead.

Disappointed, Maya wiped the receiver off on the bedsheets and hung it up. She walked lazily into the kitchen and made herself a cup of instant coffee, smiling to herself until she noticed the dried pool of blood and tears and mucous on the kitchen floor. The sight of it made her feel like calling Mr. P. back on the telephone and apologizing to him again. Instead, she opened the curtains and pulled a chair next to the window, leaning her bare legs on the windowsill as she drank her instant coffee.

It was very bright outside and the hundreds of people in the streets seemed to be animated with an odd sort of bustling joy, their arms swinging at their sides, their feet tapping the pavement. Almost all the women wore short bright skirts and the frequent flash of naked flesh gave the city something of a carnival atmosphere, a look of subtle gaiety. Maya followed a slow-moving middle-aged man up the street. He was dressed more shabbily than the others, wearing a thin short-sleeved shirt and a faded pair of chino pants, and he turned his head uneasily from left to right as he walked.

Finishing her coffee and turning from the window, Maya closed her eyes and tried to think of an excuse for her parents that would adequately cover her forthcoming departure to Etheus' lonely mansion. She could think only of telling them that she was going away, going to Europe or Japan, that she would be too busy to write to them for some ime. Then, when they never heard from her, they would think that she had simply forgotten them that she was enjoying herself too much to even think of them. And, too, they would think her so distant—Europe, after all—that it would never enter their minds to launch a search for her, and even if it did, they simply hadn't the means to pay for such a search.

Sighing, Maya stood up and walked into the bathroom. She washed her face and brushed her teeth, being very careful not to open a small cut on her lip which had resulted from the beating Peter had given her. Then she tore a small piece of toilet paper from the roll, braced one leg on the top of the orange toilet-seat, and wiped several times at her vagina, checking for her period. It never bothered her when she was late as this was the rule with her. She didn't use any birth control device—she had never even heard of birth control until coming to New York—and never gave so much as a thought to the possibility of pregnancy. When she had first met Peter, he had made constant love to her for a solid month, and she had not become pregnant. Maya had spent many restless nights with her face pressed into the pillow, worrying that she would never bear children, but then, with characteristic facility, she dismissed the problem from her mind, rationalizing that she didn't want any children yet anyway.

Maya flushed the tissue down the toilet, walked into the bedroom, and sat down on the edge of her bed. She decided that it would be best to call her parents immediately, to get it over with, out of her mind. She dressed in her bellbottoms and lime blouse of the day before—once, she had neglected to dress before calling her parents and she had been very uncomfortable for the duration of the phone call—and leaned against the bedroom windowsill while dialing her parents' number. The phone rang several times before it was answered.

"Hello?"

It was her mother's voice, distant and small. Maya pictured her wearing her green house-dress, perhaps with the gray sweater that she never seemed to take off. Maya wondered if her mother's face was still as smooth and round as it had been several years before, if the little wrinkles at the side of her mouth had grown deeper.

"Hello," Maya said. "It's—"

"Maya!" her mother cried. "Oh, Maya, it's so good to hear from you. We haven't spoken to you in ages . . . ages! How are you? Do you feel well? Is everything all right? We'd love to see you, dear . . . When are you coming up for a visit?"

"I'm fine," Maya said. "How are you?"

"Oh, we're fine, dear, we're just fine. When are you coming up to see us?"

"I'm afraid I won't be coming up. I'm going away . . ."

There was static over the phone and Maya pressed

the receiver tightly to her ear, twisting her hair in knots with her free hand.

"What did you say, dear? Did you say you're going somewhere?"

"Yes," Maya said. "I'm going to—"

"Just a minute, just a minute. Be right back..."

There was a loud noise, as if the phone had been dropped to the floor, followed by a long silence. Maya pictured her mother running to the kitchen to take some muffins out of the oven, folding her sweater around the hot pan as she always did.

"Hello, dear," her mother said finally. "Now, where are you going?"

"I'm going to Europe," Maya said.

"Europe!" her mother shouted. "Europe! That's so far away... How long will you be gone, dear?"

"A long time..."

"Well, how long?"

"I may not come back. I'll be living there for at least a year. I may stay there..."

There was a long silence during which Maya stared anxiously down at the dial of the telephone, tangling the long black cord around her fingers.

"Mother? Are you there?" she said finally.

"I'm here," her mother said. "I just don't know what to say... It's such a shock..."

"I know it's kind of sudden..."

"Well, who are you going with? Your fiancé? What's his name?"

"Peter."

"Are you going with Peter? I feel so terrible that we never met him..."

"No, I'm not going with Peter. We're not seeing each other anymore."

"Not seeing each other? That's *terrible,* Maya. What happened? He sounded like such a nice boy..."

"I don't know," Maya said. "Things just didn't work out. We weren't right for each other..."

"I'm so sorry to hear that, Maya. I'm really sorry."

There was an uncomfortable pause and Maya found herself tempted to say goodbye and hang up the phone.

"So who are you going with?" her mother said.

"Going with?" Maya said distractedly.

"To Europe," her mother said. "You're not going alone, are you?"

"No," Maya said, "no ... I'm going with a friend from work."

"A nice girl?" her mother said. Then: "What am I saying? Of course she's nice ... Well ... we'll miss you, Maya. We'll really miss you ... But ... we don't really see you now anyway ..."

"Is Daddy home?" Maya said. "I wanted to say goodbye to him."

"No," her mother said after a pause. "He's outside somewhere ... I don't know where he is ... Probably walking in the woods ... I'll tell him goodbye for you. Maya?"

"Yes ..."

"Write to us when you get a chance ... so we won't worry ..."

"I'll be very busy. I'll try ..."

"All right, Maya. Maybe ... it's just as well we won't be seeing you ... It'd just be very sad, I guess. Remember when you left for the city? Remember how I cried? I don't know ... I just get like that ... Well ... write to us once in a while, Maya ..."

"I'll try ..."

"All right ... all right. Well ... goodbye, darling. We'll miss you very much ..."

"Goodbye, Mama ... Give my love to Daddy ..."

Maya waited for her mother to hang up the phone and found herself listening to the old lady's soft crying. Over the telephone, it sounded like the mewing of a small kitten. Maya listened for a few seconds, her eyes closed, then very quietly hung up the phone, as if afraid to disturb her mother's sadness.

Maya paced about the house for a time, silently berating herself for her cruelty, then put on a pair of brown leather sandals and left the apartment building, ignoring the doorman's leering hello.

She walked aimlessly up and down the streets for a time, trying to think of some place to go. Normally, she went only to and from work during the week, making an occasional stop for groceries or the like, and on the weekends, Peter would take her to the movies or to a club. She thought of going to the beach, but dismissed the idea immediately when the memory of the man who had called himself Phil came into her mind. Finally, she thought of the park—Peter had taken her there once or twice—and she walked west until she came to the entrance nearest the zoo.

She bought an ice-cream bar at the entrance and sat down on a green bench next to an old man and watched the people on the benches opposite her feed the squirrels and pigeons. One old lady in a purple hat had at least twenty squirrels around her, some even standing on her lap, all imploring her with tiny, rapid movements for food. Two benches to the right of the old lady sat a well-dressed, fat-faced man wearing sunglasses and a low-brimmed hat. Hands folded behind his thick neck, he carried on a long, emphatic conversation with himself, occasionally pausing to gesture with one or both hands. He frightened Maya and she got up and strolled down the bench-lined lane, feeling the hot, cold, and indifferent glances of the park regulars on her back.

She passed the children's horse-cart ride and a little stand at which gaudy souvenirs were sold, then walked into the zoo and found herself staring at a huge shaggy-haired animal who was identified as a yak by the sign that hung on his cage. The yak stared at Maya with its large bloodshot eyes, then turned his back to her and chewed lazily on some bits of a leafy vegetable that had been thrown into his cage. It made Maya depressed that so huge an animal should be confined in such a small cage. She walked quickly away, hardly pausing to look at the queer miniature horses, or the camels, or the llama. She drifted around the zoo, watching children running from cage to cage, often fighting with their parents, until she came to the gorilla's cage, where she stood for half an hour watching the gigantic black gorilla pick up peanuts thrown by the crowd, scratch himself, and browbeat his mate, all with a look of the most profound boredom and disdain. He looked somehow unreal to Maya, like a man in a shaggy suit and black rubber mask. His quick eyes indicated an understanding which seemed even more than human, a resignation which was both tragic and beautiful. Finally, the gorilla stood up, urinated all over the floor of his cage, and pressed his face to the urine. It seemed a gesture intended for the crowd.

Maya walked away and bought a beer and a frankfurter at the cafeteria. She took it to a small table outside and ate to the sound of the seals that arf-arfed incessantly twenty yards from where she sat. The beer made her lightheaded, and when she had finished eating, she walked very lazily about the park, smiling at the children, the pigeons, the squirrels, and the birds. The park became a soft green blur to her as she walked, its noises like the song of wooden wind chimes. The asphalt lanes that she walked upon seemed always at a slight tilt so that the park always seemed turned to one side or the other, its hills rolling toward or away from Maya. She felt as if she were in a movie filmed at odd camera angles through very soft, hazy lenses.

"Hello."

Maya turned and stared at a tall boy with dirty-blond hair that fell almost to his shoulders. He wore scuffed brown boots and a pair of heavy dungarees patched at the knees with bits of bright-colored fabric. His yellow silk shirt was stained with dirt, the sleeves cut off at the elbow, the edges frayed and blowing in the light breeze that wafted through the park. His face was very lean and simple, scarred under one eye, and streaked with dirt, and he carried a heavy khaki knapsack strapped over his shoulders, its bulging seams threatening to burst at any moment.

"You look very happy," he said to Maya. He stood motionless at the side of the lane as he spoke, his eyes very calm, his thick-veined hands steady at his sides. "Are you as happy as you look?"

"Do I know you?" Maya said, tilting her head slightly to one side and smiling despite herself.

"I don't think so," the boy said. "I come from North Dakota. They call me Dakota."

"It's cold up there, isn't it?" Maya said.

"Real cold," the boy said. "Do you mind if I walk with you?"

"I guess not," Maya said.

With disarming naturalness, the boy stepped forward and slipped his hand around Maya's waist.

"You don't mind, do you?" he said. "I like to feel close to people."

The boy's touch made Maya feel warm and secure. She smiled up at him and slid her hand under his knapsack, hooking her thumb in his thick leather belt.

They walked in silence for a time, the boy occasionally pulling a leaf from a tree and chewing on its stem, Maya smiling to herself, her head pressed to the boy's strong shoulder.

"Do you come to this park a lot?" the boy said.

"No," Maya said. "Hardly ever."

"I've just been here a couple of days," the boy said. "I've been sleeping in this park . . ."

"You don't have a place to stay?" Maya said, looking up at him.

"Well," the boy said, "I guess I could find one if I wanted to, but I like to be outside when it's warm. I don't like the rest of this city too much anyway . . ."

A squirrel scurried into the path, stopped and fixed Maya and Dakota with his frightened little eyes. Dakota reached into his pocket and threw the squirrel a piece of a melted chocolate bar but the squirrel ran up a tree before the candy landed. Walking on, the boy stroked Maya's sun-sparkling hair and smiled.

"How come you stopped when I called you?" he said. "I thought for sure you were gonna run away . . ."

"I don't know," Maya said. "I wasn't scared of you or anything . . ."

"You know, once I said hello to a girl . . . it was in Georgia . . . prettiest little shady street I ever saw in my life . . . and this girl just started to scream and scream. She just stood there, screaming at the top of her lungs. I didn't know what in the hell to do . . . So these two bruisers come running out of the woodwork . . and *bam* . . . they did a number on me like there wasn't gonna be no tomorrow . . . Gave me this scar . . ." He traced the jagged line under his eye with his long thumb. "But . . . I never stopped saying hello to people . . ."

A little boy stood in the path, crying and reaching futilely in the air for a green balloon that had caught on a branch several yards above his head. Dakota tousled the boy's hair and took off his knapsack and climbed the tree, untangling the balloon's string and handing it to the boy. The boy accepted the balloon without a word and ran down the path, making a loud, airplane sound in his throat.

"He didn't even say thank you," Maya said as Dakota hefted the knapsack onto his back.

"Neither would I," Dakota said, slipping his hand around Maya's waist again.

They walked under a dark tunnel and Dakota stopped and clasped his hands behind Maya's neck and kissed her very lightly on the lips.

"Would you like to make love?" he said. "I haven't made love to anybody in weeks . . . I get real restless at night . . . like I don't know what to do with myself . . ."

Maya looked up at him and smiled, running her hand gently over his flat belly.

"Come on," he said, squeezing her plump bottom. "I know a beautiful place by the lake. I slept there last night and I didn't wake up till noon . . ."

They walked to the lake, then circled it until they came to the bottom of a sloping hill that ended at the water's edge. Dakota took off his knapsack and laid it against the gnarled trunk of a leafy tree.

"Here?" Maya said. "People can see ..." She pointed above her to the path at the top of the hill.

"Hardly anybody comes down this way," Dakota said. "And nobody'll bother us. If you close your eyes, you won't even know they're there ..."

He took off his yellow silk shirt and spread it on he ground, then sat down to pull off his brown leather boots, finally kicking off his brightly-patched dungarees and standing naked beneath the tall tree, his fat, thick-veined penis twitching against his strong thigh.

"Lie down," he said to Maya indicating his outspread yellow shirt. "I'll undress you ..."

Maya hesitated, then stretched herself on the ground, watching the sinewy muscles in his thighs as he walked forward and knelt between her legs. He unzipped her bellbottoms and stroked her smooth belly very gently, letting his fingers twist through her bushy triangle.

"Oh," he said very softly, his eyes closed. "I'm gonna give you *all* my love ..."

He pulled her bellbottoms down her legs, contemplated her good-and-pink pussy for a minute, then bent forward and buried his face in her slit, forcing her lips apart with his thick tongue. Maya moaned and opened her legs wide, then locked them around the boy's neck, praying, in the back of her mind, that no one would walk by and spot them.

The boy tongued her for a long time, swallowing mouthful after mouthful of her thick juice, tickling the grass-dampened crack of her bottom with his forefinger.

"Do you like to be fingered in your asshole?" the boy said, wetting his forefinger in the depths of her pussy. "I knew a girl that used to go crazy for that ..."

"Ummm," Maya said, nodding her head.

The boy ran his dripping finger up and down the cleft of Maya's rump as he tongued her, then explored the soft, tiny folds of her asshole with his long thumb. Maya squeezed her buttocks together as the boy slipped his thumb slowly into her rear opening and forced the smooth walls wide apart.

"Take off your shirt," the boy said to Maya, swirling his thumb in her hole and touching her pudgy clitoris with the tip of his tongue.

As Maya pulled the lime blouse over her head, the boy stretched himself beside her, thumb stuck firmly in her deliciously-contracting anus, and took the long nipple of her breast in his mouth, alternately biting it gently and teasing it with his tongue. Then, as Maya slid her hands feverishly up and down long his back and buttocks and thighs, the boy placed his weight on her and rubbed the plum-like head of his penis against her tongue-wetted slit, massaging lips, hole, and clitoris, with long, easy strokes. Maya reached under her thigh and grabbed the boy's long pole in her hand, pulling it to her silk-haired entrance.

"Put it in," she whispered breathlessly.

The boy gave her just the head of his penis, vibrating it expertly in the sucking vestibule of her hole, covering her neck with warm, wet kisses. Maya tried to force him into her, pulling him by the buttocks and thrusting her pelvis upward, but the boy resisted her eagerness and entered her very slowly, giving her only a half an inch at a time and occasionally pulling his organ out of her so that just the very tip of its head rested between the trembling lips of her pussy. Then, as Maya shuddered beneath him, the boy plunged the length of it into her, smiling down at her as the twitching head poked into her innermost depths and a cry of surprise escaped her lips. Without moving his body, the boy jerked his thick penis up and down inside her and Maya responded by squeezing her hole open and shut on his shaft, massaging it from tip to base. His penis swollen from Maya's powerful contractions, the boy raised himself on his elbows and rocked slowly back and forth on his out-stretched toes, his organ cutting a wide, circular path in Maya's foam-sloshing pussy. Maya locked her legs around the backs of the boy's tensed thighs, rubbing his smooth buttocks with the soles of her feet.

"That's nice," the boy said, closing his eyes. Then, pressing his belly tightly against Maya's, his sparse-haired testicles falling against her upraised buttocks: "I'm gonna make you come now..."

He wiggled his penis inside her, his buttocks shaking wildly, and plunged in and out of her as if he was scooping ice-cream from her pussy. Maya clutched his strong back and rolled in the cool grass with his thrusts, her pussy gurgling, thick vaginal foam dripping down the insides of her thighs.

Suddenly, Maya heard footsteps overhead. She looked up and saw a short, bald-headed man standing at the top of the hill staring incredulously down at them. The boy called Dakota saw the look of fear in Maya's eyes and stared upward at the man, a smile on his lips.

"Hello," he said to the man, simultaneously doubling the tempo of his thrusts and tickling Maya's sweat-drenched armpits with his fingers.

As the bald man walked quickly down the other side of the hill, Dakota bent forward and kissed Maya on the lips, forcing her mouth open with his tongue and orally imitating the movements of his penis. Tossing like a beached flounder, Maya reached her orgasm, raking her fingernails along the boy's sides and sucking his tongue deep into her mouth.

"You didn't come," she said finally, running her calves along the backs of the boy's legs and massaging his rigid pole with slow contractions of her pussy.

"I want you to have a few more," he said with a smile, rolling over on his back and pulling Maya with him. "I can come anytime I want." As he finished speaking, he began lifting Maya slowly up and down on his sky-ward pointing organ, thumping it occasionally against the smooth walls of her hole with a quick contraction of belly and buttocks.

He brought her twice more to orgasm, his biceps bulging as he lifted her high in the air and pulled her tightly to his hairy groin, her buttocks meeting his testicles with rhythmic, resounding slaps. Then he lay on his back while she sucked lovingly on his foam-covered penis, her lips pressed tightly against the shaft, her tongue tickling the underside of the plum-shaped head. Finally, he took her from behind, filling her almost immediately with his hot, thick libation and falling forward across her back, his belly pressed to her smooth rump as if glued to it.

"Shouldn't we get dressed?" Maya said as he lay on top of her, his breath hot against her ear.

Wiping the sweat from his forehead, the boy acquiesced, patting Maya's bottom affectionately before getting to his feet. As he dressed himself lazily, he cast worried glances at Maya, who stared blankly down at the grass as she pulled on her bellbottoms and lime blouse.

"What's the matter?" the boy said finally as he buttoned his yellow shirt.

"Nothing," Maya said. "I don't know . ."

"Yes you do," the boy said. "What's wrong? You looked so happy before ... Didn't you like making love?"

"I loved it," Maya said. "I really loved it. You made me feel very ... beautiful . ."

"Then what is it?" the boy said, lying down on the grass and pulling her down beside him. "You look so sad ... You look worried ... or angry with yourself ..."

"I don't know," Maya said. "I was just thinking about my parents ..."

"What about them?" the boy said.

"Well," Maya said, "I'm going away soon ... I may never see them again ..."

"It's real hard to say goodbye to people," the boy said. "You know, I hated my daddy like poison ... he'd been punching my head since I was old enough to walk ... but when it came time to say goodbye to him ... when I left home ... I cried like a baby ... and I'll be damned if he didn't cry too, the old bastard ..."

He paused, took a pouch of tobacco from his shirt-pocket, and rolled a cigarette. "You got any brothers or sisters?" he said, lighting the cigarette and inhaling deeply.

"No," Maya said, "I'm an only child.."

"When were you born?" the boy said. "May? June?"

"May," Maya said. "The twenty-fifth of May. And they named me Maya . . ."

"I thought you were born around then," the boy said, "You're a Gemini. Did you know that?"

"No," Maya said. "Does that mean anything?"

"It's the twins," the boy said. "I don't know much about it, but I just had a feeling of something . . . like . . . double . . . about you. Like twins or something. I had a brother who was Gemini, but he died in a fight with one of his friends. It was about a girl, I think . . . some crazy nonsense , . . and my brother's friend killed him . . . stuck a knife in his heart . . . but then the friend died too, a couple of days later. Drowned himself to death in the bathtub. Everybody said it was accidental . . . he'd been drinking a real lot . . . but I think he killed himself out of grief . . . 'cause he loved my brother more than anything in the world . . ."

"That's sad," Maya said.

"It sure is," the boy said. "It sure is . . ."

He plucked a tall stalk of grass from the ground and put it between his teeth, waving it up and down with a tiny motion of his jaw. The sun was sinking behind a gently-sloped hill in the distance, casting half of the boy's lean face in soft shadow.

"Where do your folks live?" the boy said, touching Maya's bare arm.

"In Vermont," Maya said, "In a little town near Keene."

"Ho-eee," the boy said. "You know, if my daddy lived up in Vermont, I'd go to see him once a week, just to get the tar beat out of me . . ."

Maya laughed and squeezed the boy's hand, then closed her eyes and lay very still.

"I'll bet your mother cried when you said goodbye," the boy said. "Am I right?"

"Yes," Maya whispered.

"And your daddy squeezed you real tight?"

"No," Maya said. "He didn't squeeze me . . ."

The boy fell silent for a time, rolling his head back and forth in the grass.

"You know something?" he said finally, running his hand lightly over Maya's belly. "I could do with another fuck or two . . . How about you?"

"No," Maya said suddenly, sitting up and looking around her. "I have to go . . ."

She stood up, tightened the straps of her leather sandals, and walked quickly away, her long golden hair blowing wildly in the breeze.

"Hey!" the boy shouted, jumping to his feet. "Where you going?"

"I'm going home," Maya called without turning, then ran quickly down the asphalt pathway and disappeared in the distance, leaving the boy called Dakota standing dumbly under a tree.

VIII

"We've got one leaving in three-quarters of an hour. Good enough?" the man said.

"Yes," Maya said, staring vacantly at a huge wall-map crisscrossed with thin black lines and dotted with little red marks.

The man put his glasses in his jacket pocket and wrote out the ticket, then inserted it in a heavy stamping machine.

"That'll be twenty dollars and twenty-four cents," he said. "Round trip, you said?"

"Yes," Maya said. "Round trip."

"Twenty dollars and twenty-four cents."

Maya gave him a twenty and a one and he gave her change, then peered over the counter at Maya's feet.

"No luggage?" he said. "You should have taken a sweater at least. It gets pretty cold up there around this time . . ."

Maya shrugged her shoulders, took her ticket and change, and stepped out of the way of a young sailor who approached the window after her.

"Don't forget," the man behind the counter said. "Change at Boston . . ."

Maya waved without turning and took the escalator downstairs, her breasts cold under the thin lime blouse, her long, erect nipples clearly delineated by the clinging fabric.

Downstairs, the terminal was alive with men, women, and children waiting for any one of fifty busses. Women sat on their suitcases, children ran around and around the cigarette and candy machines, men paced nervously about, and red-capped porters pushed suitcase-piled cars through the thick crowds yelling, "Coming through! Coming through!" Maya walked quickly through the crowd toward a sign that read: 22: BRIDGEPORT, BOSTON. Once, a small man wearing sunglasses squeezed her bottom as she passed him, and then, several seconds later, a Negro red-cap grinned at her and pointed excitedly toward his groin. Both times, Maya hurried by, trying her best not to become flustered.

A group of about forty people stood waiting for the bus to Boston, some leaning on the terminal's tiled wall, some sitting on the floor, others standing in small groups outside the door to the boarding area. A bleary-eyed, staggering drunk walked back and forth, pint bottle in hand, asking everyone for the time and screaming about a woman that was waiting for him in Bridgeport.

Maya stood rigidly beside the tiled wall, looking constantly at a large clock that hung suspended from the terminal's grimy ceiling. Suddenly, she stared slightly at the sight of a tall, awkward-looking boy who stared wide-eyed at her from under a dark stairwell. He seemed terribly nervous, his hollow cheeks flushed and twitching, and as soon as Maya spotted him, he turned quickly away, as if frightened. He reminded Maya of a rabbit, so quick were his movements, so small his eyes. He was poorly dressed, wearing a navy blue sportjacket too large for his narrow frame and a pair of unpressed gray slacks that broke several inches above his shoes, leaving his thin, white-socked ankles exposed. Maya soon felt a motherly compassion for the boy, but each time she cast a glance in his direction, he looked quickly away, shifting his weight from large-shoed foot to large-shoed foot, and pretending to smooth his lustreless brown hair.

Several yards from where the boy stood, a strange couple sat huddled together on a cordovan-colored suitcase, their arms intertwined, hands resting on each other's thighs. At first, Maya thought that they were both boys or both girls. They wore their hair at the same length—curling to the base of the neck—and both were smooth-faced and dark-eyed. They were dressed indentically in wheat-colored jeans, open-toed sandals, and dark knit shirts, their collars pulled up over the backs of their necks. Maya stared closely at them to determine their respective genders and discovered that they were actually boy and girl, their only distinguishing features being their genitals. Maya wondered if they were brother and sister, staring at the soft bulge that rested against the boys thigh, then blushed as she noticed the girl staring back at her, a strange, vaguely sinister smile on her lips.

Maya turned and walked several yards away to a red candy machine. She depositied a nickel and pulled the lever for mint life-savers, then opened the round package and popped two of the candies into her mouth. When she turned back to the 22: BRIDGEPORT, BOSTON sign, the bus had already pulled in and everyone was crowded at the door to the boarding area.

"I'm going home to my sweet angel!" the drunk was screaming, swigging from his pint bottle and wiping his mouth with the stained cuff of his jacket. "I'm going home to my sweet angel!"

After everyone's baggage had been loaded into the cut-out panels at the side of the bus, the fat, slick-haired driver opened the door and took tickets as he let the people on. Maya entered last, shivering slightly with exposure to the air-conditioning, and handed the driver her ticket.

"Change at Boston," the driver said, tearing part of her ticket off and handing the rest back to her. "You're gonna get mighty cold in just that little green thing," he said as an afterthought, staring at Maya's protruding nipples. "Want my jacket?" He smiled at her and started to take the gray jacket from the back of his seat.

"No thank you," Maya said and proceeded down the aisle.

The bus seemed filled to capacity and as Maya walked toward its rear, she prayed that she would find a vacant seat. She breathed a sigh of relief as she came to the last seat on the aisle—right next to the lye-stinking bathroom—and found it unoccupied, then felt her heart jump as she recognized the awkward-looking boy who had reminded her of a rabbit sitting in the window-seat next to it. She sat down in the seat, both amused and touched by the boy's hot blushes, took out another life-saver, and popped it into her mouth.

The driver made a few jokes over the public address system while announcing the stops the bus would make, then started the bus, turned out the dim overhead lighting, and pulled out of the terminal, following a long, winding ramp down to the street. Night was falling as the bus drove uptown past Lincoln Center and through Harlem and Maya found herself staring through the green-tinted window at crowds of black men and women standing restlessly in the streets, some talking, others watching the traffic, and quite a number dancing to music that played from loudspeakers hung over the entranceways to various stores. As she watched the flow of life in the street, Maya felt the boy next to her staring at her out of the corner of his eye, his large hands trembling slightly in his lap. It occurred to her to offer him a mint life-saver, but she decided against it, fearing that she might scare him.

Within minutes, the bus was travelling on a fluorescent-lit expressway, cars passing on either side of it. The scenery became dull and monotonous as the bus sped forward into the darkness, sign after bright-lettered sign announcing the proximity of this or that restaurant or motel, gas station after dingy gas station announcing its new give-away contest. Maya sat back in her seat and wished that she had brought something to read. She popped one life-saver after another into her mouth in an effort to take her mind off the heavy smell of lye that rose out of the rest-room beside her.

In the front of the bus, the drunk was singing, "Oh, my little angel . . I love you so much ... I want to tell the whole wide *world* ... and I love you so much ... that I can't live without you . . oh, my little angel-dear ..."

"Will you shut up?" somebody said.

The drunk stood up and broke into a fast chorus of *Yes Sir, That's My Baby* and the driver stopped the bus and told the drunk that if he didn't shut his face he was going to have to get off the bus. The drunk thought about it for a minute, then took a swig from his bottle, and got off the bus.

The bus became deathly quiet with the drunk gone and Maya closed her eyes and thought about having dinner with her parents, listening to the hushed night-sounds of the forest outside the kitchen window. She fell into a light doze, her arms folded across her breasts, then woke suddenly as she felt something drop across her lap. Blinking her eyes, she let out a tiny gasp at the sight of the boy's large, clumsy-fingered hand resting on the top of her thigh, pinky and ring-finger lightly grazing her crotch. More surprised than anything else—the boy had seemed so *shy* to her —she turned toward him and found his head pressed to the green-tinted window, his eyes closed as if with sleep. For a few seconds, she wondered if she should remove his hand from her crotch, then almost broke into a chuckle as she noticed the boy's other hand working busily on a stout penis concealed in the loose folds of his gray pants. She watched him for a few minutes, fascinated by the stealth with which he took his pleasure, touched by his innocence, and excited by the frenzied motion of the hand with which he stroked himself. Then, moving as little as possible so as not to frighten him, she undid the zipper of her bellbottoms and pulled them down to the edge of her triangle. She paused a second, staring at the boy, her lips parted with anticipation, then touched him lightly on the hand.

The boy froze, his eyes shut tightly, his hand turning cold and clammy. Very, very gently, Maya pulled his hand under her pants and pushed it down over her hairy mound. The boy gasped, then began to breathe very rapidly, the motion of his hand on his stiff organ seeming to Maya like a scene from a sped-up silent movie.

Squeezing her thighs around the boy's other hand, Maya reached over and unzipped his fly, then reached into his underwear and pulled out a long, meaty organ and stretched it against the boy's belly. Again, the boy froze, then pressed his face hard against the window as Maya caressed the soft underside of his penis, then pulled out his heavy balls and tickled them with her slender fingers.

The boy seemed afraid to stroke Maya's pussy. He left his hand exactly where she had placed it, resisting even the insistent squeezing of her thighs. Maya placed her free hand under her bell-bottoms and pressed the boy's hand tightly around her pussy, forcing his heavy fingers to explore her moist slit while she jerked his penis up and down, running her hand along the length of it. She wanted to get down on her knees and suck the boy's sturdy pole—she was willing to bet he had never had it sucked—but considered the business too risky. Instead, she forced two of the boy's thick fingers inside her hole and played with him with both hands, running the fingers of one hand around the head of his penis, and beating his bone-hard shaft with the other. Suddenly, the movement of the boy's hand on Maya's pussy became convulsive, frenzied. He whipped his fingers madly up and down inside her and scratched at her curly triangle with his thumb, his pinky lodging in the crack of her bottom. Then, in great, slow bursts, he ejaculated, spurting huge gobs of semen high in the air, the terrific pumping of his organ almost forcing Maya's hand away. Maya waited until the last drops of hot fluid had trickled down the sides of the boy's penis, then grabbed him by the wrist and forced his hand violently up and down in her pussy until she felt her own orgasm approach. Squeezing the boy's drooping penis for all it was worth, and locking her thighs around his hand, she rocked back and forth in her seat until the climax exploded within her, then dropped her head against the boy's shoulder, her eyes closed. After a short rest, she leaned forward, first casting a quick glance over her shoulder, and licked the boy's limp organ clean of semen. For the first time, the boy opened his eyes and looked at her, his face utterly pale, his lips trembling. Maya smiled at him, put his penis back in his pants, and zipped his fly, then sat back in her seat and raised her buttocks slightly to close her bellbottoms. As she fastened he zipper and sank down in her seat, she saw a pair of dark, gleaming eyes staring at her from across the aisle. It was the girl that Maya had seen earlier sitting on the cordovan suitcase, her arm aroung her identically-dressed ... brother? Lover? Maya and the dark-eyed girl stared at each other for a full five minutes, Maya sitting calmly with lips slightly parted, the dark-eyed girl smiling a mysterious smile, bracing herself on the arm of her seat as the bus zipped silently through the night. Then Maya turned away and closed her eyes, her body shivering with the cold. In a short time, she was asleep, dreaming of pine-cones falling lazily into snow.

Clouds were gathering in the sky as the bus pulled into the run-down municipal parking-lot that served as Keene's bus terminal. Maya got off the bus and walked into the shabby little bus depot to see if she could get a taxi to take her to her parents' house in Green River. Inside the depot stood a cluttered desk and a battered coke machine. Behind the desk sat a small, sleepy-eyed man who Maya remembered very vaguely from her childhood. She didn't know many of the people in Keene—it was a large town, trying to be a city—but she had come there occasionally as a child when her mother had taken her with her to shop for some new appliance or other, and later, as a teenager, to take the bus to some uncle or aunt's house in a neighboring town, her father always driving her to the terminal and warning her to be very careful and not to talk to strangers.

Maya walked to the corner and into Big Ed's Cigar, Newspaper and Candy Store. With a perfunctory smile at Big Ed's puffy face, she walked into the back to the telephone booth and found herself staring at a cardboard sign lettered in red crayon that read: IF YOU PLAN TO USE THIS PHONE, PLAN TO USE SOME MONEY TO BUY SOMETHING IN THIS STORE. She walked back to the counter and bought two packages of mint life-savers, then returned to the telephone and dialed her parents' number. The phone rang for at least a minute before it was answered.

"Hello?" It was Maya's mother, her voice breathless, as if she had been running.

"It's Maya . . . Guess what?" Maya said.

"Maya!" her mother cried. "What is it? What's the surprise?"

"I'm in Keene," Maya said. "Can you send Daddy to pick me up?"

"Oh, Maya!" her mother shouted. "What are you doing in Keene?"

"I wanted to see you," Maya said. "I miss you . . ."

"You're so sweet, Maya," her mother said. "You're really so sweet . . . ."

"Can you send Daddy to get me?" Maya said. "I'm in Big Ed's . . . you know . . . on the corner . . ."

"Well . . ." her mother said, then paused.

"Mom?" Maya said. "Can you send Daddy?"

"Well," her mother said, "all right. I'll be there as soon as I can . . ."

They said goodbye and Maya hung up the phone and walked outside. She stood on the corner watching late-model cars and bashed-in pickup trucks travel up and down the street, then stepped back and waited under Big Ed's awning as a light drizzle started to fall. She smiled at the thought of spending a night or two in her old bedroom, decided that she would take a walk through the woods later if it cleared up.

After a half-hour of waiting under Big Ed's green-and-red striped awning, Maya saw her father's wood-paneled station wagon driving slowly up the block. Her mother was alone in the car, dressed in a light green house dress and her familiar gray cardigan sweater. Maya ran to the round-cheeked old lady as soon as the car stopped, reached through the open window and hugged her with all her might. Her mother cried briefly, holding Maya tightly by the back of the neck, then took out a crumpled tissue and wiped her eyes and nose.

"Come, Maya," she said. "Get in the car. We have to hurry..."

Maya walked around to the passenger's side of the car and slid into the front seat, the long-forgotten leather-and-oil smell of the car making her feel warm and dizzy.

"What's the hurry?" she said, closing the door behind her and pressing down the plastic-covered lock.

"Well," her mother said, driving nervously up the street, "your father hasn't been feeling too well... I don't like to leave him alone for too long..."

"What's wrong with him?" Maya asked, staring at her mother's somewhat haggard face. "He's sick?"

"Well ... you know," her mother said vaguely, "we're getting kind of old ... I guess ..."

Maya looked closely at her mother's soft gray eyes, creased at the corners now and weighted with small, fleshy bags.

"It's nothing serious, is it?" Maya said.

"We're getting old, Maya," her mother said. "We're just getting old..."

She turned the car to the left and drove away from Keene down a narrow road cut into the woods. Maya stared out the window, damp breeze blowing her hair wildly in the air and felt small chills run up her back as she recognized sight after familiar sight. She almost cried when they passed the outdoor antique market that her parents had taken her to once a month for the duration of her childhood, its wizened, red-nosed proprietor still sitting in the battered rocking chair that he'd sat in when she was four years old. In the distance, jutting peaks stood like sentries over the forest, their summer-green sides dotted with birch and beech trees.

Within several minutes the car was driving through the two-block town of Green River and Maya was constantly startled at the sight of familiar faces grown slightly older. It seemed odd to her that here, where she had spent so many of her childhood Saturdays and Sundays, her memory was terribly at fault, while she had remembered Keene, which had never been a familiar place to her, down to the spit-stains on the linoleum floor of Big Ed's Cigar, Newspaper, and Candy Store. In Green River, stores seemed always smaller than she had remembered them, faces less exaggerated and the bright things that had attracted her as a child —the buzzing neon sign over the diner and the painted horse on the hardware store window—far duller than represented in her mind.

At the edge of the town, Maya's mother turned right down a steep hill that passed over rusting old railroad tracks that hadn't been used in years.

"You look so beautiful, Maya," she said. "You're getting to be a woman . . ." She smiled, brushing a strand of graying brown hair from her lightly-wrinkled forehead. "You were such a beautiful little girl ... Daddy and I always look at the pictures of you in the album... You know, your hair was almost white when you were a baby..."

As she spoke, she turned the car down a narrow dirt road and drove very slowly toward a small two-story house made of logs with an adjoining porch and a crude stone chimney rising upward at its side. Maya felt her heart flutter at the sight of the old wooden house that she had thought she would never see again. She heard the peaceful sound of the lake lapping against its stony shore and she remembered mornings spent with her father in the family's little rowboat, waiting, waiting for a hungry fish.

"Well," her mother said. "Here we are." She stopped the car under a tall oak that served as its garage and slid out, Maya following her to the red screen door, her eyes bright with anticipation.

"Maya," her mother said to her. She had a queer look in her soft eyes.

"Yes," Maya said.

Her mother stared at her for a few seconds, then turned away.

"Never mind," she said with a smile, pulling open the screen door by its rusty handle and motioning Maya in.

"Daddy?" Maya called as she walked through the darkened living room. "Daddy?"

"He's in the bedroom, Maya," her mother said, sitting down on the single wooden chair that stood near the fireplace.

Maya walked through a narrow hallway and knocked lightly on the door to the bedroom, then swung the door open and almost collapsed at the sight of her father. The sickly-sweet smell of his fast-approaching death was heavy in the air.

The old man was propped up grotesquely in bed with three fat pillows behind his back and head, his bloodless arms hanging limp at his sides. His face seemed more a skull than a face, the cheeks puckered and hollow, the eyes sunk so deep in the head that they seemed merely empty sockets, the thin lips pulled back to expose tartar-encrusted teeth. Trembling, the old man lifted his arm several inches from the blanket, reaching toward Maya who watched it drop like a dead weight to the bed.

Maya's mother filled a fire-blackened kettle with water and put it on the old-fashioned stove to boil. Then, as if struck with an idea, she pulled open the kitchen curtains and beckoned eagerly to Maya.

"Look," she said, pointing out the window.

Maya walked to the window and stared out at the tree-bordered lake shimmering at the base of the hill on which the house rested.

"It's so beautiful this time of year," her mother said.

For a brief second, the peaceful rippling of the lake made Maya feel as if she were in a soft, silent dream. She watched two fallen leaves drift with the motion of the lake, swirling in little circles as they moved ever closer to the shore. Then, as if with the passing of a cloud, her eyes became sad and her lips trembled.

"Why didn't you tell me about Daddy?" she asked her mother.

"I didn't know how to say it," her mother said. "What should I have said? Maya, your father is dying?"

"How long has he been like this?" Maya said.

"I don't know ... A few months, maybe a little longer ..."

"Why didn't you tell me? Why didn't you tell me on the telephone? Tell me to come up?"

"To watch him die? Who wants to watch somebody die? It isn't pretty, watching someone die ..."

"You should have told me," Maya said. "He's my father ..."

"You didn't marry him," her mother said. "When you marry somebody, they make you say something about loving him in sickness and in health ... You didn't marry him. You don't have to watch him die ..." She opened the old coffeepot and filled its upper section with ground coffee, then poured in the boiling water and let the pot stand. "Believe me," she said. "He didn't want you to know. What do you think, he wants you to remember him like this? White and coughing and spitting up his guts? I'll tell you the truth ... I wanted you to come up ... I even asked you, remember? I said, Maya, when are you coming to see us? I don't know.... I thought you should see each other once more.... But when you said you were going away, I was glad that you weren't going to see him ... I was relieved ..."

Her room was exactly as she had left it, colorfully-bound books arranged neatly on the bookcase, mirror tilting from dresser to wall, headboard of the bed flush with the windowsill. The thin layer of dust that covered the room gave it a hazy, soft quality. It brought an increasingly familiar dream-like feeling to Maya and she closed her eyes and stretched her arms out at her sides, as if trying to commune with a spirit. As she opened her eyes, breathing in the room's piney smell, a little white box that stood atop the dresser caught her eye. She opened it ever so delicately, not in the least surprised to find it empty. The simulated pearls it had once contained had been lost in the woods years before.

Gently, Maya placed the box back on the dresser, remembering the bright feeling of the pearls around her throat. Then, the dustiness of the room made her sneeze and she took a broom and a dustpan from the closet and gave the room a thorough sweeping. She made the bed very tidily, fluffing up the goose-feather pillow with both hands and tucking the sheets neatly under the mattress as she had been taught to do as a child. Then she pulled her bellbottoms down her smooth legs, hoping that her mother wouldn't have any occasion to notice that she hadn't worn any underwear, and pulled her lime top over her head. Naked but for her leather sandals, she lifted one leg onto the edge of the bed and wiped the slit of her pussy with her middle finger, checking for her period. Finding no sign of it, she turned and stared at herself in the mirror that stood atop her dresser, finding it strange to see the full body of a woman reflected in the wood-framed mirror of her childhood. The sight of her upthrust breasts and outward-spreading bush made her feel oddly detached from herself, as if she was neither child nor woman but some third person, observing both child and woman from a distance. Vaguely frightened, she pulled off her sandals and got into bed, pulling the covers up over her shoulders and turning her face from the fading gray daylight that seeped into the room through the window's dusty panes of glass.

Hands folded over her belly, Maya thought of Etheus and Suzanne. She didn't really miss either of them —though the thought of them, and of the smiling man, greatly pricked her curiosity—and didn't particularly wish to return to the lonely mansion in which they dwelled, but she felt bound to return by her promise to Etheus and by his rightful victory over her. She felt it obligatory to stay with her mother until her father died —the old lady would need someone to comfort her— but felt an insistent tension at the thought of missing her rendezvous at the little restaurant on Long Island. To avoid wishing for her father's death, she decided to stay with her mother in any event, rationalizing that she would somehow be able to get in touch with Etheus even if her return to New York was delayed. Then, as she thought of New York and its bustling streets, and listened with half an ear to the low murmuring of the lake below, Peter entered her mind. She saw him crying, his face pressed to hers, and she heard herself calling him a faggot over and over again.

"Faggot . . . You're a little faggot . . . Faggot . . ."

The memory filled her with such deep guilt that she dismissed it immediately from her mind, and forced herself to think of pleasant childhood experiences: rowing in the lake with her father, sitting between her parents in a darkened movie theatre. Slowly, she drifted into sleep and dreamed of riding endlessly on a bus, searching frantically for her ticket at each stop.

"I guess there's not much to do around here for a city-girl," her mother said with a smile. "You must go to so many parties in the city . . . so many shows and things . . ."

Maya shrugged her shoulders and put out her cigarette in a ceramic ashtray that her father had always used. "I think I'll go for a walk," she said, rising to her feet.

"It's so dark outside, Maya," her mother said. Then,

chiding herself: "Oh, you know me. I'm always so afraid of everything. Go ... go for your walk ... but be careful, Maya ..."

Maya kissed her mother's cheek and opened the back door.

"Aren't you going to take a sweater?" her mother said. "It's cold out ..."

"I'll be all right," Maya said, stepping through the doorway and closing the door behind her. "See you soon," she shouted.

She stood at the side of the house for a moment, staring up at the stars, goosebumps rising on her bare arms. Then, as she walked away from the house, the night became totally black, impenetrable, the branches of trees obscuring the faint light of the tiny crescent moon. Maya paused in the blackness for a time, not able to see two feet in front of her, and listened to the rustling noises of the forest's night-creatures. Over the noise of the crickets and the shooshing sound of the wind, Maya could hear the gently-rippling water of the lake. Arms held out before her, she turned to the right and descended the steep hill that led to the shore of the lake, her feet slipping on moist stones, her hands clutching desperately at branches with which to steady herself. Once, she slipped and tumbled headlong into the blackness. The crickets ceased their low rattle until she caught hold of the low-hanging branch of a tree and brought herself to balance, her sandalled feet digging deeply into the moist earth. She moved very cautiously after that, never relinquishing her hold on one object until another had come into her grasp, until finally, after what seemed hours of slow crawling, she felt the stones of the shore under her feet. She knelt down and moved on hands and feet until she came to a large stone that stood half in and half out of the water, then took off her sandals and rolled her bellbottoms up over her knees and sat down on the rock, dangling her shapely legs in the lake. She sat quietly for a time, making the water ripple with slow, circular motions of her legs, listening to the croaking of the frogs and the splashing sounds that the fish made diving about in the lake. Then, made bold by the warmth of the water, she stood up on the stone and pulled off her clothing and waded naked into the lake.

She stood thigh-deep in the water, standing on a flat piece of mossy slate and swirling her fingertips in figure-eights at her sides. The feeling of the slow-moving water between her legs—just barely lapping at the fine hairs that graced her crotch and curled upward toward the wind-tickled crack of her rump—made her feel a warmth so powerful that it became a pressure. Suddenly, she spread her legs wide apart, thrust her belly forward, and urinated into the lake, running her hands through the barely-visible golden stream and feeling the stream of her urine rise in the air. Then, still urinating, tinkle of her thin stream blending with the croaking of the frogs, she walked to the edge of the lake and dove into the water. She did the Australian crawl for a minute or two, churning the water with the kicking motion of her feet, then broke into a slow breast-stroke and frog-kick, holding her legs open as wide and as long as possible, wanting to fill her pussy with the lake's warm water. Finding that the water would not enter her, she stopped swimming and began treading water with her feet and one hand, pulling the lips of her pussy open with the other hand and suddenly flipping herself over on her back, scooping a good cupful of water into her vagina in the process. She floated on her back, watching her seemingly detached breasts rising out of the water like two sunken islands capped with bumpy lighthouses, and wiggled her buttocks so that the water in her pussy sloshed like a warm malted against her smooth membrane. She tried several times to finger herself, finding that the water inside her would not bring her to orgasm, but each time she moved her outstretched arm she sank helplessly beneath the lake's surface, her long hair swirling about her like the underwater plants that were visible during the day. Discouraged heat rising within her, she turned and swam toward the shore, doing a slow sidestroke so as not to hurt herself against the rocks. Then, as if in a dream, she made out the faint moon-lit outline of her father's rowboat moored to a wooden post. She swam to it and grabbed its hull, lifting one leg over the side and pulling her slippery body upward with hands and feet.

She sat motionless in the boat for a time, listening to the gentle splashing of the lake against its sides and feeling the water drip from her hairy crotch. Then she lay down in the bottom of the boat, her head propped against its hard wooden seat, and placed her legs over its sides, her water-seeping pussy making a gurgling sound as its lips were pulled to their limit. She toyed lazily with her clitoris for a minute, squeezing it until it stiffened, then pulling it up and down as if it were a light-switch, then moving it in a circle, rubbing it against the wet, clinging hairs that adorned her slit. She moaned softly, as if enjoying her hand for the first time, then brought her other hand to the mouth of her plump vagina and circled the eager hole with her middle finger. Gripping the sides of the boat tightly with her tautened calves, she slipped the finger slowly into her pussy and felt the smooth walls tighten around it. She fingered herself for several minutes, her buttocks grinding against the boat's damp bottom, her breath rasping through clenched teeth. Then, conjuring up an image of Suzanne bending forward and spreading the cheeks of her rump to expose the upside-down V of her red-slitted bush, Maya wrenched the finger from her pussy and held it under her nose. She smelled it for several seconds, rubbing her clitoris and remembering the taste of Suzanne's hot mound, then plunged it impulsively into her mouth and sucked it clean of foam.

Her heat made more intense by the taste of her own juices, Maya thrust two fingers inside herself and worked them deeper and deeper as if trying to force her entire hand into her burning pussy. Her extended legs banging crazily against the sides of the boat, she jerked herself to a thunderous climax, her loud gasps bringing even the frogs to silence.

She lay still in the boat for a long time, her body perfectly relaxed, thick foam dripping down the insides of her thighs and spreading beneath her buttocks. She thought of sleeping in the boat but soon began to sneeze with the dampness of the air and decided that she had better return to the house. She scrambled to the shore and located her clothing after a great deal of stumbling, dressed herself, and started up the hill toward the house. Suddenly, she felt as if someone was beside her. She stopped and waved her hand through the air, but touched only the thin branch of a tree. She was overwhelmed by a sense of *deja vu*. She felt certain that at some earlier time—perhaps as a young child—she had stood at this exact spot, felt these exact same sensations. She told herself that she was being foolish, that there was nothing to be afraid of, and proceeded slowly up the hill, then stopped frozen in her tracks, heart pounding wildly, as she heard a soft, rustling sound behind her.

"Who is it?" she whispered.

Only the low shoosh of the wind answered her. The frogs and crickets were perfectly still.

"Who is it?" she said again, peering into the blackness.

Again, no answer.

Suddenly, Maya felt something icy on her naked shoulder. She bolted forward, dizzy with fear, and scraped herself against tree after tree as she ran to the top of the hill in a matter of seconds. As she reached the darkened house she was sure that the thing, whatever it was, was only inches behind her. She threw open the back door, slammed it closed, and bolted it behind her. She listened at the door for a few seconds, hearing nothing but the wind, then crept quietly upstairs and turned on the light in her room.

She sat crosslegged on the floor, head bent forward, eyes closed, and tried to collect herself, breathing deeply and slowly, wishing that she was in the city where spooks had long-since been driven out by streetlights and all-night revelers. Then, when her heartbeat had ceased thundering in her head, she went to the crude bookcase that stood against the wall and took several of her childhood books from the shelf. Lying on the floor on her stomach, Maya leafed through book after gaily-covered book, staring fascinated at the bright pictures of princes in scarlet breeches, maidens with tiny white feet, ogres with huge green eyes, and an assortment of clear-winged fairies, red-cheeked ladies-in-waiting, malevolent magicians, and mole-chinned hags. Maya looked through the books for upwards of a half-hour, then laid her head down on the floor to take a little rest and fell immediately to sleep, overhead light burning brightly through her dreams.

Late at night, the sound of her father's coughing woke her and she got up from the floor, turned out the light, took off her clothes, and crept into bed. The coughing kept her up for more than an hour, then stopped, leaving the house peaceful and still. Maya fell asleep listening to the slapping of leaves against her bedroom window.

IX

Maya awoke with the feeling that she was pregnant. She tried unsuccessfully to remember the dream from whence the idea had come, then dismissed it as an improbable fantasy resultant of her anxiety over her father and things in general.

It was barely light outside, crescent moon still hanging in the gray-black pre-dawn sky. Maya thought of going back to sleep but felt totally awake, her senses enlivened by the freshness of the country air. She threw open the window and breathed in the dewiness of the forest, rubbing her goose-bumped buttocks with both hands, then turned to her bookcase and pulled a leather-bound bible from the shelf. She had decided the night before to read to her father from Luke since he had always liked Luke the best. She dressed quickly and walked quietly down the stairs, cradling the heavy book in her arm.

She started for the kitchen, thinking to make herself some breakfast, but stopped as she noticed a dim light glowing in the living room. She entered the room very softly and saw her mother sitting in its single wooden armchair, soft old eyes focused on the dying embers that smoked in the fireplace.

"Mom?" Maya said. "Why aren't you asleep?"

"He's dead," the old lady said.

Maya stood stock still in the doorway, somehow afraid to move.

"I just woke up and looked at him and he was dead," the old lady said. "He died all by himself ... all alone ... It made me feel so queer to see him like that ... dead ... like he wasn't real or something ..."

"Would you like something to drink?" Maya said. "Some tea? Something to warm you up?"

"But I'm glad," her mother said. "I'm really glad ... I don't feel like crying ... He was in such terrible pain ... I like to think he's with God now ... even though he didn't believe in God ... Do you think he's with God, Maya?"

"Yes," Maya said. "I think so ..."

"I guess I would like some tea," the old lady said. "I'll come into the kitchen with you ... It makes me feel funny to be so near him ..." She gestured briefly toward the closed bedroom door, then followed Maya into the kitchen.

Maya lit the green glass lamp and put on the water and brewed the tea. She felt that she should go in and look at the dead shell of her father but felt repulsed at the thought of it. She wondered absent-mindedly if he had died after the coughing seizure that had awakened her.

"So," her mother said. "I guess I ought to call Doctor Hinkle to come over and write up the certificate ... and that godawful mortician from Keene ... what's his name? The one that buried Aunt Rosie? Totsie? Tootsie? Totzer ... Mr. Totzer ..."

"Drink your tea, Mom," Maya said. "It's nice and hot ..."

"I don't think we'll have a service or anything, Maya ... He wouldn't have wanted that at all ... We'll just have him buried and we'll stand over his grave and shed a few tears if we can ... and then we'll come home and clean up. I think I'll feel better when the room is clean again. It'll just be like he's out in back or down by the lake. I guess the only time I'll really miss him will be at night when I get into bed. You know, every night ... I'm ashamed to say it ... Every night, when he got into bed he'd lift up my nightgown and kiss me ... here ... and here ... and here. .." She pointed very tenderly, as if remembering the kisses, at each of her breasts and down at her womb. "He'd kiss me so lovingly, Maya ... and then he'd get into bed ... and I'd just feel like a queen ... like a real, honest-to-goodness queen ..."

Maya and her mother talked and drank tea until the sun stood high over the forest. Then the old lady called the doctor and the mortician and told them both to come over as soon as they could and led Maya back into the living room to wait for them.

They spent the rest of the day cleaning the room in which the old man had died, taking out empty liquor bottles, scrubbing the floor, washing the windows and finally burning the soiled sheets on which he had lain for so many weeks. The sun was setting when they were done, the room somewhat restored to the state of homely cheerfulness that Maya remembered from her childhood, and Maya and her mother went into the kitchen and ate some cold leftovers for dinner.

After dinner Maya started a crackling fire and brought in a second armchair from the porch and sat with her mother watching orange flames leap into the air like the forked tongues of thousands of serpents. She thought about taking a walk in the woods the next morning to search for the grassy place where she had long ago shed the first dew of her youth.

The fire died after awhile and Maya's mother stood up, gray cardigan sweater clutched tightly across her breast and patted Maya on the cheek.

"Go to bed, Maya," the old lady said. "We'll get up early tomorrow and put your father in the ground."

Maya stood up and kissed her mother on the forehead. With a last look at the glowing embers in the fireplace, she turned and went upstairs to her bedroom, locking the door behind her at the thought of the icy thing she had met in the woods the night before. She took off her clothes and got into bed, consciously avoding the sight of her naked body in the mirror. As she lay on top of the covers, staring down at her long toes in the dim moonlight, she felt lonely for the company of a man, someone smooth-skinned and lithe, with small hard muscles, tight buttocks and a long fruit-like penis. She started to masturbate, running her fingers through the meaty lining of her pussy, but found her heat constantly dampered by the image of her father's corpse. So, listening to the light flapping of a bat outside her window and thinking of the dark-eyed boy who had taken her virginity, she fell into a peaceful sleep.

Late at night, Maya sat bolt upright in bed, her body tensed, ears straining for the sound that had awakened her.

"Maya! Maya! Maya!"

It was her mother's voice, urgent, desperate.

Naked, Maya ran down the stairs and into the living room, her hands gone cold with fear. Her mother stood at the door to the bedroom, hand clutched to her heart, face drained of color.

"What is it? What's the matter?" Maya said, looking about the lamp-lit room for some sign of danger.

The old lady stared strangely at Maya's naked body, her eyes fixing involuntarily on her daughter's curly bush.

"I . . . I was just having a nightmare," she said. "I'm sorry I . . . screamed . . . I wasn't awake . . . . I was just so frightened . . "

"Would you like some hot chocolate?" Maya said.

"No," the old lady said. "No . . . I was just frightened . . . I didn't know what I was doing. Maya . . ."

"What?"

"Would you mind spending the night with me? I feel very funny . . ."

Maya put her arm around the old lady's shoulder and led her into the bedroom.

"Don't you want a nightgown." her mother said as they got into bed.

"No," Maya said, "they make me uncomfortable..."

"You're getting to be such a ... woman ... You look like a movie star," the old lady said as she turned out the lamp at the bedside. "Your father would be so proud of you..."

"Goodnight," Maya said.

The next day Maya and her mother drove into Keene and followed a hearse back to a cemetery to the west of Green River. It was a gray, gusty day, and it started to drizzle as Maya and the old lady walked toward the plot that had been dug for the old man, followed by Mr. Totzer, his awkward assistant, and a third man who helped them with the casket.

Maya and her mother stood at opposite sides of the grave as Totzer and his assistants lowered the casket into the ground, Maya still wearing her blue bellbottoms and lime sleeveless blouse, her mother in the shabby gray sweater and green house dress. Totzer and his men left as soon as their work was done, Totzer looking as if each of the aesthetic principles by which he governed his professional life had been shattered. A little old man who tended the grounds of the cemetery came by with a shovel and filled the grave with moist earth, tongue working rapidly against the edge of his bushy white moustache as he strained his tough little muscles with load after load of dirt.

"Yeh," he said without looking up. "Next summer ... grass come up ... pretty as a picture ..."

Maya's mother gave him a ten-dollar bill and led Maya back to the car long before the grave had been filled. Raindrops splattering against the windshield of the car, they drove slowly home, neither of them speaking.

On the last day of her stay Maya awoke very early, took a hot shower and dressed herself in the grimy clothes she had worn all week. She went into the kitchen and slurped down a cup of coffee, then wrote out a note for her mother saying that she would be back by late afternoon if not before, and left the house, closing the door quietly behind herself.

Outside, the forest seemed enchanted, so still were its dewy leaves, so subtly rich the spectrum of its colors. Maya walked very slowly at first, staring up at the pale blueness of sky that showed through the tops of the trees. Autumn was approaching and the dew-sparkled leaves were already turning yellow—some even orange—at their delicately-veined edges.

But for the rare chirp of a distant bird, the only sound in the forest was that of Maya's sandaled feet stepping lightly over the springy, leaf-covered earth. She tossed her golden-silk hair from side to side as she walked, enjoying the feel of it against her shoulders, her large eyes ever alert for some landmark that might lead her toward the grassy place where she had lain with the boy. Occasionally, a falling leaf would glide before Maya and she would snatch it from the air and stroke its slippery surface with her forefinger, remembering the way the boy in Central Park had pulled leaves from the trees and chewed on their thin stems while he walked. A mosquito or two whined in Maya's ear as she wandered through the woods, but she paid them no attention, letting them bite her at will, feeling almost joyous at the thought of sacrificing her blood so freely.

After an hour's walk, Maya came to the place where the icy stream had been and found, to her disappointment, that it had gone all but dry. It was a muddy place now, its bottom filled with gray stones, an occasional dead frog sinking into its center. Maya had wanted terribly to wade through the stream, both for the feeling of its iciness and for an excuse to disrobe. Instead, she took off her sandals and rolled up her bellbottoms and squished across the floor of the dried stream, thick mud cool on her sinking feet.

Once past the muddy ditch, Maya was at a loss as to which direction to take. She wandered aimlessly through the woods, stepping over fallen trees and touching the twisted branches of wild bushes, ever watchful for some clue as to the direction of the grassy place.

As the muscles of her calves began to ache and the noon sun urged droplets of sweat down her sides, Maya grew depressed at the thought of not finding the place. She sat down on a large gray stone and caressed the tautened arches of her feet, breasts falling heavily against her knees, and almost decided to go back but was pushed, at the last moment, by some burning force within her, to seek farther for the hidden spot.

Then, in the distance, she saw a hill and she knew that over the hill stood three tall trees around a small field of soft grass. She ran to the bottom of the hill, strands of hair blowing wildly across her face, and took off her clothes, folding them into a bundle and laying them beside the trunk of a tree. She stood for a minute, arms outstretched and legs spread wide, feeling the forest's light breeze raise tiny goose bumps on her naked skin, then ran quickly up the hill, hands grasping tree trunks and branches, breasts and buttocks shaking freely. At the top of the hill she parted the wiry branches of two bushes, looked down and gave voice to a long, piercing scream.

Below was a highway, a battered khaki pick-up truck pulled over to its shoulder, a beefy, red-shirted man raising the truck's back end with a grimy jack. The beefy man looked up at the sound of Maya's scream, dropped the black tire that he held with one hand and started slowly across the road, his small eyes fixed on Maya's long nipples, one hand running slowly across his hanging belly.

Maya froze as she saw the man come toward her, then ran down the hill as he broke into a heavy-footed trot. At the bottom of the hill she searched frantically for her clothing, then turned to the sound of crunching branches and rolling stones to see the red-shirted man come crashing over the top of the hill, his grunting plainly audible from twenty yards. Maya took off into the woods, branches scratching her bare belly, sharp stones cutting her feet, as the man followed close behind her, his heavy boots kicking up huge clods of dirt as he ran. As the pounding of her heart almost erased the sound of the man's panting pursuit, Maya turned, praying that the man's weight had slowed him down, then went mad with fear at the sight of his sweating face not three yards behind her. Redoubling her efforts, Maya stumbled on an unseen branch, gasped and fell face-forward to the earth. The man came to a crashing halt at the side of the fallen girl and stood over her, his small eyes darting over her long legs and protuberant buttocks, his hand stroking the stiffening member concealed beneath the leg of his grease-smudged pants. Then he stooped and pulled Maya's rump cheeks apart with his rough hands and gave the fleshy mound that peered from between her legs a swift slap.

Maya lay with her face pressed to the moist earth, her eyes shut tightly. As the man let go of her bottom, she rolled slowly over on her back and stared briefly up at his chase-purpled face, then closed her eyes again and spread her legs wide apart.

The man pulled his pants down over his boots and tossed them to the side, then pulled off his boots and stood naked but for the red shirt that flapped over his hanging buttocks. He toed Maya's nipples for a second, then toed her bush, then plopped down between her legs, stiff organ held proudly in his hand. Without a word—there was something about his speechlessness that made it seem as if he didn't think Maya capable of speech—he grabbed Maya's pussy in his hand and jammed the nozzle-like head of his organ into it as if fitting an attachment to a vacuum cleaner. Then he threw her legs up over his shoulders and with one grunting push, thrust the length of himself into her. For lack of lubrication, Maya's hole made a squeaking sound as it was forced by the man's stout organ, and Maya turned her head to the side and bit her lip to keep from screaming.

The man tore his penis in and out of her for a few

minutes, then grabbed her by the buttocks and moved her circularly around his organ. When she had mastered the motion to his satisfaction, he let go of her buttocks and stood perfectly still but for an occasional twitching movement, holding one of her ankles and rubbing her belly in encouragement. Maya worked desperately on the man's penis, eager for him to be done with her. She squeezed her pussy snugly around it, twisted it in ever more violent circles and finally, with a gurgling giggle, the man filled her with semen, his hand squeezing her belly like so much dough.

The man left his penis inside her until it wilted, then pulled it out and lay down beside her, one heavy arm flattening both her breasts. He lay still for a long time and Maya, thinking him asleep, tried to slip out from under his arm. Without opening his eyes, the man grabbed her by the nipple and twisted it between his knuckles until she lay still.

After a time the man stood up, grabbed Maya by the waist and rolled her over on her stomach. He pulled a few clinging leaves from her buttocks, knelt beside her and rubbed his penis against one of her soft cheeks until it was completely stiff, then pulled her buttocks apart, straddled her with his hairy legs and stuffed the head of his organ into her asshole. It was as if he was trying to show her that it was only the hole that mattered to him, that he was impartial as to its location.

Maya suffered the rape of her asshole in silence, feeling the man's bludgeon-like penis rend the walls of her hole, feeling his hairy belly press like a sack of peat moss against her back. The man spent himself with the same childish giggle as before, pulled his organ roughly out of her anus and wiped it very scrupulously on the back of her leg. Maya held her breath as she waited tensely to see what the man would do next, then let her whole body go limp at the sound of his slow dressing.

When the man had finished dressing he walked over to Maya and rolled her over with the heel of his boot.

She stared up at his watery little eyes and the man looked down at her, an oddly serious look on his face, and rubbed her muddy bush with his boot.

"You be here tomorrow," he said to her in a high-pitched voice. "I'll do you some more. You come over to them bushes, all set like you was today and I'll come up and do you some more."

Then, tucking his shirt into his pants, he walked slowly into the distance and disappeared over the top of the hill.

Maya lay for a long time staring blankly up at the darkening sky through the leafy tops of the trees, her lips parted, her legs opened wide as the man had left them. She sat up finally, clutching her belly, and retched, her head hanging between her knees, soiled strands of her hair lightly sweeping the moist ground. Then she got to her feet and wiped clinging leaves and clods of earth from her back and belly, finally cleaning her pussy and rump-crack with her hand and discovering a tiny trickle of blood from her asshole.

She found her clothes where she had left them and pulled them on, pausing once to vomit again, and made her way home, traveling as quickly as her throbbing intestines would allow her, frightened that the growing darkness would catch her lost in the woods.

They walked out to the wood-panelled station wagon, the old lady leaving the green glass lamp burning in the kitchen, and got in through the same door, both of them shivering slightly in the cold night air.

"You forgot your things, Maya," the old lady said as she started the car. "Your slacks, and the nice top you were wearing when you came up . . . "

"I don't want them," Maya said. "They'll be here when I come back . . ."

The old lady nodded, released the emergency brake, and drove into the black night, huge moths swooping continually across the twin beam of the headlights.

The roads were empty and they got into Keene very

quickly, the old lady pulling the car to the side of the shabby bus depot and turning sadly to Maya.

"Should I wait with you till the bus comes?" she said, her voice thin and shaky.

"No," Maya said. "That would be just sad, Mama..."

"You're right," the old lady said. "It would be..."

They stared at each other for a few seconds, then reached forward and clutched each other, their breasts pressed fiercely together.

"I love you so much," the old lady said, a tremendous burst of emotion in her voice. "I love you so much..."

When Maya awoke, the bus was pulling into the Port Authority Terminal, the driver barking crisp instructions over the public address system concerning the pick-up of luggage. Maya found herself sprawled over two seats, her feet hooked under an armrest, her green pleated skirt bunched up around her thighs. She blinked her eyes and sat up, hefting herself into the aisle seat as she pulled down her skirt and straightened her sweater which had twisted so far to the side that one of her breasts threatened any minute to spill over its stretched V neck. She felt betrayed by her sleep, her deliberate look of innocent girlishness destroyed by the unconscious movements of her body.

When the bus stopped, Maya was the first to get off, practically pushing a wrinkled spinster out of her way. She was sure that everyone on the bus was laughing inwardly at her, that everyone had seen her unsatisfied womanhood exposed. As she ran through the terminal, she thought continually of Etheus, of his power, and she prayed in her mind that his guidance would release her from the torment to which she had awakened.

Outside, the streets were burning hot, objects in the distance wavily distorted by the heat that rose from the pavement. Delivery boys wore T-shirts, businessmen removed their jackets and loosened their ties, and droplets of sweat carried bits of make-up down the cheeks of well-dressed women. It seemed to Maya as if the city was melting. Her blue sweater was drenched with sweat within moments after she walked out on the street. It clung scratchily to her arms and breasts and back, increasing her self-consciousness to the point of mania. She grabbed the first empty cab that passed and gave the driver the address of her apartment.

When the cab arrived at the plate-glass entrance of the building, Maya paid the driver hurriedly, entered the lobby without waiting for the doorman's assistance, and took the stairs two at a time to the floor of her apartment.

Inside, she double-locked the door behind her, tore off her clothes in the hallway, and ran into the bathroom to take a cold shower. The thin jets of water stung her flesh like tiny bits of ice and she quit the tub before half of the sweat had been washed from her body. She started to dry herself but found the smallness of the white-and-black tiled bathroom maddeningly confining and stepped shakily out of the room, her feet leaving wet prints on the blue carpet of the hallway.

She tramped restlessly through the suddenly narrow rooms of the apartment, pursued by long-forgotten demons who played wickedly on the periphery of her consciousness without ever fully revealing themselves to her. The sounds of the city seemed to conspire to drive her mad, her ears constantly assaulted by the blaring of horns, the screeching of brakes, and the dissonant hum of multiple voices, footsteps, building constructions, radios, clocks, even watches ... Yes! She could hear the sounds of watches from the street! They ticked, they ticked, and they ticked ...

Maya threw herself on the floor, hands pressed to her ears, faces drifting fluidly before her mind's eye, words and phrases repeating themselves in endless echoes through her brain. Pressure building in her head, she gave voice to a short scream, then smashed her fists against the wall's cold plaster until a sickening weakness came over her, turning her extremities cold and itchy, making her feel as if she would vomit and urinate and defecate all at once.

She lay very still on the floor, her eyes lost in the wiggly texture of the carpet, her breath coming very slowly through her parted lips, saliva trickling from the corners of her mouth. For a long time, she thought that she was dying, and she wondered if perhaps she should try to get up and call an ambulance or a doctor or the police, but then, very gradually, the weakness left her, seeming to seep out through her fingers and toes, and she sat up and leaned against the wall, her hands trembling slightly, her vision somewhat blurred. After a long time, she rose shakily to her feet and made her way into the bedroom, her hands braced against the walls. She fell down on the bed, legs pressed tightly together, hands clasped rigidly across her belly, and remained motionless for the rest of the day, turning her head every few minutes to stare at the clock that ticked atop her dresser.

She felt mad lying on the bed like that, turning from the clock to the ceiling and back to the clock, but she felt that the madness was nothing to the horror that might possess her were she to stand and try to function. Continually, she felt the demons in her mind insinuate themselves through long-closed doors, merely suggesting their presence, tickling her fears with their formless tentacles, and continually, she drove them away with the thought of Etheus. She pictured herself kneeling before him, eyes lowered to his thick-veined feet, her shoulders receiving his absolution through his cool fingertips. And she would know of nothing but his house, and its halls would be her streets and highways, and its rooms would protect her from all manner of unholy things, and she would wander silently through the house, playing simple games of make-believe with the redheaded girl with the thick black bush. Etheus, with his stallion's sceptre, would deliver her from her torment. *His* was the power, and *his* the way . . .

When it was half past six, Maya rose up slowly from the bed and walked to her closet. She rummaged through her clothing for several minutes, then found herself growing weak from the business of selecting a dress and pulled out the first thing that she touched, an austere black shift. She wore neither underwear nor stockings, and chose for her feet the plain leather sandals that she had worn in the country.

She walked into the bathroom and lifted her shift over her hips to perfume herself, but as she lifted the bottle to her vagina, it slipped out of her hand and smashed into a thousand bright slivers on the black-and-white tiled floor. Thick smell of perfume rising heavily in the air, Maya quit the bathroom, repeating the name of Etheus over and over again in her mind to keep the ghosts of panic from overtaking her. She walked into the kitchen and arranged her hair in a loose bun at the top of her head, staring at her distorted reflection in the side of the toaster.

As she walked into the dining-area to take the red card out of her purse, the doorbell rang. Maya went to the door, thinking somehow that Etheus had sensed her discomfort and sent for her immediately. As she pulled the door open, she started slightly at the sight of Peter, then turned away from him as he entered the apartment.

He looked healthier somehow, his arms and face somewhat fuller, his eyes more alive. He wore a navy Ban-lon shirt that set off the pinkness of his cheeks, and a pair of gray slacks that accentuated the suppleness of his thighs.

"I've been trying to get you in all week," Peter said, touching Maya's shoulder.

Maya moved away from him, clutching her purse tightly in her hand.

"I don't want to fight with you, Peter," she said.

"I don't want to fight, Maya," he said. "I love you."

"Everything is different now, Peter," she said. "It's just all different."

"All right," Peter said. "That's all right. I just wanted to apologize to you ... for always being suspicious ..."

"It's too late for that," Maya said. "Everything is different now..."

"You look so beautiful, Maya," Peter said. "I never saw you in that dress..."

Maya stared down at her sandalled feet, pale against the blue carpet.

"What do you want, Peter?" she said.

"I just wanted to talk to you," he said. "I just wanted to look at you... be with you..."

Maya lifted her eyes and stared up at Peter's smooth-featured face, dark locks of hair falling over the sides of his forehead, his blue eyes sparkling with earnestness.

"I have to go, Peter," she said. "I'm sorry..."

"That's all right," Peter said. "I'll wait for you... I'll wait until you come back."

"I'm not coming back," Maya said. "I'm going away."

Peter was silent for a time, his hands thrust deep in his pockets.

"I'll wait for you, Maya," he said. "I love you."

"I'm not coming back, Peter," Maya said. "I'm sorry..."

"I'll wait for you," Peter said softly.

"*I'm not coming back.*" Maya shouted, frustration mounting within her.

"You have to come back, Maya," Peter said. "I love you... I can't lose you..."

Maya stood for a minute, imagining the sort of life she might have had with Peter, suddenly sad at the thought of leaving him. Suddenly, she rushed forward and threw her arms around his neck, kissing him fiercely on the mouth.

"Goodbye, Peter," she said, then let go of him and rushed out the door.

"I'll be here, Maya," Peter said softly from the doorway as she rushed down the stairs. "I'll be here..."

Outside, Maya hailed a cab and gave the driver a

twenty-dollar bill when he squawked about the distance of the restaurant.

As the cab left the city and pulled onto the Expressway, the ride began to seem interminable to Maya. She watched trees pass the window in slow motion, shiny cars shoot by the cab and disappear into the distance, black fumes of their exhausts swirling into the air.

"Can't you drive any faster?" Maya said to the driver. "I'm in a hurry..."

"I don't want no speeding tickets, lady," the driver said. "I'm doing the limit..."

Maya closed her eyes and thought of Etheus, pale memories of her past slipping from her like so many wisps of drifting smoke. Once, she thought of Peter waiting quietly in her apartment for her to return, but even as she pictured him, the outlines of his face grew blurred, indistinct. And then, all that was past seemed dead to her, seemed a solid chunk of stone, cold and dead as her father's corpse.

As the car turned off the Expressway, Maya found herself staring at quiet residential streets shaded by oak trees and measured into neatly tended squares of lawn. Everything seemed unreal to her, the houses like strange boxes that had been dropped from the sky, the dark-suited men with newspapers under their arms like automatons, flashing programmed grins at the sight of their children and wives. Maya turned from the window and watched a fly walk along the dashboard of the car.

Dusk was falling like a dark feather as the taxi approached the isolated restaurant, the pale orange sun sinking slowly behind a distant hill. Etheus' limousine, gleaming in the fading rays of sunlight, seemed a heaven-sent chariot to Maya, and as the taxi pulled beside it, she threw what was left of her money at the driver and jumped out of the cab before it had come to a full halt.

The chauffeur did not leave his seat to open the door as Maya approached the limousine, and even when she peered in the window, a bright smile on her face, he seemed not to notice her. She opened the door herself and slid into the back seat and the chauffeur turned quickly around, his eyes wide with surprise.

"You see," Maya said. "I'm not late this time . . ."

"Oh, you must allow me," the chauffeur said, half-muttering to himself

"Allow you?" Maya said.

His movements jerky, eyes fixed on some distant point, the chauffeur got out of the limousine and pulled open the back door.

"You must . . . allow . . ." he muttered, then bent his head and laughed. "You've gotten in for yourself," he said after a pause, his hands trembling as he spoke. "You've really no need for me at all, then . . ."

"Is anything wrong?" Maya said. "You seem . . ."

"No . . . no," the chauffeur said, pulling off his cap. He bowed, sweeping his cap before him. "But," he said, "But, but, but . . . We must go to the house, we must go to the house . . ."

He jerked himself into the car and started the engine, tiny droplets of sweat trickling down the back of his neck. The woodenness of his movements frightened Maya for a time, and she made a mental note to mention the man's strange behavior to Etheus. Then she relaxed with the steady motion of the limousine and pictured Etheus standing at the door to his mansion, green eyes gleaming with solemn love, black robe open to expose the length of his massive organ. She would run to him, hold him in her arms, fall to her knees and kiss his thick-veined feet . . .

Maya sank back in her seat, her breath easing slowly through mouth and nose, her body tingling with anticipation. Very soon now . . . just a matter of seconds . . . and she would be with him . . . She was done with the world, her torment at an end . . .

The gate to the mansion was open, swinging on its rusty hinge, and the chauffeur laughed as he passed the deserted guardhouse.

"Gone for a little walk," he said, turning around to

face Maya. "Gone into the woods to shoot a squirrel for his dinner..."

Faster and faster, he sped down the dirt road, then jerked the limousine to a screeching halt, headlights illuminating the darkened front of Etheus' house. Maya waited for him to open the door but he sat motionless in his seat, his hands clenched tightly to the steering-wheel.

"Go," he said without turning, "Go. You don't need me to help you... You don't need me... Anyone can open a door... just anyone..."

Maya stepped out of the car and walked quickly toward the house, shivering slightly in the coolness of the night air. She took the stone steps slowly, clutching the gnarled wooden handrail for support, then stood for a moment before the huge oak door, her hands trembling with excitement. She knocked twice, remembering Etheus' anger at her entering his study without being bidden to do so, and waited for the butler to come to the door. After several minutes of waiting—during which she wondered if the simplicity of her black shift would be appreciated by Etheus—she opened the door and stepped into the vestibule.

The vestibule was empty and dark, wood panelling pulled back to reveal a single flashing red light on the metal intercom.

"Hello," Maya said, her voice low. Then, louder: "Hello! Is anyone here?" Her hands turned cold and clammy. "Is anyone here? It's Maya! Is anyone here?"

She ran to the metal plate, her face lit by the flashes of red light, and pressed buttons and flicked switches, shouting stupidly at the machine.

"Hello!" she hollered. "This is Maya! Where are you? This is Maya! I'm in the little room by the door..."

Multicolored lights flashed on and off as she flicked switch after sweat-slippery switch. Then, with a sharp crackle, the machine went dead.

It was a test, Maya decided, Etheus was testing her. She must remain calm. She must bear him always in her mind. Somewhere, behind the dusty walls, he stood and watched her, gauged her every move.

Slowly, Maya pulled her dress over her shoulders, then bent to unstrap her sandals, her body curved sensuously, breasts grazing her knees.

"I'm naked," she whispered to the walls as she stood up, holding her breasts out for invisible eyes to see. "I want to be one of you. I'm naked .. " She paused for a response, then began again, very haltingly. "Etheus?" she said. "I want to find you, Etheus. I'm going to come looking for you, so if that's not all right, I want you to say something. I'll wait here all night if you want .. naked. I'm naked. Can you hear me? Are you there?"

Overhead, there was the creak of a floorboard.

"I'm coming, Etheus," she said, taking a candle from the wall and lighting it. "I'm coming to be with you. If it's not all right—if you want me to wait—just ... do something ..."

She paused a second, then opened the door to the hallway and peered into its musty darkness.

"I'm coming," she said. "If you don't want me to, just say so, just do something ..."

The flame of the candle flickered madly as Maya walked down the corridor, waxing and waning as if with the flow of her thoughts. As she started to mount the stairway, she was startled by a noise to her left, and she turned to face a narrow door, its dusty latch imprinted with the marks of slender fingers. She opened the door very slowly, then almost dropped her candle as her eyes met those of a furry rodent who ran at the sight of her and took shelter beneath an overturned purple chair. Maya closed the door and took the thinly-carpeted steps quickly, a picture of Suzanne in her mind. She saw the redhead lying beside her in bed, Egyptian eyes opened wide with mystical delight.

"Etheus!" Maya screamed suddenly. "Where are you? This is Maya! I need you, Etheus! I'm afraid ..."

She began running through hallways and up flights of stairs, clutching with her free hand at the wood-panelled walls, her feet making a dry, scraping sound against the dust-covered floor. Then, stumbling forward, candle slipping from her grasp, she came to the familiar door to Etheus' study.

"Oh, thank heaven," she whispered, bowing before the door. "Oh, thank heaven . . ."

Crawling forward, she opened the door and peered into the wine-colored room in which she had first been taken by Etheus and his disciples.

In one corner of the room, a small bulb burned, casting its feeble light over a scene of chaos and destruction. Everywhere, photographs were torn from the walls, some crumpled to the floor, others hanging limply by their edges, naked couples creased and twisted in folds of cracking cardboard. The window had been smashed, splinters of glass twinkling on the sill, and the heavy curtains had been pulled from their rods.

Maya rose slowly to her feet, droplets of sweat trickling down the valley of her breasts. She walked to Etheus' desk and ran her finger over the rim of a half-filled cup of coffee, then felt the coldness of the coffee with her thumb. The acrid odor of tobacco lingered in the room, and as Maya searched for its point of origin, her eyes came to rest on a crumpled tan raincoat tossed sloppily over the back of a leather armchair. Trembling, she advanced, lifted the coat lightly in her arms, then dropped it suddenly to the floor at the sight of the black robe that lay beneath it. She felt as if there had been a play, and the play had ended, and the actors had left their costumes behind. Gently, she lifted Etheus' robe to her face and sniffed its elusive fragrance. Frightened by the robe's coldness, she placed it once again on the back of the chair and stared miserably down at her small naked feet. Beside her was the crumpled raincoat of the smiling man. Its frayed hem formed the outline of a jagged grin against the deep wine color of the carpet.

A nameless horror gripping her by the throat, Maya turned and walked from the room, her legs shaking beneath her. She walked endlessly through the deserted corridors of the dark house, holding back the helpless tears that welled up in her eyes for fear that were she to let one salty droplet fall, she might cry for all eternity. Once, she screamed, "Etheus!" and heard a ghost-echo repeat the name in subtly-decreasing volumes until the house was still once more.

"Yes," she whispered, "Yes," and continued through the hall, her flickering candle illuminating the hundreds of dust-blurred footprints that formed chaotic patterns on the bare wooden floor.

As she walked, she opened doors and stared into cold, lamp-lit rooms that seemed frozen in time as if caught in three-dimensional photographs. Here was the bedroom she had slept in a week ago, huge portrait hanging crookedly on the wall, the face of the blue-uniformed officer slashed with a knife. Further down the hall, was a woman's room, a thin whip lying curled on the floor like a snake, an emaciated kitten mewing at the window, and through the room, a bathroom, its tub filled with stale water, a towel fallen from the rack. From the window of the bathroom, Maya could see the beams of the limousine's headlights focused steadily on the front of the house. She didn't want to see the chauffeur. She didn't want to know what had happened.

Downstairs, Maya found the room in which the men had slept, the grim athletes who had performed so unfailingly on the stone platform in the woods. The floor was littered with empty packages of cigarettes and green jugs of wine. Discarded black uniforms were strewn across chairs and night-tables, their elastic openings puckered like the mouths of fish. The sleep-creased sheets of the beds were stained with semen, and Maya paused at the edge of one of the beds to breathe in the dying odor.

She paused in the vestibule, hands on her naked hips, and smelled the ancient perfume of the house, then stepped outside and descended the cold stone steps, night wind raising goose-bumps on her uncovered flesh. She skirted the black limousine and walked zombie-like toward the woods, determined not to look back at the house lest she lose her mind to the demons that followed her, calling her by name.

"Wait!" came the scream of the chauffeur. "Wait! You haven't heard!"

Maya continued walking, counting her footsteps silently as she approached the edge of the woods, and the chauffeur bolted from the limousine and caught her by the arm, spinning her around and fixing her with his tiny red eyes.

The chauffeur seemed a dwarf to Maya, his face like pale wax melting in the glare of the headlights.

"You haven't heard," he said. "You haven't heard the story . . . Oh! It will make you sad . ."

"I don't want to hear," Maya said. "Leave me alone . . ."

She walked trance-like into the woods, stone-and-wood house looming like a painted backdrop behind her. She walked in widening circles for many hours, barely noticing the long branches that scraped at her arms and thighs, until finally she found herself in the road next to the black-and-white striped guardhouse that stood beside the gate to Etheus' house. She curled herself on the wooden floor of the guardhouse, her muddy feet pressed against its baseboard, and fell into a frozen sleep, her ghost-filled dreams punctuated by the rusty creaking of the wrought-iron gate as it swung open and closed, now showing, now hiding, the way to Etheus' house.

MORE EROTIC CLASSICS FROM CARROLL & GRAF

☐ Anonymous/ALTAR OF VENUS	$3.95
☐ Anonymous/AUTOBIOGRAPHY OF A FLEA	$3.95
☐ Anonymous/CONFESSIONS OF AN ENGLISH MAID	$3.95
☐ Anonymous/CONFESSIONS OF EVELINE	$3.95
☐ Anonymous/COURT OF VENUS	$3.95
☐ Anonymous/THE DIARY OF MATA HARI	$3.95
☐ Anonymous/DOLLY MORTON	$3.95
☐ Anonymous/THE EDUCATION OF A MAIDEN	$3.95
☐ Anonymous/THE EDUCATION OF A MAIDEN, PART II	$4.50
☐ Anonymous/THE EROTIC READER II	$3.95
☐ Anonymous/THE EROTIC READER III	$4.50
☐ Anonymous/THE EROTIC READER IV	$4.95
☐ Anonymous/FANNY HILL'S DAUGHTER	$3.95
☐ Anonymous/FLORENTINE AND JULIA	$3.95
☐ Anonymous/INDISCREET MEMOIRS	$4.50
☐ Anonymous/A LADY OF QUALITY	$3.95
☐ Anonymous/LAY OF THE LAND	$4.50
☐ Anonymous/LENA'S STORY	$3.95
☐ Anonymous/THE LIBERTINES	$4.50
☐ Anonymous/LOVE PAGODA	$3.95
☐ Anonymous/THE LUSTFUL TURK	$3.95
☐ Anonymous/MADELEINE	$3.95
☐ Anonymous/MAID'S NIGHT IN	$3.95
☐ Anonymous/THE OYSTER II	$3.95
☐ Anonymous/THE OYSTER III	$4.50
☐ Anonymous/THE OYSTER IV	$4.50
☐ Anonymous/PARISIAN NIGHTS	$4.50
☐ Anonymous/PLANTATION HEAT	$4.50
☐ Anonymous/PLEASURES AND FOLLIES	$3.95
☐ Anonymous/PLEASURE'S MISTRESS	$3.95
☐ Anonymous/PRIMA DONNA	$3.95
☐ Anonymous/ROSA FIELDING: VICTIM OF LUST	$3.95

- ☐ Anonymous/SATANIC VENUS — $4.50
- ☐ Anonymous/SECRET LIVES — $3.95
- ☐ Anonymous/SENSUAL SECRETS — $4.50
- ☐ Anonymous/SWEET TALES — $4.50
- ☐ Anonymous/THREE TIMES A WOMAN — $3.95
- ☐ Anonymous/VENUS DISPOSES — $3.95
- ☐ Anonymous/VENUS UNBOUND — $3.95
- ☐ Anonymous/VICTORIAN FANCIES — $3.95
- ☐ Anonymous/THE WANTONS — $3.95
- ☐ Anonymous/A WOMAN OF PLEASURE — $3.95
- ☐ Anonymous/WHITE THIGHS — $4.50
- ☐ Cleland, John/FANNY HILL — $4.95
- ☐ Perez, Faustino/LA LOLITA — $3.95
- ☐ van Heller, Marcus/THE FRENCH WAY — $3.95
- ☐ van Heller, Marcus/THE LOINS OF AMON — $3.95
- ☐ van Heller, Marcus/ROMAN ORGY — $3.95
- ☐ Villefranche, Anne-Marie/FOLIES D'AMOUR — $3.95
  Cloth — $14.95
- ☐ Villefranche, Anne-Marie/MYSTERE D'AMOUR — $3.95
- ☐ Villefranche, Anne-Marie/SECRETS D'AMOUR — $4.50
- ☐ Von Falkensee, Margarete/BLUE ANGEL NIGHTS — $3.95
- ☐ Von Falkensee, Margarete/BLUE ANGEL SECRETS — $4.50

Available from fine bookstores everywhere or use this coupon for ordering.

Carroll & Graf Publishers, Inc., 260 Fifth Avenue, N.Y., N.Y. 10001

Please send me the books I have checked above. I am enclosing $_____ (please add $1.00 per title to cover postage and handling.) Send check or money order—no cash or C.O.D.'s please. N.Y. residents please add 8¼% sales tax.

Mr/Mrs/Ms _____
Address _____
City _____ State/Zip _____
Please allow four to six weeks for delivery.